FATAL INTUITION

MAKENZI FISK

Thank you
Makenzi Fisk

Mischievous Books

2015

First Mischievous Books Edition 2015
Cover Design: Makenzi Fisk
ISBN: 978-0-9938087-8-4

ACKNOWLEDGMENTS

Stacey, thank you for your unwavering
support and encouragement.

DEDICATION

Despite our pasts, we are strong enough.

CHAPTER ONE

Boots scuffed gravel behind her, and a muscled forearm snaked around Erin Ericsson's neck. Pungent male sweat stung her nostrils. She tried to twist free but it was too late. The assailant squeezed her throat between forearm and bicep. Starbursts crackled in her vision. Blindsided, her brain registered the fleeing footsteps of her quarry.

There had been two suspects, not one. She hadn't seen *that* coming when she'd arrived on scene with her partner.

A sharp tug at her waist was followed by a metallic scrape and her pistol clattered into a storm drain with a sickening splash. *Escape!*

She drove her head backward, anticipating the satisfying impact when her skull would crush the soft cartilage of his nose. There was no impact, just a dancer's fluidity as he moved with her. She dug her fingers into his forearm, searched for the pressure point near his elbow. He grunted and squeezed tighter. *I have to breathe!*

This call had gone sideways. It should have been easy. She and her partner, Agent Clark Davis, were supposed to apprehend a bank manager, a white collar criminal with no violent past. The hardest thing about this arrest should have been talking the arrogant fraud artist out of his luxury office.

Complacency was her first mistake. Her second was not trusting her instincts enough. Erin's skin had prickled when they'd approached the bank. No customers exited and none entered. It was a dead zone, except for a window blind at the side office that flicked open and closed. Something was off.

She held her palm out toward Davis, even a guy without street experience would know what that meant, and slunk toward the window. A peek inside might allay her suspicions. She should have called out to warn him, should have pulled him away.

More comfortable behind a desk in an air conditioned office, he'd stared at her in disbelief when she'd signaled. "You scared? Subject doesn't even know we're coming." He'd smoothed back his impeccable hair and sauntered up like a Jehovah's Witness with a message from the Lord. That's when the first suspect had bolted out the front door with a duffel bag, and knocked him on his ass.

Erin took off in pursuit and hoped that Davis wasn't still sitting on the sidewalk with a puzzled expression. She hoped he'd gotten to the car radio and called for backup. Focused on catching the blond-haired robber, she'd missed the hulking figure emerging from the shadows who had clothes-lined her mid-stride. Now here she was, fighting for air.

She spiked her elbow toward her assailant's spleen but he squeezed her into his chest. He was wily and strong. Her remaining breath wheezed from her throat. Her ribcage compressed.

One-one thousand, two-one thousand...

Erin could hold her breath for up to two minutes underwater, but this was different. The pressure was unbearable. Her lungs burned. She tucked her elbow and jabbed it into his ribs, any sensitive organ would do.

Flinch or something, damn you!

This guy was a machine. His body was solid, too hard. Her elbow met a ridge in the fabric between his armpit and flank. He was wearing a ballistic vest. She should have known.

Okay, Plan B. Make a little space between them. She might still take him down if she gained room to maneuver. Without warning, she dropped her weight and a hundred and twenty-five pounds of desperate energy plummeted in his arms. Just a moment of imbalance and she could use her Judo skills.

He was too smart. Grip tight, he anticipated her move and countered. Her feet dangled like a child's. If she was still in uniform, she'd have access to any number of tools on her belt but disarmed, and wearing plain clothes, she'd have to rely on her wits. She drove her heel toward the top of his foot, aiming for sensitive metatarsals. Without leverage, her soft shoes glanced off steel-toed boots.

Where was Agent Davis? The commotion should have brought him running. *What was he doing?*

Her view of the street blurred. Time was running out. Finally, he shifted his weight and an unmistakable shape pressed against the base of her spine. The barrel of a pistol. She'd been captured. This was how it ended. It was all over.

* * *

Allie drummed her fingertips on the rental car's steering wheel. She stared at the digital clock until it ticked forward one minute. Through the main entrance, not a single vehicle entered and none exited. In her lap, the illuminated screen of her E-reader dimmed and went black. No fabricated story could keep her mind from the real-life worry that consumed her thoughts.

Erin was in trouble. She should have been here an hour ago. As if electricity crackled across the space between them, Allie sensed her girlfriend's fear, her panic and despair. Wherever she was, Erin was trapped.

On the passenger seat, the dog kicked his legs in his sleep and she reached out to reassure him that his dream was only that. "It's okay, Doppler."

He opened one eye, sniffed the air and curled into a ball. The sensitive little Chihuahua usually picked up on her emotions long before she did, but he wasn't the least bit concerned. Was her intuition off?

She picked up her cell phone and activated the screen. Should she call someone inside the gates? She'd been uneasy ever since Erin had joined the FBI. No matter how many times she'd been reassured, a kernel of worry remained embedded in her subconscious. It grew into a looming specter at times like this.

At her feet, her computer case yawned open and the corner of a rumpled envelope mocked her through the half-open zipper. *Winnipeg Youth Detention Centre* was stamped across the sender's address. As if its contents could be transferred by touch, she poked at it with the corner of her phone until she zipped it shut. She didn't need to think about *that* right now. She'd never considered herself a worrier but things had changed. Ever since Lily.

A trickle of sweat ran down the back of her neck. Was she losing it? She unsnapped her seatbelt to relieve pressure on the scar across her abdomen. The puffy pink line was a constant reminder of the savage thirteen-year-old girl, and it still itched with the memory. She reached for it but caught herself. Her hands trembled and she wrapped them around the steering wheel instead. Seeking release, the confined tremors rippled from her hands to her spine. The numbers on the digital clock blurred to a glowing smear of blue.

The dog leapt to his feet and his triangle ears sprang upright. He shook his coat and put a paw on her lap until she stroked his fur. Doppler, the pup they'd rescued from a Winnipeg storm grate, had grown into his oversize ears about the same time he'd worked his way into her heart. His soft brown eyes glistened with intensity. Even though he was technically Erin's dog, he'd become Allie's best buddy, and her emotional weathervane.

She took a deep breath. *No.* She would not give Lily this much power over her. The girl's sentence wasn't up for another year and she wasn't going anywhere. The ominous letter could stay tucked away in her bag until she was ready.

Right now, she was worried about Erin and was powerless to do anything but wait. The dog wagged his tail and prodded her with his wet nose. He'd be acting like a nutcase if there was anything actually wrong, wouldn't he? He always picked up on stuff like that. Erin was fine. Doppler was only worried about Allie. She needed to relax.

"Come on, *Chorizo.*" She smiled at Erin's silly name for him, and scooped up the wiggly dog. His legs paddled air before his paws hit the pavement and he rocketed to the nearest tree. While he nosed his way around the shrubs, Allie stared at the gate.

…sixty-one, sixty-two, sixty-three…

Counting, when had she started doing that? More than the counting, she resented its accompanying anxiety. At home, she checked the locked doors, over and over, and then there was the alarm. Sometimes she got out of bed to make sure it was set. It was so old she couldn't be sure it worked any more, but it made her feel safer. A little.

She stopped and exhaled. Lily. She'd come full-circle, right back where she didn't want to be. Doppler nosed at her pant leg and she gathered him into her arms.

"I know you're a real dog, and you can walk on your own feet, but this is for me. Okay?" Carrying him around like a teddy bear bent the house rule about treating dogs like dogs, no matter the size, but

4

dammit, right now she needed a hug.

Her gaze strayed back to the gate. What crisis could make Erin this late for their rendezvous?

She set the dog on his feet and he took off, nose to the ground, his short legs deceptively fast. He'd scented a wild animal, or something. She chewed her lip for a moment and then locked the car door. Maybe he'd flush out a rabbit, or even a deer. That would be a good distraction. Allie ducked through heavy brush at the side of the road and followed him into the woods.

CHAPTER TWO

Erin slumped in her captor's arms and his grip loosened enough for her to inhale. Sour realization, along with his rank body odor, filled her lungs. Cops don't bargain for cops. Her hostage value was nearly worthless. Her badge might as well be made of tinsel, for all the good it did her now.

Agent Davis rounded the corner behind them. "I called for—" His jaw slackened at the sight of the huge stranger squeezing the life from Erin, and his eyes dropped to the pistol at her back. He scrabbled for his shoulder holster.

"FBI. Drop the gun." Davis's voice squeaked like a young man toying with puberty. There was no doubt he'd rather be in computer crimes, investigating faceless strangers in faraway places, strangers without guns.

"Don't even try it. I'll finish her if ya don't raise yer paws right now." Erin's captor jabbed the pistol's barrel into her vertebra.

Davis's empty hands shot into the air. "Okay."

"Get lost, or her brains will be all over yer pretty shoes." The big man growled something unintelligible, and Davis turned and ran.

Erin's final hope vanished with him. He'd call for backup, and they'd come. Of course, they'd come lights and sirens, might even call out the Special Weapons and Tactics Team, but would it be too late?

Across the road, a battered green pickup rumbled from the lane. Behind the wheel sat a man with an intense stare, a shock of blond hair and a familiar face, the face of the suspect who'd escaped. He spotted Erin and shook his head. The truck halted halfway into the street and the big man stiffened beside her. He wasn't letting go of his prize.

The driver glared for a moment and then pulled the getaway vehicle closer. Pistol in her ribs, her captor shoved her through the passenger door and pinned her between them. She fought the insane impulse to clip on her safety belt when the driver hit the gas and they snapped back in their seats.

"What're you thinkin' Elton?" The blond man appraised her with blue eyes before turning them back to the road. "This screws up everything."

The big man chuckled softly. "Don't worry, Wesley. I kicked her Glock into the sewer, and look how teeny tiny she is. She won't be no trouble." In contrast to his unpleasant body odor, his benign expression and bald head reminded her of the man from the cleaning commercial. A man who loved his momma and might own a cat. Not at all like a desperate criminal.

"Humph." Wesley gunned the engine on a straightaway and the old motor hiccupped before all eight cylinders roared.

Erin shuffled her feet around the bulging duffel bag, and used her fingers to probe the space at the back of her seat. Was there anything usable? A ballpoint pen? Something sharp? Even a damn straw would be a godsend right now. An innocuous item could be turned into a valuable weapon. She dug deep but came up empty-handed.

"Ain't no big deal, Wesley. I wanted some fun for a change." Elton winked at her and she narrowed her eyes.

"This wasn't the plan, you big schmuck. Hit the bank. Get out clean. That's it." He glanced at the bag on the floor and then up at Erin's chest. "A hostage. Seriously?"

"Nobody said we couldn't." Elton held out gorilla-sized palms in an innocent gesture.

Wesley shook his head. "You're such a pain in my ass. If you weren't my only brother…" The corner of his fake mustache twitched in an amused half-smile. "You check for her backup gun at least?"

"Course I did." Elton quickly ran rough hands around her waistband and down to her ankles. "She ain't got one."

"Okay, then." His brother relaxed and rolled down his window. He stuck out his elbow as if it was a hot summer day and they were on their way to the beach. Wind buffeted the interior, and with it came the sound of sirens. They were coming. The two men exchanged meaningful glances.

Elton bounced on his seat. "This is gonna be fun."

Wesley jutted his chin toward a windowless warehouse fronted by a row of roll-up doors. "Here we are. The Alamo." Aside from stenciled numbers above each entrance, there was no business name, no address or identifying marks on the gray exterior. He stopped, got out to lift the door, and pulled into 1107B.

The interior was smaller than Erin expected. There was a door to a walled-off area on one side, and boxes stacked in neat rows on industrial shelves as far as she could see. She craned her neck, but the only exit appeared to be the space through which they'd entered.

Wesley jumped out again, pulled down the door, and pitched them into darkness.

"Don't get no ideas," Elton growled, closing his fist around her taut bicep. He hauled her off-balance out the passenger side and she stumbled against him.

It was totally devoid of light. No matter how hard she concentrated, she couldn't see a damn thing. Where was the big man's gun pointed? Her abdomen? Her head? The floor? How far could she get in the dark before he, or Wesley, took her down? Without sight, escape was a risk too great to take. These men must be familiar with this place if they could navigate it unseen.

"Ouch! Who put that there?" A thud and scuffle indicated that Wesley didn't know his way as well as she'd thought.

"Hurry up, goddammit," Elton grunted. "I'm getting flashbacks to when you locked me in the closet that time." He snorted and pulled her toward the sound of his brother's voice.

The lights flickered and glowed for a moment before blazing to life, washing everything in fish-belly yellow. They stood beside the interior room and waited while Wesley fiddled with the locked door.

Erin blinked until her vision adjusted. While neat shelves filled the bulk of the main area, heavy wooden boxes formed random barricades around this particular room. The Alamo indeed.

She exhaled at the whoop of sirens outside. That was fast. Soon the perimeter would be established. The next step would be to attempt contact, and then negotiate surrender. If it got that far.

"I asked them last week to replace this crappy knob." Wesley yanked the key out and booted open the door. He dumped the duffel bag onto the desk and went to a cabinet affixed to the wall.

Rows of blued-steel barrels glinted from the interior. These men were pros, this was the armory, and they had their choice of weapons, from shotguns to assault rifles to semi-automatic pistols. She took a mental inventory while he retrieved a set of police-issue handcuffs from the top shelf.

At least two MP5s, an AR15, a Mossberg 12 gauge shotgun like her dad's, a half dozen semi-automatic pistols and even a couple of .38 revolvers. Were those canisters of CS gas?

The contents of her stomach turned to lead. Half a decade ago, the department's misguided training officer had decided that all members needed to experience the effects of nerve gas. An outhouse-sized gas shack was set up and canisters of CN, a lesser agent, were deployed in the enclosed space.

Nervous, and eager to get it over with, Erin had been the first volunteer shut inside. Her burning mucous membranes were nothing compared to the psychological terror that ensued when she repeated the exercise with CS. She'd nearly taken the door off its hinges, and punched the training officer holding it shut, in her panic to get to fresh air.

Holy crap, what were these two planning? She'd run bare-chested into the line of fire before she'd allow herself to be gassed with CS again.

Wesley tossed the cuffs to Elton. "Get her out of the way," he ordered. "This ain't no time to babysit. Company's coming."

Elton ducked his head and steered Erin toward a conduit pipe attached to the wall. She deliberately tripped.

"Oops, you okay?" His tough-guy persona faltered for a split-second when he caught her. In the instant their eyes met, she saw his vulnerability. Now she had a plan.

Erin tensed her forearms and bent her wrists when he snapped the cuffs around them. She'd seen a slight thirteen-year old girl do this once, and she'd later been able to slip free. Would it work for a grown woman?

The sirens silenced with the screeching of tires outside, followed by a subdued hum of activity. "Hurry the hell up, bro!" Wesley hollered.

"You're shaking." Elton frowned and backed away without

cinching the ratchet tight. His bald forehead furrowed in concern.

"They're here. Get into position." Wesley crouched behind a wooden crate, a gunslinger-style holster with one of the revolvers on his leather belt. Old school.

Elton armed himself with the other revolver, and tucked it into the back of his jeans. He joined his brother behind the crate, shotgun in his hands.

Thank God they hadn't chosen the gas. She twisted her wrists and was relieved to find slack. These could slip off and… She tasted metal in her mouth at the thought of what that thirteen-year old girl had done when she'd freed herself. Erin had relived every detail of that night, over and over, for the past year and a half. The scar above her girlfriend's navel was still raw after all this time. She'd been lucky she hadn't lost Allie, and it had taken every bit of self control she possessed not to beat the girl senseless.

No, Lily was still out there, doing easy time in a Canadian youth detention center. Erin didn't want to know when she was getting out, didn't want to hear that name ever again. She had a new career, a new start with Allie away from those memories, and she was going to make this work. First she had to get free.

The office phone jangled and Wesley hurried to answer it. With both men's attention diverted, Erin strained tender wrist bones against metal. How had Lily done it? She adjusted the angle, clenched her jaw and shredded the top layer of skin. A wet trail trickled down to her fingertips. So much for her career as a hand model.

"We've got one of yours." Wesley spoke matter-of-factly into the phone, a greasy businessman making a simple transaction. He listened for a moment and shook his head. "No deal." He held the receiver toward his brother and waited calmly.

Elton pointed his shotgun at the ceiling. "I'm gonna kill her!" He screamed like a crazed lunatic. "Swear to God, I'll do it." *BANG!* He fired a round.

Erin's ears rang from the blast. Her hands trembled. She tugged one last time and was truly surprised when she pulled free. The clang of the cuff as it swung against the conduit pipe was swallowed up by maniacal laughter. She concealed it in her fist. Elton was overdoing it. Was he insane?

Wesley brought the phone back to his lips. "Hear that? I don't know how long I can keep him under control. Call me back in five minutes and I'll give you a list of our demands." He slammed it into its cradle and smiled at Elton. "He's shitting bricks."

The two men sat side-by-side on a crate and waited. Elton held his shotgun and swung his legs like a little boy.

Wesley kept an eye on the door, and leapt on a thin cable when it snaked under the crack. "No cameras in here," he said and threw a box over it. He turned to his grinning brother. "I told them to phone. Should we kill our hostage to punish them?"

Elton shrugged. "Maybe."

Neither of the men had given Erin so much as a glance since she'd been cuffed to the pipe. They might not even notice. The door release dangled a mere twenty feet away. Was she fast enough? If she avoided being shot by her captors, would she open the door to a hail of friendly fire? Should she stay put and wait to be rescued? From what she'd overheard, that might be impossible. She tucked into a crouch, ready to run for it. Was there a hope in hell?

The phone jangled again, and Wesley turned his back to answer the call. Elton's head followed. This was it. The best chance she'd ever have.

She exploded from her crouch and covered the distance to the door in a few bounds. Like a basketball player executing a lay-up, she launched herself at the release and pulled it with all her weight. It screeched open.

"Hey!" Elton was the first to pursue her. He tripped and tumbled to his knees, a growl rumbling in his throat. "Crap. Sorry, bro. Thought we had this one." He'd already given up.

She rolled under the door crack and came to her feet, sprinting for the first set of flashing lights.

Bug-eyed, Davis stared at her when she dove for his shielded position behind a car. "You're bleeding." His Glock shook in his hands as if they were on their first date. "We were going to negotiate. We would have gotten you out."

"Sorry to ruin your plans." Erin glanced down at her scraped wrists. They'd heal. She gingerly released the remaining cuff with the key he handed her.

The roll-up door squealed on its bearings, and all attention focused on the two criminals in the doorway. Palms high, Elton and Wesley sauntered out.

"Freeze!" Davis shouted. He was joined by a cacophony of

commands from a half dozen other agents barricaded behind their cars.

"Get on your knees!"

"Don't move!"

"Stop!"

"We surrender!" Elton recited a well-rehearsed line. He grinned at the flurry of activity as agents adjusted their positions. "We should have held out for pizza," he muttered to his brother. "I missed lunch."

"Whatever," Wesley retorted. "It's past quittin' time, and I'm gettin' too old for this."

Two of Erin's classmates broke cover to take the men into custody.

One man in khakis and black polo shirt separated himself from the rest, and his voice boomed above the activity. "Let's wrap this up, people. Good work. Make sure all the vehicles and equipment are properly returned."

He leveled a stern gaze at Davis. "Watch where you're pointing that thing. I don't care if it's not a real firearm, treat it like it is."

Davis's face reddened. "Yes, s-sir." He holstered his bright orange training pistol and hurried to make himself useful packing equipment into the trunk of a dented Crown Victoria.

"Boys, boys." The instructor shook his head at the grinning *criminals.*

Elton and Wesley, the role players hired for this FBI training scenario, leaned casually against the hood of a car. Uncuffed and relaxed, they looked like anyone you'd meet on the street. Maybe Elton really did love his mama and own a cat. Maybe the two weren't even brothers.

"Took it a bit far today, didn't you?" Harsh sunlight created shadows in the craggy lines of the instructor's face, lending him a sterner than usual appearance.

Erin rubbed her sore collarbone where the hard edge of Elton's steely forearm had squeezed her. He sure didn't pull any punches when he played his part. His crazy lunatic routine had seemed real, too believable.

And then there was Wesley, the mysterious man with the peeling mustache. He'd played the cold mastermind of the duo, yet here he stood like a normal human being. The game was over. He probably had a wife and kid at home and was eager to clock out.

"You aren't authorized to go off script," the instructor growled. "Whose idea was this?"

"No one said we couldn't," Elton blurted. He dipped his head at the training officer's glare.

Wesley stepped forward. "It was all my idea. I wanted some fun on my last day. I'm sorry if I screwed up your trainees." He reached into his pocket and handed over his ID card. "Consider this my notice. I'm done."

"Aw, Wesley. No." Elton's face crumpled like a sodden paper bag. "I liked this job."

The instructor considered him for a moment. "You'll be on notice if you decide to stay."

Erin held her breath when the instructor turned his attention to her.

"E-ric-sson," he stretched the word into three agonizingly long syllables. "What am I going to do with you?"

"I had the opportunity to escape." She tucked her abraded wrists deep into her pockets and squared her shoulders. "I took it. I—"

"That's not the problem."

Elton huffed.

"You walked right into a robbery-in-progress without so much as a glance over your shoulder. I don't know what it was like in your sleepy little hometown, but here anything can happen. Out there," her instructor pointed somewhere in the distance, "*everything* will happen. You need to keep your head up."

Erin's shoulders slumped. She had sensed something awry, from the moment she exited the car, before she'd taken a single step toward the bank. Even in this simulated town, there was a pattern of activity, and it was off.

Accustomed to working alone, she'd been distracted. Davis, the man with the impeccable hair and shiny shoes, her partner in the simulation, had changed everything. He didn't have a clue how to behave on the street. Back home, Morley Falls crew members sometimes teamed up, but she preferred to work alone.

"And don't even consider blaming your partner. Davis is green, but you are all trainees here. You were fully aware of each other's strengths," he looked her in the eye, "and limitations. You are not the *Raging Ranger* here. We are all on the same team."

Erin's jaw clenched at the loathed nickname. She'd left Morley Falls PD behind, but the stupid moniker dogged her even now. Would she never be free?

She'd been saddled with that after she'd hunted down a fellow police officer, and discovered that he wasn't a child molester, or a killer. Derek Peterson was just a bad cop, and a poor excuse for a father. Lily's lies had sent him to prison, and he'd served time before the truth had disentangled itself.

Now the girl was in detention and he had to rebuild his devastated life. Lily would be nearly fifteen by now, probably honing her criminal skills in juvy. Erin frowned.

"Don't give me that look, Ericsson," her instructor barked. Erin snapped to attention and his expression softened. He jutted his square jaw toward her concealed wrists. "You'll need to take care of that." He pivoted on his heel and strode away.

* * *

Allie stood still and listened. Save for a squirrel chattering somewhere in the distance, the woods were silent. *Unbelievable.* How would she explain this to Erin? *Honey, I lost your dog. I'm a terrible parent.*

Why had she brought him? It wasn't as if she hadn't gotten two separate dog-sitting offers from Erin's family. No, she insisted on bringing Doppler, *because Erin missed him,* and crammed him into a tiny kennel under her airplane seat. The truth was that Allie needed him. She'd been relying on his calming energy ever since *that night.*

It didn't hurt that the little dog was a great traveling companion. He'd slept through the entire flight and enjoyed riding up front in the rental car from the airport. The trip had been smooth, until now. Now he was gone, lost somewhere in the woods near Quantico's FBI training facility.

She rubbed her throbbing temple. It was as if the signals were mixed up. She thought about the dog, and up popped thoughts of Erin. She couldn't seem to focus. Doppler wasn't in danger or she'd surely have felt it by now. No, the Chihuahua who thought he was a bloodhound was probably happily following some rabbit trail back to Minnesota. What was she going to do?

She imagined his wagging tail, his soft ears, and closed her eyes. She inhaled as if she were in yoga class and rotated toward the tattling squirrel. *Of course.*

She opened her eyes and Erin materialized from the woods like a sexy apparition, with the dog's legs dangling over her bandaged forearm.

"Looking for something, Miss Brody?" Erin wore the adorable grin she reserved only for her.

"You found him!" She rushed into her arms and squeezed the Chihuahua between them until he grunted. It had only been a few months but Erin seemed different. She stepped back and looked at the bandages. "You're hurt."

"It's nothing, only scraped a bit. I'll be fine."

"We waited. I let Doppler go for a walk and... How did you find us?"

Erin's grin faded. "I'm sorry, Baby. Our training exercise went late." She shrugged and the corner of her eye twitched. "A couple of guys from class dropped me off at our meeting spot on their way to town. The rental car was here and I knew you couldn't be far. You told me you were bringing the dog, so I followed the sound of the nearest yakking squirrel."

That made sense. Why hadn't Allie realized it was that simple? She'd had to focus her intuition to figure out where the dog had gone.

"Let's go for dinner. The food's not horrible, but I'm so tired of the same sauce on everything. I know a good pub where we can get a mouthwatering bacon burger and home cut fries. And beer. I need a beer." Erin led the way back to the car.

"I'm glad you came," she said, once they'd turned back to town. "I've been super busy, but I earned weekends off since I aced my PT test and I wanted to at least take one night off." She reached over and took Allie's hand in hers. "I booked us a room."

A warm flush crept up Allie's cheeks. They'd been together for years, but suddenly it seemed like a reversal of their first real date. Back then, Allie had been confidently mischievous while Erin betrayed her nervousness with pink cheeks and an adorable stammer. Now the tables were turned, with Erin the confident one, and Allie's uncertainty laid bare.

"How's Z-man? Gina? L'il baby Z?"

"Good, good, a handful of toddler energy. That kid can empty all our cupboards in two minutes flat." She smiled. "He's irresistibly adorable."

"I'm betting that our godson gets away with everything." Erin laughed. "I'm starving. I don't think I can wait until dinner. Do you have any treats that aren't for Doppler?" She unzipped Allie's bag, cocked her head and pulled out the envelope. Her eyes widened at the return address. "What's this?"

Allie braked and eased the car to the side of the road. She couldn't concentrate on driving when something this big needed to be discussed. "It came in the mail after you left." The skin on her forehead suddenly seemed too tight. "It's from *her.*"

Erin looked at Allie, looked at the envelope, and reached inside to pull out the single sheet of folded paper. Doppler whined on her lap but she stared at the letters long and hard before she spoke. "Lily's coming back? What the hell does that mean?"

"I don't know," Allie croaked. She swallowed hard and got out of the car, bending to hold her knees. Blood and oil swirled in her memory. It transformed into smoke. Smoke filling her lungs, consuming her oxygen. "No!" She coughed, as if she could expel it all and breathe again.

Erin was already beside her, concern puckering her brows. "You're still not sleeping, are you? Are the nightmares back?"

"It's not the nightmares. I just can't sleep, and I don't trust myself."

"What do you mean?"

"I guess, and then I second-guess. I'm so afraid to be wrong, I can never make a decision. It's driving me nuts." Allie swept her hair back from her face. Where was her ponytail elastic? Couldn't she remember even the little things? "I'm sorry, I didn't want to ruin our one weekend together by talking about *her,* but I'm worried sick. Does this mean she'll be out early?"

"It can't be. They promised to let us know her release date, and Z-man's keeping an ear to the ground for any info. Don't worry, she's blowing smoke."

Allie coughed again. Of all the words Erin could have chosen, why had she used that one? As sure as the itch that was spreading from her gut, she knew Lily meant what she'd written. Somehow, she was getting out and she was headed back to Morley Falls.

Erin squeezed her elbow. "Come on. Let's get some dinner and relax tonight. When I'm studying tomorrow, you can take the official

Quantico FBI family tour. That'll take your mind off things. You can buy little FBI T-shirts for the kids at the gift shop. *As if* you need to bribe them to love you more."

"Well..." Her spirits lifted with the tug at the corner of her mouth. Kids always made her feel better. "The cat could use a new outfit for the next Auntie Allie sleepover party..."

Erin shook her head. "That poor cat." Her twin nieces and nephew often begged to stay over with *Auntie Allie*. While Sophie and Victoria doted on Wrong-Way Rachel, and dressed the reluctant cat like a fairy princess, Jimmy loved the dog best. He'd been the one to name the Chihuahua Doppler, and took dog-sitting responsibilities seriously.

Allie shrugged. "Oh, don't worry about Rachel. She loves every single minute of attention. Maybe I'll pick up a tiny FBI vest for the dog too." She patted him when his ears perked up.

"That's the spirit, Baby. Let's go get a burger. I'm starving."

The scent of smoke embedded in her memory wafted through her thoughts. She clenched her teeth and put the car back into gear. Lily wasn't getting out, not for a while.

CHAPTER THREE

Winnipeg Youth Detention Center

"Get the fuck outta my chair." The fat-ass loser stares down at me, hands on her hips. Another new kid's trying to prove herself but she's picked the wrong person.

Kiss my ass. I curl my lip but keep my eyes on the TV.

She moves to block my view. "Get out." Her fat fists clench into meatballs.

I stare up into huge black pupils that disappear into dark irises. Her eyelid flinches when she meets my glare and the skin on her neck goes pink. One of her fists rises and I narrow my eyes.

"Angel, no!" Shonda, the skinny meth-head, buzzes past and takes fat-ass with her. There's a hiss of whispered conversation and then silence. Angel bends to peer under the corner of the shirt sleeve Shonda peels aside. She shoots an alarmed look back at me and they both shuffle away.

That's right, Shonda, you twitchy bitch. Tell her. Tell her what I did to you when you tried to push me around. Did you ever dig the tip of that sharpened pencil out of your skin? I bet you sleep with one eye open now.

Both hands behind my head, I weave my fingers together. I am the bad-ass panther. Kids in here are smart enough to understand. No one messes with me. No matter whose turn it is, everyone knows I pick what we watch on TV, and right now it's a show where they DNA test guys to find out if they're the daddy. Those people are so messed up that it's entertaining.

Who cares, unless yours is rich and can buy you stuff? Mine isn't. I couldn't care less if I ever see him again, and my mom's dead so there's no one to tell me what to do.

"Lily Schmidt, come with me."

Sheisse. Well, no one except the workers in the secure custody unit. I roll my eyes. It's the middle of my show. He motions me to follow him and the door hasn't even closed behind me when someone steals my chair.

"I've been talking with your counselor, Lily." This guy has been here less than a month and he's already trying to ruin my world. I examine his name tag where it never gives a last name, just AHMED.

"We'd like you to take a more active role in your rehabilitation."

Twitchy Shonda didn't rat me out. I make my face do the happy thing.

"The librarian has consented to let you come in for a couple of hours a day and help out."

Double schiesse. My days of invisibility are over. That means no more daytime TV. "The library?" Then I remember checking that little ticky-box on the form when I first came. I chose the jobs that seemed easiest. I didn't imagine they'd ever happen, but I sure as hell didn't want to work in the kitchen scraping food off someone else's plate. "What do I do, Ahmed?" I say his name like a sneeze and he tilts his head, but he'll give me points for trying.

"Put books away, help out with odd jobs, whatever Mr. Angotti needs." He fake-smiles back at me. "It will be good for you." His smile fades and he shrugs. "It never looks bad on a Day Pass request."

"Okay, Ahmed. That sounds great." Actually, it sounds like slave labor. "When?"

"You can start tomorrow morning. Oh-nine-hundred."

"Perfect. See you tomorrow, Ahmed." *Fuck.* Tomorrow's the grand finale of the *Who's Your Daddy* show. I pull my lips back from my teeth and hope it looks right. He takes a half-step back and I head off toward my bunk. I don't want to watch the rest of this episode if I have to miss the end. My life is ruined. I am so done with this place.

The next morning, Ahmed herds me and another kid down the hall right after breakfast. Ugh, greasy eggs and toast are still swimming in my gut, and I didn't have time to finish my coffee. The only good part was when Angel, the fat-ass new girl, left her bowl unattended and I poured a mound of salt in her cereal.

Why do I have to go so goddamn early? There is no way this is gonna be fun. The other kid being herded happens to be the one girl in this place who has managed to avoid me the whole time she's been here. She's smart, keeps her head down, and stays off the radar. In another life, maybe she could have been my new minion.

Ahmed scoots her into the janitor's cubby where Smelly Joe is waiting. She'll be mopping floors with him all day, and holding her nose. I almost pity her. Almost.

Down to the main floor and through another set of security doors is the library. Mr. Angotti is writing on the white board.

Today's Schedule:
Pool Party 1:00. Bring your own water wings.
Bus to Disneyland 5 p.m. All ducks half price.

Ahmed points at it and slaps his knee. He takes me by the elbow and I wish I could crush his fingers with a hammer. "A new helper for you, sir."

The jokes were so stupid that I can't even pretend to smile. I keep my eyes on my shoes so he'll think I'm shy. This sucks.

Mr. Angotti looks me up and down as soon as Ahmed leaves. "Do you know the Dewey Decimal System?"

"Is this a math quiz? Nobody told me to study." *What the hell?* Shelve books, do easy crap, that's what Ahmed said.

The librarian squints one eye. "It's the numeric system we use to file books." He waggles a finger at me and then puts his hands on his belly and laughs like Santa Claus. "You're funny. We're going to get along great."

For the first time, I notice that behind him is a single glass door marked *Emergency Exit.* Outside is a field surrounded by a puny eight-foot chain link fence, and no razor wire. A baby could climb that.

"Come," Santa says. "Let me show you how the Dewey Decimal System works."

"I'm so glad to be here." I meet his eyes and he seems pleased that I'm getting over my shyness. It's not a lie. I *am* glad to be here, because now I see a way out. As soon as I'm free, I'm going back to Morley Falls. I'm going home.

An hour later, I'm halfway through re-shelving a cart of books when one catches my eye. Wilderness Survival. On the cover is a picture of a campfire and a shelter made of branches. The title of the book is printed with raised letters and the picture looks three dimensional. I can almost feel the heat on my fingertips when I trace the shapes.

My heart pounds in my ears, and I flip through the pages for more pictures. Is this what Twitchy Shonda feels like when she wants her fix? I find the chapter on lighting fires without matches, and my heart slows to normal. It's all black and white drawings, and they're too neat. I take out my pencil and draw jagged lines and shooting sparks until my heart speeds up again. I'd give my right nipple for a lighter and a can of gasoline right now. No, I'd give Shonda's right nipple. A gurgle of excitement wiggles up from my belly.

I don't see him until he's right in my face, leering like he's at a strip-joint. "Are you having a sexual experience with that book?" He's tall, taller than Santa, and his brown eyes shine like marbles. We hardly ever cross paths with anyone from the boys wing without a worker around.

I slam the book shut but the pages are still rippled from my sweaty hand. "What the fuck are you lookin' at?"

"You don't look so scary up close." The dark hairs on his upper lip curve when he smiles, almost like a real mustache. "Did you really kill someone?"

I count off five or six fingers. "More than you'll ever know, so get outta my face."

He pulls a book off the shelf and opens it wide. My jaw drops at the photo of a firefighter battling a blazing inferno. In color.

He leans against the shelf to watch me. Blood races through my veins and he leans closer. I don't even care that his breath stinks of coffee. If he had a match… "Yes, this is Santa's workshop. You can have everything you want, but you have to know how to find it."

"You call him Santa?"

"Everyone does, obviously." He peeps at Mr. Angotti's desk between books on the shelf. Santa's white-haired head bobs as he hums.

I cover a snort with my fingers and he reaches out to grab my hand. Breath freezes in my lungs until I realize he's given me something. A piece of folded paper. It's soggy.

"You're welcome." He backs away.

Gross. "What the fuck?" Just when I thought he wasn't an asshole. I drop it on the floor between us but he ducks to pick it up.

"No, silly." He unfolds the paper and shows me a white puddle in the middle. "Liquid correction fluid, from Santa's desk." I still don't get it until he cups his hand around it and inhales. Pure bliss glazes his shiny eyes. "Why else would anyone wanna work here?"

"Oh," is all I can manage. I put away the fire book, but I've committed its location to memory. "I need to finish."

"No, you don't. Santa never checks up on us. That's why this is the best job here." He hands me the soggy paper again. "Do it."

"Fuck that. I'd rather have a beer."

"This is the closest you'll get to that in here." He juts out his chin.

What could it hurt? It might even make my day suck less. I do what he did. It smells weird, and it stings. Pain scours my sinuses and enters my brain, but with it comes the need to giggle. I clap my hand over my mouth and saliva spills between my fingers. The numbers on the books weave in and out.

"Shh." He coughs in his throat.

"Again." I hold my nose over it and inhale even deeper until he pulls it away.

"Take it easy. You're gonna be sick."

I don't care. My feet are suddenly on backwards and my neck is made of spaghetti. It's amazing. "You got a name, big guy?" It's like I'm in a movie and I'm asking him out on a date. I'm not even sure what to do with boys.

He slides his hand under my shirt so I grab his crotch. We stare at each other for an unflinching moment before he removes his hand and I release his balls.

"Well played," he whispers.

"Fuck, yeah."

"Shh. Santa's coming." When he grabs my shoulder, I don't even want to punch him.

Then it hits me. The headache that threatened me the first time I inhaled. This time it crashes behind my eyes and I want to barf. I'm bent double, looking at my ankles when Santa's shoes appear in front of me. Funny, I thought they'd be black boots. With shiny buckles. "Buckles!"

"What's going on?" Santa does not sound impressed.

"I don't know, Mr. Angotti. I found her like this. I think she's trying to say something about a headache. Maybe she's having a migraine attack. My mom gets those for no reason at all, and they can be terrible."

Santa's shoes, which are not black boots with shiny buckles, shift to the right and his hands slide under my arms. He sits me on the carpet and I slump with my hands over my eyes. I honestly do have a headache now.

"Stay with her while I call the nurse," Santa tells the nameless boy, and he squats beside me.

My face is on the floor, drooling like a garden slug in the dirt, when the nurse comes. She's brought a wheelchair and thank God I don't have to walk because my legs are mush.

The boy leans over when they load me into it. "T, my name's T," he whispers into my ear before she wheels me past the emergency exit. Even though the door is closed, I can smell the freshly mowed grass and dandelions from here. They smell like home.

This boy is nothing like anyone I've known. Not like my grandfather, or my father, the useless prick. If he was stupid enough to 'fess up for stuff he never did, he deserved to go to jail. He could have ratted me out, but I knew he wouldn't. Not his only child.

No, T is a whole different animal. He saw the real me and he understands what I want. I can use a guy like that, and now I have a plan to get out.

Is T for Tom, or Tyson or Travis? Probably T for trouble. I might like that guy.

CHAPTER FOUR

"Well, Mr. van Gogh, you're finally legit." Parked side-by-side, the lawyer handed a card out his window to Derek Peterson, who snatched it from his manicured fingers. The smaller man drew back, as if frightened of losing them.

"I told you, don't call me that. If you do it again, I'll shoot you between your little piggy eyes," Derek snarled.

The lawyer smiled nervously and adjusted himself in his seat. "Um, about that problem we discussed…"

"Your wife." Derek shoved the P.I. license into his wallet. "I'll have something truly salacious for you by Monday." He toed an empty vodka bottle under the seat. He meant it. He'd do it as soon as he found the time.

"B-but court is in two days. She's going to make me pay." His last syllable rose an octave.

"Don't whine, Dick. You cheated on her first."

"I don't want her to take my stocks, the lake house, my c-car. That's half of *everything*." The barrister's face reddened. "And m-my name is Richard. Why can you…"

"I'll call ya." Derek hit the window switch. "Dick." He shook his head. Pathetic. So what if the pussy lawyer had to play by the rules and give his wife half of everything in the divorce? That was only fair. Derek would never try to cheat a woman out of what was rightfully hers. He'd once been a great cop and was still a standup guy, not like he'd had a choice when it had come down to it. His ex-wife had sold everything and divorced him as soon as he'd stepped foot in prison.

He pressed his foot to the gas, and the car's tires chirped. The only thing he really missed was his Mustang. This economy rental was a gutless piece of crap.

He dialed his contact at the police station and left another message. How long did it take to check a license plate, for frig's sake? With his P.I. creds fresh off the printer, he couldn't wait for his business to take off so he could bill some real clients.

First order of business was to get the lawyer off his back. Derek would get what the man wanted and jettison him. He didn't wield enough power to be of much use anyhow. His buddy at the police station was more promising. Soon they would both be cashing big paychecks.

He took another drive by the lawyer's residence but the cheating wife's silver Porsche was absent. She wasn't going to make it easy by taking her boyfriend home, was she?

Derek rolled the empty vodka bottle from under the seat and unscrewed the cap. The half-mouthful of residual liquid trickled down his throat, but left him trembling for more. He almost regretted giving his last twenty dollar bill to the motel manager, but the man had not given him up to the rental company goons when they came to collect their car, so that deserved a reward. If he could hold out a little longer, there'd be clients, and he'd be rolling in cash. Yeah.

He stared at his hands on the steering wheel until his knuckles turned white, and nearly leapt on his phone when it buzzed.

"Hey Derek. I got what you asked for." Officer Ernie Jenssen, his old police buddy, wanted to meet.

He hit the speakerphone and rolled down his window for extra background noise. "Ah, um. I'm working a case. Really busy." He straightened his fingers and then clenched his hands into fists.

"I'm off duty in an hour and I won't have time until tomorrow. If you want…"

"All right, I'll put everything on hold for you, buddy," Derek lied. "Meet me by the train bridge." Ernie would believe anything his old training officer told him, wouldn't he?

He chomped down a mouthful of breath mints and ran a hand through his greasy hair. He didn't want to look like he'd been sleeping in his car, which he had to admit, he sometimes did. Ten minutes later, he nosed his car alongside a marked patrol cruiser in a back alley.

"Hey Ernie, how's it hangin'?" Derek quipped when the young officer rolled down his window. He forced a smile. *Relax, you're trying too hard.*

"Low. It's hangin' low." He glanced in his rear-view mirror.

"Don't worry. There's no one around." Derek leaned out to take the papers from him.

"Can you hear out of that ear, boss?" Ernie's eyes fixed on the mass of scar tissue that used to be a nicely-shaped ear.

"Yuh," Derek grunted. At least he hadn't called him fuckin' Vincent van Gogh.

Ernie cleared his throat. "So, are those the records you wanted?"

"Damn straight. This is perfect." After two weeks of tailing the lawyer's wife, he'd come across the boyfriend's car, hiding behind her silver Porsche at a local dining spot. What he'd needed from Ernie was a name and address.

"Registered owner of that car is a guy named Randolph Keller." He squinted at Derek. "Know him?"

"Nope." He damn well *did* know who that guy was, and Dick would not be happy to hear that his wife had been screwing his business partner. The same guy who was being so helpful with his divorce. Now all he needed was photo evidence. He looked up into Ernie's questioning eyes.

"Next time buddy," he said. "I'll pay you what I promised next time."

The skin around Ernie's eyes tightened.

"Swear to God, I'll throw in a little extra. You and me, buddy. This could turn into a good thing."

Ernie gave his head a half-shake. "I'm not so sure. I kind of thought this was a one-time thing, Lieuten... uh, Derek. Kind of like a personal favor."

Derek grinned. His student still saw him as teacher. That would work in his best interest. "Don't worry, it's little stuff. And nothing you don't want to do." The lies slid off his tongue as smoothly as they had when he was still on the job. "Hey, I was thinking, buddy. I left my wallet at home. Would you lend your old boss a couple of bucks? A twenty would do."

Ernie hesitated and then reached for his wallet. He drew out a bill.

"Or fifty, fifty would be better."

Ernie frowned, but fished out a couple more bills.

"Son, you're a saint. I'll have a nice bonus for you next time." He watched the police cruiser drive down the alley and exit onto the main street before he tucked the money behind his shiny new P.I. license. This partnership with Ernie would work out fine.

Derek turned off the engine, got out and locked the door. The only thing of value he owned was a digital SLR camera and a couple of fast lenses. He couldn't risk losing them now. He'd ordered the equipment with his credit card right before they'd canceled it.

He'd pay their overdue bills. He'd pay everyone as soon as those checks rolled in. He'd get his Mustang back, and he'd get his family back. He'd be happier than ever. Right now, he needed to find Tiffany, the love of his life and Lily's doting mother, and this was the last place she might have been.

He opened the back gate to a dilapidated townhouse and rapped on the screen door. Inside, a small dog broke into frenzied barking and a middle-aged woman cracked the door open enough to peer at him. The dog bounced at the opening, all teeth and bluster.

"I'm not buying any." She closed the door.

He knocked harder.

She wrenched it open, glaring at him from a prematurely wrinkled face. Ash dangled from her cigarette, smoked to its filter and pinched between stained fingers. "I told you…"

He wedged his shoe in the door so she couldn't slam it in his face again. "Tiffany Schmidt. Early twenties. Beautiful. Had a young daughter. Ring a bell?"

The woman's yellowed eyes widened. She clucked her tongue and the dog sat obediently at her feet. "I remember her. She lived next-door. Haven't seen her for years. She came back to visit me once, said she moved in with her father. Her and… the little girl."

"She came back? What did she say? Did she tell you where she was going?" Derek leaned forward. He wanted to hear every word.

"You're missing an ear!" She took a step back.

"Yes, I know," he growled. "Can we get back on track?"

The woman hesitated, as if unsure if she should stay or flee. "Tiffany came to tell me she was getting married, finally found her prince, I guess." She twisted her mouth. "That rock on her finger was puny, if you ask me."

Derek's cheek twitched.

She tapped her ring finger to emphasize her point, and the ash dangling from her cigarette broke free. He followed it with his eyes until it landed on her slipper.

That had been all he could afford. He'd planned to get her a better one, as soon as he finished paying for that damned new boat. There was always something back then, but he'd lost it all to his wife anyways. He should have married Tiffany in the first place.

"She was a pretty girl. I told her she could have done better, but she insisted he was *the one*. I guess he wasn't, because I haven't seen her since." She leaned forward and whispered. "The ladies at bingo said she up and ran off one day, left her child behind. It must have been because of her *problem*."

"The drugs." No sense beating around the bush.

"Yeah, she had a real hard time staying away from that stuff. She'd be gone for days and was always looking for someone to take care of the girl. She kind of wore out her welcome, and Mitsy never liked her, did you Mitsy?" She bent to pat the mop-haired dog. "Sometimes she'd get me to babysit, and the dog would hide the entire time. If my dog doesn't like someone... well, you know."

She peeked out the door as if to check on eavesdroppers. "I heard that the fellow three doors down had a cat go missing and blamed the girl. Wilsons' cat disappeared too." She puckered her bottom lip. "And Ramona in 5A said she caught her going through things in her bedroom. Imagine that, a thieving little girl."

"You're wrong!" Derek exploded. "Lily would never—" He stopped mid-sentence, and tweaked his anger into what he hoped was a look of interest.

"Lily, you're right. That was the girl's name, pale as a ghost, no respect for her elders, always playing with matches."

Derek couldn't stomach any more gossip, and this was going nowhere. Tiffany had not been seen, or heard from, since the day he'd proposed. Had she really panicked and run off? Who could disappear without a trace? He eased his foot out and stepped back to let the screen door swing shut. "Thank you for your time."

Back in the car, he slouched behind the wheel. His guts curdled like sour milk and his nerves jangled. He put the car into gear and headed for the nearest corner store. Beer might do the trick.

At Gina's Stop 'N Go, he parked beneath the new illuminated fish sign. Since the fire, it had been rebuilt better than before. You could get anything you wanted, from snacks to headache remedies to live bait or even a couple of beers for the road. Since high school, he and Gina had never seen eye-to-eye, but he didn't care about that right now. Right now, he needed a drink to calm his trembling hands.

"Hey, Derek," Gina greeted him as he strode past. "Nice weather we're having, eh?"

He grabbed a case of Budweiser from the cooler and returned to the counter before responding. "Yup."

"How's the P.I. business?" She rang up his purchase.

"Great. Really busy." Gossip traveled faster in Morley Falls than in prison. He'd barely gotten his license and it was all over town. He handed her one of the twenties he'd borrowed from Ernie. If everyone knew everything, why the hell hadn't anyone heard about Tiffany?

Gina plucked two chicken kebabs from under the warming hood. She wrapped them in foil and tucked them into the bag. "I've got this free promo going on."

When was the last time he'd actually eaten anything? "Fine. I'll take 'em off your hands if you're givin' 'em away."

"We don't want them to go bad." Gina's voice was gentle.

He gave her a second glance. Even with her tattoo, and the hard edge of her jaw, she seemed softer somehow. The curves of her body were comfortable, like a man could fold his arms around her and— what the hell was he thinking? This was Gina. The fierce bitch who'd stood up to him in high school. Wouldn't let him get near sweet little Erin Ericsson. He'd never forgive either of them.

His eyes took one last sweep of Gina's face, the straight line of her nose, the curve of her mouth and the smooth skin at her throat. He had to admit that Gina had changed since the fire. Her rough edges had been polished smooth.

"No, we can't have that." He lifted a shoulder and took the bag when she held it out. He'd always thought Officer Chris Zimmerman had sold out when he'd married tough Gina. Maybe Z-man wasn't such a loser after all.

Derek popped the tab on a beer and had his first sip before he reached the car. He sat behind the wheel and downed it in a few more gulps. He opened a second can and put the car into gear. His hands would stop trembling soon. *Goddammit.*

The sun had set by the time Derek reached the row of luxury condos near the river. He backed into a concealed spot across the street and attached the telephoto lens to his camera. How long would it take for Randolph Keller to come home? It was like fishing.

A half hour later, there was a tug on the line when Keller's red Corvette eased into the garage. Minutes after that, the silver Porsche pulled into the driveway. The fish was on the hook. Dick's wife skipped up the steps and inserted a key. The affair had been going on for a while if she had her own key to the place. All he needed to do now was to expertly reel in this fish.

The kitchen light went on, then the back deck. Drinks on the patio, they were going to make it easy for him. Derek got out of his car and found a trail along the river with a good view.

There they were, acting like a couple of newlyweds. Dick was going to freak out. His wife was an exhibitionist. It's a wonder she'd never been caught before now. Derek's camera snapped multiple frames as she straddled Keller on the deck chair, red wine spilling from her glass. Her laughter carried over the gurgling of the river. If that was his wife, he'd want to squeeze the life from her. He put down the camera and took out his cell phone.

Dick answered on the first ring. "Do you have what I need?" He sounded so desperate that Derek wanted to slap him.

"I got more than you need." He said through clenched teeth. "Listen, I know you're gonna piss yourself when you see who she's with."

Dick groaned.

"I'll make you a time limited offer on this, man-to-man. If this was my wife, I'd want to make her pay. For an extra five grand, I'll kick the crap out of this guy for you."

The phone was silent.

"Don't worry, nothing will lead back to you. Listen, I'll do it for twenty-five hundred."

"I-I don't think that's a good idea. Just what we agreed, the photos I already paid you for." Dick's voice wavered.

"Well, buddy. My price went up. Considering who I'm lookin' at screwing your wife right now, you're going to pay me another five grand and you'll thank me for it when you don't give her a dime." Derek disconnected. *What a pussy.*

He took a few more photos. With the patio lights casting shadows across the couple, the images were as good as the ones he'd seen in an art show once. He'd have another look at them once he got back to his car. And he'd have another beer.

Derek rubbed bleary eyes and tore off his sweat-soaked jacket. Through the windshield, the town spread out before him from his vantage point at the top of the hill. He took a mouthful of vodka from a half-empty bottle and swished out the foul taste in his mouth before swallowing. His teeth were covered in moss. When he set the bottle down, it clinked against the empty one from the day before. When had he bought more? And where was his beer?

He held up his hand and examined torn, bloody knuckles. There was a fuzzy memory, or was it a dream, of shooting through his open car window. A fox, or something. He checked his shoulder holster. Empty.

Frantic, he scrabbled with raw fingers under the seat. Nothing. He picked up his jacket and froze at the obvious spatters of blood across the front. Had he gotten into a bar fight? What had he done last night?

Sure, he'd had blackouts before, but not like this. What if he had gone back to the condo? Derek put his head in his hands. Fragments of memory sank out of sight. Where was his pistol? He jumped out and checked the trunk, sighing when he popped the lid on his camera case and found it nestled safely in its foam cocoon. At least he hadn't been stupid enough to pawn the one thing he really needed.

Back behind the wheel, he opened the glove compartment and was immensely relieved to find his gun. He gripped it in his hand like an old friend, but his blood ran cold when he ejected the magazine. Two cartridges were missing. Two shots fired. So it hadn't been a dream. A memory then. Had he hit the fox?

On his knees, he searched every inch of the interior for the expelled brass. Sweat dripped from his temples and drenched the neck of his shirt. If he'd fired his pistol from the car, why couldn't he find the empty cartridges?

His phone buzzed in his jacket pocket and he cleared his throat before answering. "Peterson Investigations."

"I received your emails from last night." Dick's voice was tense, as if he spoke through a tightly clenched jaw.

What a helluva blackout if he couldn't even remember emailing the lawyer. "Uh huh," he muttered.

"The photos were... My own partner! And my wife!" Dick sounded mad enough to act like a man for once. "I called Keller, that bastard, to come in for an emergency meeting."

Derek relaxed. Keller was fine. It had only been a fox.

"He's in for the surprise of his life. I've had the accountant go through the financials this morning. All this time, Keller's been funneling off cash to spend on *her*. Tens of thousands. She's not getting a dime out of me. And he'll be lucky if he's not disbarred for embezzlement."

"Glad to hear it. My bill is in the mail." Derek disconnected. Somehow, he'd pulled it off. Even in a drunken blackout, he could get the job done. He was that good.

He started the engine and drove back to his motel. With an extra five thousand coming in, he'd be able to get the manager off his back. Hell, he'd even get up to date on the rental car before they managed to reclaim it one of these days. Things were looking up.

Ernie pulled him over as soon as he hit the main road, and Derek swore when he saw the red and blue lights flash in his rear-view mirror. He kicked the liquor bottles under the seat and stuffed the bloody jacket after them.

"Rough night, Lieutenant?" Ernie leaned down and inhaled the boozy odor wafting through the window.

"I'm headed home, buddy. Are you coming off night-shift?" Derek tucked his bloody knuckles out of sight.

"Yeah, sorry to create such a production, but I didn't want the other guys to get the wrong idea if they saw us together." He let the rest hang.

Derek's gut churned. By wrong idea, Ernie meant he didn't want to be viewed as conspiring with the disgraced ex-cop. "No problem, buddy. Do what you gotta do." He snorted when Ernie's cheeks flared pink.

"We had a helluva night, and I wanted to see if I could get your take on it. Well, since you did time in the same prison." Ernie shifted his weight.

"What are you talking about?"

"You haven't heard." He bent to look him in the eye. "We had a murder last night."

Derek was light-headed with confusion. A murder in Morley Falls was a rare occurrence and a big deal for the local department. "Who?"

"A guy named Ethan Lewis was shot in his room at the Sunset Motel. Whoever did it, beat his face to a pulp first. Someone really must have hated him. Word is that Lewis was in Stillwater Prison the same time as you. Evil little dude got out a week ago. Walked with a limp. Did you know him?"

Ethan Lewis, aka Badger. "Nope, can't say as I did." Derek had given him that limp in prison when a guard had turned his back one day. The ex-cop had no choice but to disable the other inmate when he'd attacked him. Sure, they'd had their differences, but he never imagined that Badger would head back here. Now he was dead.

"That's weird." Ernie cocked his head. "Our local records show you arrested him for aggravated battery. Officer Ericsson backed you up on that call."

Derek avoided eye contact. Friggin' Erin Ericsson. The little bitch who'd sent him to prison. The super cop who left Morley Falls PD to join the FBI. His anger burned at the mention of her name.

"You two sent him down for quite a few years. I would have thought he'd make his presence known when you were in there."

He shrugged. "I arrested so many dirtbags, I guess he wasn't memorable."

"Okay, then." Ernie straightened. "There's cash in it if you hear anything on the street. This thing we got going can work both ways, right?"

"Alrighty." Derek got it. Ernie was trying to work him the same way he worked Ernie. And why was Erin Ericsson's career golden when his had crumbled before his eyes?

He sat in his car and stared at his torn knuckles long after Ernie was gone. His hands were shaking again. Back in his shoulder holster, the pistol, minus two rounds, weighed heavy. He reached under the seat for the rest of the vodka.

CHAPTER FIVE

"Wow, you are hungry." Allie pushed her plate toward her girlfriend, who polished off the rest of her fries. When had she started ordering junk food? What she'd really wanted was a salad. She took the lighter from her bag and clicked it. The spark flared and died. A little ripple of excitement wriggled down her spine. She did it again.

"Our physical training schedule is grueling," Erin said. "Today was ground-fighting. Davis forgot to take off his ring and cut open Garrett's nose. It was a good punch too. Never thought he had it in him." She nodded at a pair of men in black polo shirts two tables over. One of them sported a white bandage across the bridge of his nose. "Guys from my class," she mumbled between mouthfuls. "Garrett, the guy with the busted nose, passed his PT exam on the first try too. He could have weekends off like me, but everyone spends most of it studying. There are so many things to remember in Fundamentals of Law. Did you realize that every state's penal code is unique? That makes it tricky."

Allie focused on the flame spurting from the lighter. An ache gnawed at her subconscious. She rolled her thumb over the spark wheel, reveling in the feel of its rough edge against her skin. Oily smoke filled her nostrils.

"Allie?" Erin was staring at her.

"Um hmm?" She put the lighter down.

"What are you doing?"

Allie looked down at the plastic lighter on the table. She'd been playing with it at the gas station but hadn't realized she'd actually bought it, and she didn't remember taking it out of her bag just now. How could she not remember? Cold sweat prickled the back of her neck.

One of the men at the other table got up and approached them. He nodded to Allie before addressing Erin. "Sorry to intrude."

"What's up, Davis?" Her smile was strained.

He ducked his head in deference before he spoke. "I'm sorry about today, Erin. I should have, well, I have a lot to learn."

"We both made mistakes. Let's be glad it wasn't for real."

"Yeah, not for real." His eyes traveled to the bandages on her wrists. "Um, we wanted to talk to you about something." He stole a glance over his shoulder at Garrett who waved encouragement. "We've run into some trouble qualifying at the shooting range, and we've noticed that you are a pretty good shot."

Erin gave a curt nod.

"But uh, you're not doing so great in law."

"Yeah, I'm totally bombing that class." Erin pushed her plate away. "I'm studying, really. It's just so much."

"That's where we come in." Garrett got to his feet and joined Davis at their table. "We've developed an effective study strategy. If we work together, you can help us pass firearms, and we'll help you pass law."

Erin's eyebrows shot up.

"No pressure or anything." Davis glanced sideways at Allie. "If you don't have the time…"

"That's a great idea." Erin stood to shake their hands. "I'll meet you at the range first thing tomorrow morning." They exited and Erin sat back down, her frenetic mood buffeting Allie with sheer energy. "I might pass after all."

"Why was he apologizing?" Allie's intuition hadn't been wrong. Something *had* happened when she'd been waiting. And how much coffee had Erin consumed today? She was vibrating like an out of gamut color on a TV screen. It was giving her a headache.

"He messed up, I messed up, the role players messed up. One of them actually quit afterward. It wasn't the best day." Her clear blue eyes met Allie's. "You don't want to sit here and talk all night do you?"

"Not even a little bit." She'd come for personal time. A refill on all the hugs she'd been missing and some long-awaited intimacy.

Erin gulped her beer and set the mug on the table. "Ready."

"The dog is probably tearing up the motel room by now." Allie handed her credit card to the waiter.

"You're awfully serious for a girl who's flown halfway across the country for some naked time." Erin grinned. "Where's my smart-ass girlfriend?"

She flinched. There hadn't seemed to be much to laugh about lately. It wasn't only their separation. It was something more. Her phone rang.

Erin plucked it off the table when she saw the call display. "Z-man! How did you find me?" She greeted her former crew-mate Officer Chris Zimmerman.

Allie got up from the table, eyes on the lighter. She turned away, hesitated, and then turned back. While Erin was distracted by the phone call, she snatched up the lighter and stuffed it into her bag.

"How's Gina and Li'l Z?" Erin followed her out to the parking lot, phone still pressed to her ear. "Do you have any suspects?" She tugged on Allie's jacket sleeve and whispered, "There's been a murder. I think he wants me to help him solve it." After a moment, she frowned and handed over the phone. "Z-man wants to talk to *you.*"

Allie gave her the car keys and got into the passenger side. "Hello Chris."

"Hi Sweetie, my favorite psychic, best godmom ever."

She squinted at a road sign in the distance but couldn't quite make out what the letters spelled. "What can I do for you today?"

"I need your insight on this case." He didn't give her a moment's pause before he rattled off the details. "Ex-con gets whacked in a motel room, two bullets in the chest and a face like hamburger."

Allie groaned. Erin glanced over and turned the car onto the highway.

Zimmerman immediately apologized. "Sorry about that. I meant he'd been struck in the face many times with a blunt object."

"That mental image is not any better." Allie's greasy dinner churned in her stomach. A burger and fries. What had she been thinking? Why hadn't she ordered the salmon?

"Okay, I'll skip the rest of the crime scene details. Here's the thing. Derek Peterson's name was written on a piece of paper in the dead man's pocket. His name and a time. Possibly a time for them to meet."

"Derek Peterson?" she repeated, and Erin's eyes widened.

"Well, not his *real* name. His prison nickname. The paper said *van Gogh*. Everyone in Stillwater Prison called him that, since he lost his ear and all. Word is the dead guy was responsible. So, did Derek do it?"

Allie closed her eyes. This was not the way her gift of intuition worked. After all they'd been through, he should know better. "I don't have a crystal ball."

He sighed. "I guess not. Well, maybe you can keep the channels open, or fine tune your space signals, or something, and call me if the answer somehow comes to you."

"You'll be the first to know if the skies open up and I'm struck with the knowledge like a bolt of lightning."

"That could happen?"

She couldn't tell if he was serious, or kidding her back. "I'm on a date with my sweetheart, whom I haven't seen in months. Say hello to Gina, and let her know my plane lands at five on Sunday. Goodbye, Chris."

"Right, one of us will be there." He hung up.

Erin tapped her fingers on the steering wheel. "So…" She wanted every gritty detail but there wasn't much to tell.

"Derek Peterson's name came up in the murder of a guy he knew in prison. The guy who ripped off his ear."

"Derek?" Erin gaped at her. "Murder?"

"Yes, and Chris wants me to wave my magic wand and solve it for him, but I don't have a clue."

"I can't believe…" Erin's finger tapping became drumming. "This is dangerous stuff to get you involved in. Too dangerous."

"Honey, please stop that noise. He wants advice, not backup." Allie massaged her temples. It was as if her brain had stretched sideways. Erin was often intense, but today she'd reached new heights. "Your energy is out of control and I'm getting a headache. How much coffee have you been drinking?"

"A lot."

"You might want to limit your intake before you spontaneously combust."

Erin laughed. "I've missed good coffee so much, and suddenly there's this new café in the Student Center, and their dark roast is amazing, and now my heart is beating a mile a minute, and then I find out my best buddy Z-man would rather be *your* best friend."

Allie leaned back in her seat and stared at the upholstery. "You're not jealous." The speed at which Erin's energy was vibrating assaulted her.

"Don't worry," she gave Allie a wink. "I'm a big girl. Give me a minute. I'll get over the sting of rejection. I can share."

"Thank goodness, you're kidding. Honey, I think we need to detox you from all that caffeine so you can speak in full sentences."

"Right-o." Erin saluted her. "I'll take Doppler for a run as soon as we get to the motel and burn some of this off."

* * *

A half hour later, Erin opened the door to their motel room. At her feet, the dog panted heavily and sank to his haunches. "You did great today." She patted his head. "Come on little buddy. Let's get you a drink." In the kitchenette, she filled a bowl with water and set it on the floor.

Allie's bag lay open on the bedspread, its contents spilling out. Erin narrowed her eyes at the letter from Lily, crumpled and tossed on the floor. It was quiet. Too quiet.

She knocked on the bathroom door. "Baby, we're back! Are you in there? Can I come in and shower?"

Click. Click.

"Allie? Are you okay?" She turned the knob. "Why is the door locked? Suddenly modest?"

Click.

Erin hurried to the bed and rifled through Allie's bag. There must be something she could use. A paperclip. *That's it!* "I'm coming in." She straightened it, inserted it into the knob and twisted.

In front of the mirror, Allie stared at her reflection. One hand clicked the lighter under her open palm. The spark flared and went out. She clicked it again.

"What are you doing?" Erin snatched it from her hand. "Allie!"

"What?" Her eyes were dark, confused. "Did you go for your run?" She was compliant when Erin turned on the tap and thrust her scorched hand under the cool water. "Ouch! That stings." Lucidity returned and her mouth opened in horror. "Oh my goodness. I zoned out, didn't I?"

"You must have." Erin pulled her hand from the water and inspected it before wrapping it in a wet towel. "You might get a blister. What were you thinking? How long has this been going on?"

"You know I've zoned out before, but it was only a few seconds. More like a daydream." She cradled her wrapped hand. "*This* has never happened."

"I'm concerned about you, Baby." Erin touched her forehead. "You're burning up." She took her by the hand to the bed. Doppler whined and circled their feet.

"Wait. Don't lay on that. They're disgusting." Erin tore the bedspread off before she helped her under the sheet.

"I felt weird at dinner." Allie pressed her fingers to her temple. "The headache got worse. Usually Doppler lets me know something's wrong, but..."

Erin grimaced. "But we left him behind. And then I took him for a run." He might have picked up on Allie's odd behavior earlier if she hadn't taken him. He could have warned her it was coming.

"I guess he's become my unofficial service dog, ever since Lil... ever since *she* stabbed me." She pressed her hand to the scar on her abdomen.

Erin grabbed the crumpled letter from the floor. "This is bullshit. Lily can't threaten us. That goddamn kid is in closed custody in another country. She's not getting out of juvy!" She thumbed the lighter under the paper and tossed it in the kitchenette sink when it caught fire. "Good riddance."

Allie stared at the smoke trail as it swirled upward.

CHAPTER SIX

I click the bright red plastic lighter, holding it under my palm until the pain makes me stop. I love the hiss and smell of the fuel, the flash of light when the spark ignites. I do it again. I can take the pain a little longer this time. The flame's fiery tongue licks my hand. "Oh, yeah!" I whisper back. This panther has missed you so much.

"Are you purring?" T leans over and takes the lighter from me. "Ow!" He drops it on the floor of the bus. "It's burning hot! How were you holding this in your bare hands?" He examines the tip of his finger and frowns at me.

"Pussy." He should know better than to touch the metal. I scrabble through the litter under the seat to retrieve it. "Why couldn't we hitchhike straight south?"

"No way, I tried that the last time I went AWOL," he whispered. "They watch for us at the border. I was back in custody the same day."

He watches my face when I hold the lighter under my hand again. I try not to smile.

"This is better," he says. "Trust me. By the time we hit Brandon, they'll forget all about us. We can cross the border south from there and go all the way to California."

"I'm sure you can talk *someone* into taking us across." He's good at convincing people. A couple of hours ago, he talked two ladies into giving us enough money for lunch plus bus fare to Brandon. I probably would have taken their purses and run for it.

His eyes are still boring into me so I turn my head and stare back.

Does he see my predator's eyes? He doesn't even flinch, and the corners of his fuzzy baby mustache lift when he reaches over and puts his hand on my thigh. Not even two seconds later, he slides it toward my groin.

I narrow my eyes. Does he know how dangerous I am? When he reaches my crotch I hold the burning lighter to his forearm. Fine hairs curl back from the flame, and his nostrils flare.

"Fuck!" He pulls his hand away.

"Checkmate."

I was right. Once we reach the Brandon bus station, it doesn't take long for T to find his mark, and a white-haired lady with a pickup truck agrees to take us across the border. It helped a lot that T looks like her grandson. Swear to God, she almost pinched his cheeks.

We're nestled under an orange tarp in the back of the truck, bent like pretzels beside a heap of bags containing some damn blankets for a competition. When she hits the highway, I tear one open and make a pillow out of the one with the cat face design. T scoots over and I let him put his bristly chin on a corner.

"What's the first thing you're gonna do when we get to California?" He's got a pathetic sappy look in his eyes when he reaches out to touch my cheek.

I shove his hand away. "I don't want to go to California."

"Sure you do. Everyone does." His fingers crawl back toward me like a spider, and latch onto a lock of my hair. "The first thing I'm gonna do is buy a surf board. Can you imagine living on the beach? Ahhh." He curls my hair around his finger.

"There are seagulls at the beach. I hate birds."

"I'll chase them away for you." He lays his head back and stares at the underside of the flapping tarp. "It's gonna be great."

The truck slows, and T slithers under the bags. I poke my head out the side of the tarp in time to see the big Customs sign. We both lay still as corpses when movement stops.

"Well, hello Verna. Nice to see you again so soon. Another quilting weekend?" The man's voice sounds way too friendly to be official, and I'm tempted to peek, but T stops me with a soft "shhh."

"I think I'll win a prize this time. I've got a kitty design that'll knock their socks off, the old fuddy duddies."

Verna doesn't sound nervous at all. She's pretty old. Maybe she forgot we were back here.

"Good luck," he says, and Verna grinds the truck into gear.

When we pick up speed, T starts laughing. I push the tarp down enough to see that the Canadian border is the size of a Lego on the horizon. We did it. They'll never catch us.

A mile down the road, Verna stops and lets us ride up front all the way to Rugby, where we pass a monument bragging that this town is the center of North America, a fact she's very proud of. She pulls over on the main road and T kisses her cheek before we get out, as if he was her real grandson. Her eyes get all watery and she gives him twenty bucks, 'for pretending,' before she pulls away in her old pickup truck. We're left on the side of the road wiping the grit from our eyes.

"I'm hungry. Let's get a Big Mac."

T holds his arms wide and turns in a circle. "This piss ant town isn't big enough for a McDonald's." He flashes the twenty at me. "But I'll buy you a hot turkey sandwich at the truck stop."

When I reach for it, he stuffs it down the front of his jeans, but I ain't goin' in there for a twenty. I follow him down the road, him rooster strutting up ahead, the setting sun glinting off his dark hair. He thinks he's all that.

"What were you in for anyway?" Why hadn't I ever thought to ask him that before? He always asked about me and how many people I killed. I told him a few things that were true, but mostly made up lies to watch his expressions.

He hesitates when I ask him, and his shit-eating grin disappears. "Break and ent... robbery. I went down for robbery." He sticks his chest out.

"Bullshit." He hadn't been arrested for robbery, or break and enter either. It must be something stupid, or embarrassing, or sick. "What did you really do? Rip off old ladies? Kill puppies?"

He glares at me through slitted eyes and turns his back. "Robbery," he spits over his shoulder, "and escape lawful custody."

That last part I believe. He knew how to get out of juvy. After he pointed out the errors in my emergency exit plan, he showed me how easy it was. We stalled in the library until old Mr. Angotti got tired of all the extra help and sent us back to our units.

We took our time, and happened to be passing the kitchen right when the delivery truck arrived. With the back door wide open, there was too much activity to track everyone. We simply walked out the freight door and climbed the fence. No attack dogs, no armed guards and no sirens, but my heart hammered like it had come to life. I could have kissed T right then, but I didn't.

"Two hot turkey sandwiches," he tells the waitress as soon as we're seated in a corner booth. "And a couple of beers." He doesn't even wait for a menu.

"We have meatloaf on special."

Her boobs are too big for that outfit. T can't take his eyes off them. I kick him under the table and he clears his throat.

"Hot turkey." He turns back to me and shrugs.

"I want a cheeseburger and fries." I stare straight at T when I say it. Who does he think he is to order for me? I don't know if I even like hot turkey sandwiches. I've never had one.

"I can't serve you beer without ID."

T rolls his eyes. "Whatever. Bring us Cokes or something."

The waitress scurries off and returns a couple of minutes later with the sodas. We both drain our glasses and order refills before she's had a chance to walk away. She tucks her hair behind her ear when he winks at her. Stupid bitch is probably still pining for him when we finish and walk out the door without leaving her a tip.

"Let's get some wheels." T points across the parking lot to the Chevy dealership.

We're barely out of earshot and I shoot a look to the waitress, but she's busy cleaning up our mess. Why the hell would he want to screw around breaking into a business, when there's bound to be someone right here who left their keys inside? "Why bother? Let's take this one." I jut my chin toward a little car left running while the owner runs in to pay for gas. It can't get any easier than that.

"Do you want to get your ass hauled back to Winnipeg?" He looks at me like I'm an alien. "That guy will report it stolen right away, and we won't get two miles before the cops catch us. By tomorrow, you'll be back in juvy looking at the same stupid faces you did this morning."

I hadn't really thought past taking the car and making a run for it. T's got a point. "So, what's your big plan?"

"I used to wash customer cars at a repair shop." He starts walking, and I have no choice but to follow. "Most of the guys, like me, were too damn lazy to put the keys back on the pegboard in the office. We left them for the next guy." He pulls his T-shirt up to cover the bottom half of his face. "Cameras everywhere."

I lower my head and tuck my chin into my shirt. T thinks of things I don't. Maybe it's time to be more careful.

He checks one long row of cars parked outside the service bay doors, yelps when he finds a set of keys on top of a back tire, and turns a triumphant smile on me. "It's a weekend. They won't even notice until Monday morning." He unlocks a gray four-door and holds the passenger side open for me.

"I want to drive."

"You drive?" He jangles the keys in his hand for a moment before handing them over and getting into the passenger side.

Behind the wheel, I settle into the fabric seats and slide the key in the ignition. We've got a half tank of gas. That'll take us miles away. I spin the tires and squeal out onto the highway. We're not even up to highway speed when he clears his throat. He's staring at my seatbelt. I knew someone like this before. Always made me wear the damn thing. Fuck her, she got what she deserved.

"I'm not putting that deathtrap on."

"Fastest way to get pulled over is with simple shit like that. Don't give them a reason."

Blood sizzles in my veins. *Don't tell me what to do.* I sear him with my stink-eye before I clip the buckle into the slot. When I yank the shoulder strap back under my arm, I'm a trout tangled in a fish net. I hate it. "Whatever."

He smiles at me when we take off again. "You're cute."

I swallow down the spit I want to spew in his face, and ease off on the gas. The speedometer wavers around sixty-five. *Don't give them a reason.*

Four hours later, the sign announcing that we've entered Montana blurs past. T has his head back, and I've turned up the radio twice to try to drown out his snores. They're like a goddamn bull moose in rutting season. I crunch his jacket into a wad and shove it against his face.

"Ungh!" He jolts awake, fists up, and looks confused at the jacket on his lap. "Where are we?"

I shrug. "Fuck if I know. Somewhere in America, I guess." The headlights cut a bright path down the highway, to the right of the dotted yellow line.

"It's dark. Holy crap, it's dark." He peers out the side window, but there is nothing to see except weeds and a few stunted bushes in the ditch. In the distance, a speck of light winks from someone's farm.

"There's no moon tonight. Shitty fishing."

"Fishing? Now?" Still not quite awake, he rubs his eyes with the back of his hand.

"No, stupid. I meant that it *would* be a bad night to fish, if you were gonna." For a smart guy, he's such an idiot. "I'm tired. You wanna drive?"

"Uh, okay." He rubs his face again and slaps his stubbly cheeks while I pull over. Behind the wheel, he tilts his head at the instrument display. "You didn't think to tell me that we're almost out of gas?"

"Yeah, whatever." I make a pillow out of his jacket and lean against the door. "Figure it out." I drift off a few minutes after we're back on the highway.

Somewhere in my half-asleep awareness, T stops by a barn. I hear him spit and cough, as he siphons fuel from a tractor into our tank. When I wake up, the sky is pink and we are surrounded. T is lying in the back seat with his knees bent double. Outside my window, inches from my face, a black and white dairy cow squashes her huge tongue against the glass.

"Fuck me!" I spring forward and twist my arm in the fishnet seatbelt. A trail of slime and mangled grass oozes down the glass. "Disgusting!" I lean over and press on the horn until they bolt away.

"What's going on?" T, the useless bastard, is awake.

"Why the hell are we in the middle of a field? You're supposed to be driving." I'm beyond pissed.

"Car broke down. I didn't want to wake you. You are so adorable when you sleep."

As if sucking up will make me any less pissed at him. "You were supposed to get gas." Did I dream the part where he siphoned it somewhere? Have we been sitting in this cow field all night?

"I did." He blinks. "But it must have been bad or something. The car sounded rough, and then it broke down not long after. I barely got it off the road."

"Did you put diesel in the tank?" Does this city boy not know the goddamn difference?

"I dunno what was in the tractor." He wrinkles his nose like he ate cow shit. "It tasted weird."

"Diesel." What a screw-up. "Now you'll have to hitch us a ride."

T makes a face. He knows it's all his fault we're in the middle of nowhere. He gets out, and angrily throws his ball cap at the cows. They stand in a solid herd and it bounces off the back of the one that licked my window. He screams, and runs at them until they scatter across the field.

With the filthy cows gone, it's safe to get out of the car. On a whim, I check the glove compartment before I leave, and what I find makes my day.

How did I miss this beauty before? I guess I was too tired to snoop through all the car's hiding spots. Ahh, a jackknife. The imitation ivory handle fits my hand perfectly. I extend the blade and slide my thumb along the edge. It's sharp enough.

When T returns from chasing the cows, he retrieves his trampled hat and slaps it against his thigh until it's back to its original color.

I pocket my treasure without a word. It's mine.

By the time we return to the highway, he looks a little less like a raving lunatic.

"Come on, cow whisperer, use your *favorite grandson* routine and get us a ride." I punch him on the shoulder.

He flashes his thumb, and a five-hundred-watt smile, at the next car and it pulls over immediately. Damn, T is good at that. We run to catch up and slide into the middle seat of a faded red mini van.

At the wheel is an old man, and his wife turns to us as soon as we get in. "What's a nice couple of kids doing way out here? You're miles from anywhere." Her face crinkles in all directions when she smiles, and T smiles back.

"We're on our way to visit our grandma and our car broke down," I say, but her eyes stay on T's. What is it about him that melts old ladies? Is she planning to take him home and feed him milk and cookies?

"Yeah." T bobs his head, grinning like an idiot.

The old lady glances at me for a second, and then back at T. With his dark features, he is the exact opposite of my pale skin and green eyes. We're as different as salt and pepper shakers, but she swallows it. "You're good kids. Where does your grandma live?"

"Billings," T blurts out the same time I say, "Butte". We turn to each other, and there's panic in his eyes. He thinks we've blown it.

"Grandma actually lives halfway between, and we always argue about which place she's closer to, don't we, bro?" I nudge him with my elbow and he nods.

"Yeah, sis." His big weird smile is back.

The old man is not buying it. "In a pig's eye! You two are about as related as a duck and a cow. You're in some kind of trouble, aren't you?" He had to say cow. The van slows and I can feel it coming. He knows we're not who we say.

"What are you kids up to?" His eyebrows bunch up under his checkered old man hat.

If we don't 'fess up, he'll pull over and kick us out. That's not going to happen. "Turn right on that next road." I flick open the blade of my new jackknife.

T's eyes bug out when, without warning, I leap off my seat and hold it to the old lady's throat. She makes a whiny noise in her nose, so I slap her with my other hand. "Shut up."

"No! Leave her alone." The old man almost swerves into the ditch before he gets control of the van.

"Then do what I say." I prick her skin and a drop of blood appears. She's panting like she's about to have a heart attack.

"You don't have to do this," the old man pleads. He reminds me of my grandfather when he was trying to talk me out of doing something I really wanted to do. He knew he wouldn't be able to change my mind, but that didn't stop him from trying. Stupid.

This old man needs to understand that he can't fuck with me. I push the knifepoint into his wife's neck, and she surprises me by batting my hand away. "For the love of God, what are you doing, child?" I didn't figure her for a fighter, but it's too late. Blood runs down her flowered shirt, and her eyes widen at the sight of it.

"Wait! Don't. Please don't." The old man's face goes white. The van's tires grind onto the gravel and back to pavement.

Beside me, T's having a seizure or something, his shoe banging against the floor. I shoot him a look and his foot stops, but he keeps the weird grin on his face. He's not watching the old lady, he's watching me.

"Our Father, who art in heaven." The lady presses her hands to her throat and blood drips between her fingers. She's making a big deal over nothing. It's only a nick. It looks worse than it is.

"Do what I say," I hiss through my teeth.

When the old man gets control of himself, he puts on his signal light and turns off the highway. His whole body shakes and he's having trouble holding onto the wheel. I make him drive at least five miles before I figure it's far enough.

"Get the fuck out." I leave them standing like two crooked sticks on the road. T, always such a considerate guy, throws the old lady's cane out the window before I spin the tires, and swallow them in a tornado of dust. When they finish coughing, it'll take them hours to hobble back to the highway and we'll be long gone. How's that for thinking ahead? I'm smarter than T.

"You stabbed her." He's sitting in the passenger seat looking at me like I'm a juicy cheeseburger with extra fried onions. "You're giving me a boner, Lily."

"Keep your little friend in your pants. I ain't got time for your hormones."

He takes a deep breath and lets it out. "We need to look for a new car. How long would it take two oldies to walk out and call 9-1-1?"

"I dunno." There's a full tank of gas in this van and the engine runs smooth. "We can change plates somewhere. My old man is a cop. He said lots of guys on the run avoid getting pulled over by changing the license plates. You gotta find a similar car though. They hardly ever check the serial number."

"Your dad is a cop?" T doesn't believe me.

"He used to be, but he did some shit and went to prison. He's probably out by now. We should go to Minnesota. He's rich. We can stay there and he'll give us all the beer and cash we want."

"No, we're going to California." T folds his arms across his chest. He's stuck in his fairy tale dream. As if he could ever live on the beach and surf.

"Look over there." I point to a lot lined with retired farm equipment. Half-hidden behind a building is an old red van a lot like ours. "We can switch the license plate."

He uses a quarter as a screwdriver and swaps plates. Useful. This guy is useful. He leaps back in and puts on his seatbelt.

"Damn." I pull mine on too. Maybe he's on to something. If I don't think about the cows, we've done pretty well so far.

T bends the brim of his ball cap into a curve. "What did your dad do to end up in prison?"

I knew this was coming, sooner or later. I tell him a version of the story where my dad and I were best friends, and it was all a big misunderstanding. I guess it's my own fairy tale.

CHAPTER SEVEN

Derek gunned the four-cylinder engine on his rental car and blew the stop sign. Car horns honked and tires squealed before he heard a metal crushing impact. He glanced into the rear-view mirror, and smirked at what he'd created behind him. That unmarked police car wouldn't be tailing him again. Not without extensive body work.

How could they imagine they'd beat him at his own game? He'd worked plainclothes too long to miss the telltale signs of a retired cruiser, the patch where the roof antenna had been removed, the cheap rims, and the empty screw holes where the bumper's push bars had been. They must think he was an idiot.

There wouldn't be a second or third car surveilling him. Morley Falls was too small for that. He'd learned firsthand that you had to make do with what you had. Right now, he'd make do with an undersized engine and an economy-sized car. Economy meant small, and small was easier to hide.

He cut down an alley, took a side road and was almost there before he realized where he was headed. It was as if he was programmed to follow the homing beacon to Gunther's old property by the river. He'd spent so much time driving back and forth on this road, first looking for Tiffany, then hoping to spend a little time with Lily.

His chest burned. Tiffany was gone. Hope demanded he keep searching, but he might never find her. His daughter too was as good as gone. Beyond his beer, his money and his cigarettes, she'd wanted nothing from him.

After what had happened to Gunther, he'd sure never trust her to fetch him a drink or he might end up poisoned too. At least Lily's grandfather had survived. The old guy was a lucky man. Not only had he defied the odds, he'd done well when he'd sold his property and moved to a retirement home.

The closer Derek got, the more he was convinced that this was probably the best place to hide out. It was familiar, and only a few would know the connection. Erin Ericsson was gone, but there was still that goddamn keener Z-man.

Derek pulled into the roadside turnout, right after he passed the billboard advertising a new development of luxury riverfront condos. As he got out of the car, he had a pang of regret at losing his prized Mustang. He used to park it in this very spot when he came to see his daughter.

The old trail through the woods was torn up by heavy equipment and what had been dense forest, rich with animal and bird life, was now a muddy mess. He skirted deep ruts in the earth, and vaulted a drainage ditch recently dug between the bog and the river, before he reached the clearing for the house. He stopped dead. It was flattened to rubble, pulverized by a backhoe, or whatever demolition monster had killed it.

An abandoned dredging machine sat out in the middle of the bog, its suction hoses dry. Beside it was a bright orange hydraulic excavator, submerged to its muddy tracks. Attempts had been made to free it, and the bucket had scraped a halo of mud around the cab.

He shook his head. Even with most of the water pumped out, this swamp still had an appetite. The company should at least come get their equipment before it sank to the earth's core, like that kid's four-by-four truck he'd heard about. They didn't even have a chance to get a chain on it before it went under. He snorted. Stupid amateurs.

The town children said this place was haunted. They told stories about the bog monster that howled at night. Lily didn't seem scared, in fact she was the opposite of afraid. He used to find her out here, squatting on her haunches, staring out at the little pool of water, and smoking his stolen cigarettes. Haunted or not, one thing was certain. The bog kept its secrets. Whatever went in, didn't come out.

He stood on the end of a plank that provided foot access to the area, mud sucking between the board and his shoes. There had been dry years, and wet ones, but he'd never imagined the land could be torn up like this. The little open pool at the center was all but gone, its water pumped out to the river. All this for a string of luxury condos, and cash in some developer's pocket.

The corner of something metallic glinted at him beyond his reach, but he couldn't quite tell what it was. It was probably some guy's broken belt buckle. Dredging a bog was rough work. He stared at it for a moment, and then turned back toward the shed.

An electric line sagged between the power pole and the little building, now appropriated as the construction company's site office. He bent to read the Stop Work order taped to the padlocked door. It appeared the company's development permit had been denied and there would be no luxury condos after all. Protection of wetlands was taken pretty seriously around here. Who wouldn't know that? Somewhere, someone was extremely pissed off about losing money.

Derek smiled. If he'd had the cash, he might have bought the place himself. A nice new house out here would be perfect for his family, as soon as he got them together. Maybe he still had a chance.

It took five minutes, and two scraped knuckles, before he managed to smash the lock off the shed door. He threw the rock aside and sucked his bleeding fingers as he stepped inside. Had they discovered the hidden room beneath the floorboards, or was it still harboring its secrets?

A row of yellow hard hats, work gloves, and rolled-up site plans replaced Gunther's neatly organized tools. He leapt forward when he spotted the beer fridge under the work bench, and eagerly opened the door. The wire shelves were bare.

He used to bring the old man a six-pack every other week, but now he realized that Lily had probably taken it for herself. He licked his parched lips. The kid had been what, eleven years old back then? She already took after her father.

On his knees, he checked the bottom shelf under the work bench and rifled through the cabinet. Lily was good at hiding things. He shoved his arm into the dark corner and had a flicker of pride when his fingers closed around the smooth shape of a bottle. It was where he might have hidden it himself. Should he drink it or put it in the fridge to cool first? Ice cold beer had its appeal but he needed a drink *now*.

He twisted off the cap and brought the bottle to his mouth. When the amber liquid touched his lips, he stopped himself. He took a sniff. It smelled fine, but were those scratches on the cap?

Maybe prison had made him overly suspicious. He set the bottle on the bench so he could examine it like he was at a crime scene. Was one crimp bent? Had it been poisoned by Lily and intended for her grandfather? No, she couldn't have meant to harm him. She was only a kid. She didn't understand what she was doing.

If it had been opened long ago, surely it would smell bad by now. It had to be okay. He tilted it back, filled his mouth and filtered it between his teeth. Old Gunther had survived his granddaughter's attempts to poison him, but Derek might not be so lucky. He spat it out and poured the rest beside the step, smashing the bottle against a rock, as if that would end the matter.

Inside, grime from a dozen pairs of muddy work boots coated the floor, and he stomped until his motion betrayed the loose board. With the tips of his fingers, he pried up the hatch and peered into the darkness. A narrow ladder descended seven feet into a cinderblock-lined room with a dirt floor. He put his weight on the creaky ladder and climbed down until he could reach the light switch.

The TV and army cots were still there, along with two slightly moth-eaten blankets. For a time, many years ago, Gunther had used this room to hide illegal liquor during the prohibition years. Throughout its history, it had alternately concealed stolen property, criminals on the run, and who knows what else. The paranoid old man had nearly died down here, trying to hide Lily from the authorities.

He flipped on the TV and slapped the dust from the cot before settling down. It wasn't the Hilton, but it would do. Add one more chapter to the hidey-hole's history.

He went over what he remembered about the night he'd blacked out. The last thing he was sure about was buying beer from Gina's Stop 'N Go, and taking photos of the lawyer's wife in a compromised position with his business partner. What the hell had happened after that?

He wasn't averse to making a man pay for what he'd done. After all, he himself had smashed a few noses, and broken a rib or two in his day, but murder? It seemed out of the realm of possibility. Still, there was the matter of the two missing cartridges from his pistol magazine.

Had he really been firing at feral animals out his car window, or something else? If he'd ever wanted to kill someone, Ethan 'Badger' Lewis would be right at the top of the list. The inmate had made his time hell in Stillwater Prison.

He rubbed his eyes with trembling fingers. It made no sense. He hadn't even known Badger was out. In his drunken blackout, had he somehow discovered this, and gotten rid of the little bastard once and for all?

He needed a drink but couldn't risk going out. Not until the heat was gone. His chest felt tight. He lay back and closed his eyes.

Derek woke up when he rolled over and his knees struck the brick wall. It was pitch black and he was back in prison. The bars were closing in, crushing him to death. A man kneeled on his chest, a shiv at his throat. There was not enough air.

He gasped and sat up. The blanket was drenched in sweat and his entire body shivered. It took long seconds before he got his bearings. Had someone been in here with him? He was certain he'd left the TV on, but it was so dark he had to feel his way to the ladder. Panicked, he climbed up and shoved open the trap door to gulp fresh air.

Once he'd filled his lungs and convinced himself that he wasn't suffocating, he leaned in and toggled the light switch a few times. The power was off. The development company, now fully aware that the project was dead, had stopped paying the bill. Their timing was unfortunate for him.

When his nerves calmed, he climbed back down for the cot and set it over the trap door, as if that would keep his demons locked inside. It was too much like prison. Another second in that hole and he'd have lost his mind. Besides, a real man would sleep up top. He crawled onto the cot, pulled the rough blanket around his shoulders, and shivered himself back to sleep.

When morning broke, Derek sat up and banged his head on the underside of the work bench. How the hell had he wedged himself into this tight space? It was too small for an adult, more suited for a kid. His body still trembled. He needed a drink soon, or he'd do something stupid, like turn himself in.

Above him, dizzying pencil swirls marked the wood, and a child's scrawl claimed the artwork. Lily. He smiled. His daughter had played here when she was little. She'd drawn a picture of herself, smiling and holding her mom's hand. The vision of a fair-haired, happy, young girl blurred when he realized what he was looking at.

Horrified, he pushed himself out, knocking the cot over in his haste. The little girl in the picture hadn't been holding her mother's hand. She'd been stabbing her with a knife, while flames swirled around them both.

His chest was on fire, and his breath caught in his throat. No, he'd been mistaken. It wasn't a picture of Lily and Tiffany at all. The child must have seen something disturbing on TV.

CHAPTER EIGHT

Erin Ericsson slid into a seat in the back row of the classroom. Davis looked up and gave her a nod, but she could barely blink back. She wanted to lay her cheek on her notebook and sleep for a week.

Only hours ago, she'd kissed Allie goodbye at the airport and sent her back to Morley Falls, but it hadn't been the romantic weekend they'd planned. Allie's zone-out had scared them both. What if she'd really hurt herself? She said she couldn't remember anything about the incident, aside from a pervasive sensation that Lily was up to something.

Now Erin had to let her go, trust that she would be okay. With the end of training fast approaching, there was still so much to do. All weekend, she'd felt split three ways. The new study club, helping Davis and Garrett at the shooting range and evenings with Allie. The weekend of passion had become a weekend of worry, but she'd rather have a bad weekend with Allie than a great weekend with anyone else in the world.

She held up her left hand. What would a wedding ring look like on that finger? Would it be such a bad thing? Wouldn't it simply be a natural progression of their relationship? Was she overreacting because she was worried and wanted to protect Allie? Was that bad? She wanted to protect her because she loved her. More than anyone else, ever.

And, why did the thought of getting married scare her so much anyway? She'd only had a few serious relationships in her entire life and she'd been the one to bail as soon as feelings soured. Was that it?

Was she simply afraid to fail? She'd already been through a lot with Allie, and bailing out had never once occurred to her. She couldn't believe it ever would. So what was it, then?

She aligned her notebook until it was precisely parallel with the edge of the desk, and then she did the same with her pen. It was clear. The solid, confident Erin Ericsson was a chicken.

"—Ericsson?"

Erin jerked upright. Her notebook clattered to the floor and she snatched it up, placing it carefully back into position. She'd been daydreaming like a fifth-grader and had no idea what she'd been asked, but now all eyes were on her. She glanced at Davis's blank notebook. No help there. Well, she might as well come clean.

"My apolog—"

"It's pretty clear that this still falls under the Federal Kidnapping Act." Davis slapped his notebook shut and got to his feet. "It applies regardless of whether the person was alive when transported across state boundaries." He strode confidently to the white board and picked up a dry erase marker. When he was finished, he'd drawn an intricate diagram from Point A, to B, to C, using dotted lines and text labels, to illustrate his point.

If only he was that confident at the range, he'd graduate with flying colors. As it was, he would have to work a little harder with the pistol. Erin smiled her thanks when he finished. With only the occasional nudge from Davis, she made it through the rest of the class.

When she reached the driving course, her fatigue faded with the influx of adrenaline. The instructor, her favorite, reminded her of her Uncle Roger. Unfortunately, she had mentioned this to one of her classmates, and it had stuck. Now everyone called him Uncle Roger, but he seemed to like it.

"Today, we are going to practice skid control and high speed collision avoidance," Uncle Roger said. "For those of you new to pursuit driving, this is not like Sunday cruising in your grandfather's Buick. Modern cars have very advanced skid-control features. We'll practice progressive squeeze and anti-lock braking. We'll also do an exercise to prepare you in the event that this technology fails."

Erin rocked on her toes. One of the best parts of driving a police cruiser was responding to emergency calls.

Uncle Roger's class didn't consist of fancy digital presentations, whiteboard drawings or online research, merely a series of rudimentary diagrams scraped into the dirt with the toe of his shoe. "You see those three pylons out there?"

They all turned and looked.

"That's grandma and the kids. Grandma is the big vulnerable pylon in the middle, you get the idea." Flawless teeth caught the sunlight when he smiled with glee. "You will accelerate to a minimum speed of fifty miles an hour before you hit that second marker." A white stake had been pounded into the side of the paved track. "Aim straight for grandma. When it's time, the light on the portable display will indicate the direction you will swerve. Use the techniques we've discussed to avoid a collision. Don't pump your brakes like in the movies. Not unless you're driving a car built in 1970."

Davis tapped her on the shoulder. "Team up with me, Erin. This looks scary as hell." The wind blew his impeccable hair into his eyes, and he smoothed it back with a trembling hand.

"What are you talking about? You had the best score yesterday when you backed through the pylon serpentine."

"That was at two miles an hour. This is highway speed." He spread out all his fingers. "Big difference."

"Okay." Erin shrugged. It didn't matter who she teamed up with. No partner could make this exercise less than fun.

The instructor walked them to the track. "Pick your coffin, trainees."

"What?" Davis took a step back.

He laughed. "I'm kidding. Unless you do something really stupid, you'll be fine. Don't worry, you're with Erin. She's done this before."

"Come on, Davis. It's not that hard." Erin snatched up the keys for the Chevy. Garrett and his partner hesitated and ended up with the battered Ford, the oldest in the fleet.

The instructor called out as they headed to their cars. "Whoever hits grandma or the kids is buying the first round in the Boardroom tonight."

"You go first." Davis opened the Chevy's passenger door and got in.

Erin shrugged and got in the driver's side. "Watch how I do it. It's fun." She pulled on her seatbelt, started the engine, and checked the radio. "Ericsson and Davis. Ready."

"I don't normally exceed the speed limit." Davis clipped on his safety belt and tugged to make sure it was secure.

"You're first up, Ericsson." The instructor's voice answered over the speaker, followed by a hiss of static. "Proceed."

Erin stomped her foot on the gas pedal and smiled at the rush of excitement in her chest. The speedometer steadily rose while she talked. "The key is to maintain control. When that signal lights up, brake hard, and maintain steering control through the maneuver. The ABS system will hammer like crazy, but that's normal."

"If you say so." Acceleration rocked Davis back in his seat, a nervous grin on his lips. "This is like a carnival ride."

"Soon," Erin warned as the speedometer reached the target zone. Grandma and the kids were directly ahead and in mortal danger. Davis grabbed his seat with both hands.

The right arrow illuminated on the portable signal trailer, and Erin slammed her foot on the brake. Davis's shoulder bumped hers when she steered sharply, and her inside tire clipped one of the smaller pylons. "Oh, no!" She slowed at the end of the run and skidded around. The end pylon teetered, but they all remained upright.

"Grandma and the kids are okay." Davis waved at them as they passed on their return to the start. He high-fived Erin when they switched drivers. "That was a blast."

"You can do it."

Despite his initial trepidation, Davis had no trouble executing the maneuver. Garrett and his partner were not as lucky, and both men were on the hook for a round of drinks.

"Come on, hummingbird," Davis said when the class ended. "Let's go get a bite to eat. You look starved half to death, as usual." He snickered at his jibe about her quick metabolism.

She nodded. It was true. She was usually hungry.

"And coffee. You need more coffee."

When had they become best friends? "Um, I'm not so sure I should drink more than a few cups a day. I can't afford to get as fidgety as I was last weekend. You remember the kidnapping scenario and my crazy escape stunt?" As if she needed to remind him.

"That wasn't from coffee, little bird. That was pure inner gung-ho, and I don't think it's always a bad thing." He pulled on her arm. "Let's skitter through the gerbil tube and we can make it back for next class."

Apparently they *were* besties. She reached up to tousle his carefully arranged hair, and he shot her a dirty look. Maybe that was too far. "I could use a waker-upper," she said, and followed him to the glass-enclosed walkway that connected the buildings.

Erin set her steaming black coffee beside the computer and logged in. "I would never have figured you for a sprinkles-on-your-coffee kind of guy."

"They're not sprinkles, they're dark chocolate shavings." Davis took a sip of his foamy latte and licked his lips. "De-licious."

"It's not real coffee with all that fluff in it." Out of habit, she checked the local and nation-wide activity. For years, she'd started her work day with Briefing, her uniform pressed and boots shined. The sergeant on duty informed them of the daily BOLOS and local warrants. Change was not so easy. She missed the array of useful equipment on her belt, but it was a small trade-off for a future of possibilities.

She slouched in her seat and scrolled through the alerts. A child abduction in Florida, a gang murder in California and bomb threats in the Capital. Minnesota was quiet today, but Montana was looking for a pair of teens involved in a carjacking.

She clicked the link for more information. A female teen had instigated the carjacking, and had stabbed the disabled female passenger, who was now recovering in hospital. The husband had not survived. He had died of a heart attack while seeking help.

Erin sat upright. Local troopers were in contact with Canadian authorities regarding the recent escape of two teens from the Winnipeg Youth Detention Centre. Before she reached the end of the message, she knew Allie was right. Lily was out, and she was as dangerous as ever, but what the hell was she doing in Montana?

"Sir? I need to speak with you." Erin motioned for her instructor's attention. Davis raised his eyebrows and leaned over to see her screen.

"Are you having trouble with the assignment?" The instructor looked at the monitor. "You're on the wrong screen. You need to—"

"I know this kid." She pointed to the name at the bottom of the screen. "I helped put Lily Schmidt away. She's diabolical."

He peered closer and scanned the alert. "You're from a Minnesota police department, right?" He patted her shoulder. "You must be mistaken. These fugitives hopped the border from Canada. It can't be the same."

"It's a long story about what happened in Canada, but it's her. There is going to be a body count. Look, it's already started." She pointed to a related update.

"Says here the male victim died of a heart attack. Let's not waste our time on a couple of kids who stole a van, and scared an old man with a bad ticker."

"Can I at least contact the agents assigned to this case? I might be able to—"

"I'm sure the situation is well in hand. Let's get back on task, shall we?"

Erin swore he muttered something that sounded like *Raging Ranger* as he walked away. She shoved her chair back, but Davis tugged her sleeve. He silently shook his head until she sat back down.

"What the hell is going on?" he whispered. "Is it the coffee?"

"It's not the coffee." She picked up her cup and headed out. She needed to talk to Allie.

CHAPTER NINE

Hurry up! What the hell is T still doing? I'm already behind the wheel of the new car, but he's still back there in the church. Maybe he's asking God to talk me into going to California. What if I took off on my own?

T comes barreling out the side door as I slip the shifter into drive. His hat's on sideways, like a friggin' cartoon, with his body going faster than his legs. He spots me and grabs at the door handle like he robbed the place. "Open the door! Open the door!"

I hit the unlock button.

He wrenches the door open and folds his long legs into the passenger seat. "Go! Go! Go!" This time he doesn't get all picky about his safety belt. He watches over his shoulder until we're clear of town and starts laughing when we hit the highway.

"What took you so long?" It took me less than a minute to find a set of keys in a jacket in that church lobby. What could he possibly have been doing?

"This." T digs in his pocket and shows me a handful of fat white envelopes.

I still don't get it until he starts ripping them open and the money spills out. "Donations." The tires hit gravel on the shoulder of the road and I fight the car back onto the pavement. That is the sweetest sight I've seen in a while. Money isn't allowed in the detention center, and this is a lot.

He rubs a twenty dollar bill on my cheek, and I inhale the smell of ink and paper, like they do in the movies. "Let's party," he says in a low voice.

"Let's get beer." I'm all for getting totally drunk and passing out.

"Yeah." He leans back and crumples a few bills to toss at me. "We got maybe an hour before someone reports this car stolen. Let's get as far away as we can and find a spot to hide out."

An hour later, we're at a truck stop and T piles the counter high with junk food and beer. The cashier doesn't bother to ask him for ID when he pays with wads of cash from his pocket.

"It helps when you don't look like you're twelve." T gives me a nudge toward the door. "But that's what I like about you."

It's Sunday morning, and you'd think it would be quiet, but the diner is packed full of old ladies and big men wearing ball caps. T's eyes drift over the customers and settle on a skinny guy seated at the counter. The guy looks up and notices us standing there. He reminds me of twitchy Shonda.

"Wait in the car. I gotta take a leak." T heads for the washroom, and leaves me standing there with the grocery bags. I'm not surprised when the twitchy guy gets up and brushes past me to follow him.

Twitchy guy comes out first, tucking his hand into his bulging pocket. He heads straight to the exit. Two or three long minutes later, T surges through the door. His eyes shine like wet stones, and he's got a snotty nose that he wipes with the back of his hand. He's high.

"What took you so goddamn long?"

"I had to crush them before I could…" He swipes at his nose again. He couldn't wait five freakin' minutes until we got out of there before he got wasted.

I shove him and he staggers off balance. "Don't tell me to wait in the car like I'm your pussy wife."

"Yeah, pussy." He's a laughing idiot. I've never seen him sweat like this, and his pupils are like pee holes in the snow. Whatever he's on, it's not anything like the crap we inhaled in the juvy library.

People are turning to stare at us, so I grab his arm and haul him out to the parking lot. I stuff him into the car and grab a beer from the grocery bags before I throw them in the back. T twists in his seat, his knees sprawled over the backrest.

"What did you take?" As long as he keeps his grasshopper legs on his side, I can drive.

"It's good, Lily. So good." He's upside down, looking through the windshield at the sky. "I got blue ones, and pink ones, and little wee yellow ones."

"Did you spend all my money on mystery pills? What if I need more beer?"

"Was that *your* money? I'm sorry, I thought..." He screws up his eyes as if considering what I said, but the words don't come.

"We have to find a hideout." The cops will be looking for us soon, and I swear I can see his heart pounding through his shirt. As usual, I have to do everything myself. I find another car and switch license plates. Then we cruise the streets looking for a house that looks vacant. Someone's gotta be away on holidays, or something.

I'm thirsty for another beer, and T's asleep by the time I find a place that looks promising. The driveway is bare, and there's a week's worth of unclaimed newspapers on the step. I leave him in the car a block away, and go in on foot to check it out. The neighborhood is quiet, no one on the street, and nobody peeking out the window when I walk up to the front step.

I cut around back, check for alarm stickers, and use my knife to pop the cheap plastic lock on a basement window. When I slide it open, there's a whiff of old people and moldy carpet. Excitement bubbles in my throat when I squeeze through and land on soft cat's feet. Like a panther, I prowl each room. As I thought, this house is packed full of junk someone has been saving their entire lifetime. I can barely wade through the basement.

Upstairs is a totally different story. Little crocheted doilies decorate everything and the TV is a million years old. I hope they have cable, but at this point I'll take what I can get.

The door to the garage is off the front room, and I click the opener. In a couple of minutes, the car is tucked inside with T still snoring in his seat. Whatever he took, he should take half as much next time.

He wakes up an hour later and stumbles into the living room, where I'm watching an action flick on pay-per-view. I've drank three cans of beer and eaten so many potato chips I wanna barf.

He pulls the curtains shut and sits beside me with his head in his hands.

"Karma," I tell him.

"What?"

"You spent all my money and got wasted without me. Karma bit your ass."

"You want some? Here." He spills a handful of multicolored pills onto the coffee table. "The guy said they were Oxy but I'm not so sure about that."

"You're not used to it. It's been a while." I pick up a blue one, put it down and choose the yellow one instead. "Which one did you take?"

"It hits you faster and harder if you snort it." He leans his head back. "Holy shit, I have a headache. Now I need one to get rid of the headache." With the edge of a candy dish, he crushes a blue pill onto the glass top and rolls up a five dollar bill.

I crack another beer and hold the pill in my hand. "Let's do it together this time."

He flashes me a wicked grin and leans over the table. "Okay."

I pop it in my mouth the same time as he snorts the mound of dust up his nostril. His head reels back and that stupid grin spreads across his face. "Fuck, yeah."

Soon, he's having a great time but I don't feel a damn thing. He's gone through all the cupboards in the kitchen, and told me a half a dozen times that he's going to cook us a big steak dinner. There is no steak, but that's not stopping him.

I'm about to tell him to cut it out when it sneaks up on me. "T, anyone ever tell you you're not bad looking?"

He stares at me with glassy eyes, and the next thing I know we're curled up on the sofa. The movie is over, and somehow my shirt has disappeared. T is sleeping with his head on my stomach, his hand cupped around my bare shoulder. My knife's in my pocket but I can't be bothered to slit his throat with it. Besides, this isn't so bad.

I want another one of those pills. Maybe this time I should snort it like T did. Beside the scattered pills, my attention snaps to a Smith and Wesson revolver.

I bolt upright on the edge of the sofa. "T! Wake up."

His unfocused eyes crack open. "Hey, sugar. Let's do it again."

"Scheisse! Cut that out." I slap his ear and point to the gun. "Where did this come from?" As the words tumble from my mouth, scattered memories drift back to me. Us running around a field shooting at stuff. My muscles tense when I remember a swooping bird. I tried so hard to shoot that bastard, but he got away. I hate birds.

"We found it in the cabinet last night, remember? After we

danced." He slides an arm around my waist.

I push him away. "I did not fucking dance." I've never danced in my life, probably not even as a toddler.

"Yeah, well I danced for both of us and... and I think I made steak." The kitchen is a mess, every pot and pan pulled onto the floor, and the contents of the freezer melting on the counter. I'm pretty sure T's steak was a hallucination.

"I like this gun." I reach out to touch the cool metal.

"It's beautiful and dangerous. Like you." He picks it up and points it at the TV. "Bang, bang," he says without putting his finger on the trigger.

"Is it loaded?"

"Yeah. There are three bullets left from the box. *I* fired a couple and *you* wasted the rest on that crow." He puts it back on the coffee table. "There's no more ammo."

The rest of the puzzle slams together. I remember T driving out of the garage, and then running back in to close the door. I remember staring at the revolver in my lap the entire way. I remember the field outside town, the bottles and cans shattering, the stupid bird I tried to kill before T took the gun away.

He answers as if he's heard my thoughts. "I needed to save a couple of bullets so we can get more money."

"What happened to laying low until the heat dies down?"

He looks away. "You really, really wanted to go shoot that gun."

Another slice of memory slides by, along with an intoxicating skitter up my spine. Me, pointing the revolver at T's face until he agreed.

As if it was meant for me, the gun feels good in my hand, almost as good as my knife. Suddenly I'm hungry. I tuck it into the back of my jeans and head for the garage. "Let's get the hell out of here. Is there any money left?"

T scoops the rest of the pills off the coffee table and meets me in the car. He pops a yellow one in his mouth, and hands a blue one to me. "For luck."

"Why not?" My head's pounding and we're out of beer. I drive with two tires up on the sidewalk until I get to the main road, and then pull to the middle. The alignment must be messed up.

T stares at me silently when the car straddles the yellow line.

I turn the steering wheel and somehow we're riding the shoulder.

"Just checking to see if you're paying attention." In a minute, I get the hang of it, and we make it to the highway. For some weird reason, I can't seem to make the car go over thirty miles an hour. Vehicles swerve around and whiz past, honking.

"It's my turn to drive." T prods my arm.

I let the car roll to a stop. Goddamn, when did keeping the car on the road get so hard? We switch places, and he puts his foot on the gas. Everything is passing so quickly that I might barf, or am I hungry?

"Get me food." I double over and lay my head on my lap.

"Up ahead." He slows for a turnoff, and drives into a gas bar with a little restaurant attached. "Gimme the gun."

I don't have the energy to protest when he yanks the revolver from the back of my pants. "Cheeseburger," I groan.

"Wait here." He pumps gas into the tank, pulls the neck of his T-shirt up over his nose and goes inside.

I've gotta pee so bad my teeth are floating. There is a washroom sign not ten feet from the car, so I kick my door open and stagger past the gas pumps. I exit a few minutes later, and T is in the middle of the lot screaming his head off.

"Lily! Where are you?" He spins in a circle, revolver in one hand, takeout bag in the other. Dollar bills spill from his pocket, and his shirt has slipped down so it only covers his chin.

It's a scene right out of a movie, and I'd laugh if I wasn't dizzy. "What the fuck are you doing, T?"

He steers me to the car and shoves me inside, gets in the other side and tosses over the bag. Inside are two foil-wrapped burgers and a package of fries.

"Where's the beer?" It sure would be nice to have a beer with my burger.

T rips open the bag and his neck turns red. "Two fries. I said two!" He gets out, and like an angry robot, stalks back inside. The pistol is in his hand before he reaches the door and he doesn't bother to cover his face.

I stuff fries into my mouth while I wait. If he's going to drive like a madman when he gets back, I might not have another chance to eat.

A siren wails in the distance, and I roll up my window as if that will keep them out. T returns with a six pack of beer and more fries.

His mouth is stretched into a thin, hard line.

"Let's get you home, sugar."

I was right. He does drive like a madman. I'm flung from side to side, until finally he slows for our street and pulls into the garage. There are no sirens, and the street is as quiet as usual. Once again, we're home free. T hops around to play the gentleman and open my door. No one has *ever* tried that before, but I let him get away with it because I'm stoned.

"That was amazing!" He digs in his pocket, and dumps money and the rest of the pills onto the coffee table.

The mountain of cash is impressive. To celebrate, we both pop one more pill into our mouths. I like the blue ones best but they make my tongue dry as sand, so I chase it down with a beer while I watch T spread out the pile of cash.

"That's not as much as it seems. It's mostly ones and fives." I've finished my fries and steam escapes when I unwrap the foil package to take a bite. It's the best burger I've ever had.

He spreads his arms wide. "Look at that. *Nobody* messes with T. I am a god."

"Are you gonna eat that cheeseburger, God?" I reach for it and he slaps my hand. My mother used to do that. I hated when she did. Before I know it, my blade is in my hand, and it's pressed against his throat.

He freezes, but his eyes flash excitement. "If you're really that hungry, take it." He puts his hand behind his back.

"Ha, just kidding." I lower the knife, and fake like I was messing around. Before I have it back in my pocket, his revolver is pressed to my skull. Unless he shot someone to get those burgers, there are still three bullets left.

"It appears we have a standoff." I can't remember what movie that was from, but that line seems to fit this situation. I nod at my knife pressed to the crotch of his jeans and his eyes follow.

"Well-played, sugar." He drops the gun on the carpet, and kisses me on the mouth.

The blue pill is kicking in, and a warm sensation fills my belly. The knife falls from my fingers. I kiss him back and it's not so bad.

CHAPTER TEN

"Mikey? Where are you?" Allie opened the closet door, peered inside and closed it. She hurried to the living room where Erin's nephew Jimmy was playing with his twin sisters. "Has anyone seen the baby in the last thirty seconds?"

"We haven't seen Li'l Z for hours." Eleven-year-old Victoria winked at Sophie. On the floor between them, Wrong-Way Rachel was dressed in their dolls' best finery. The cat, wearing a string of plastic beads and a pink tutu, slunk into a corner to groom herself.

Jimmy put his hands on his hips and stepped away from a bundle of blankets. The bundle wiggled and a shiny black Chihuahua nose emerged. Doppler shook off the rest of the blanket to reveal the giggling curly haired toddler. Mikey grabbed his toes and rocked onto his back, tiny feet in the air.

"There you are." Allie picked him up and settled him on her hip. She shook a finger at the snickering girls. "You shouldn't make me worry like that."

"Aw come on, Auntie Allie," Victoria protested. "We try and try, but we can never fool you."

She smiled. "Don't forget that I grew up in a foster home with tons of mischievous kids. Kids like you."

"It's like you're *psychic* or something." Sophie giggled and both girls ran out of the room.

"I'm not psychic." Allie looked down at Jimmy, who still had his hands on his hips.

"Of course not," he said. "Psychics aren't real. You just know stuff sometimes."

"Exactly."

"Can I take Doppler to the park?" The dog's triangle ears perked up when Jimmy jingled his leash.

Allie glanced at the clock. "Not by yourself, Jimmy. That park is pretty far. Ask the girls to go with you."

He put his hands in his pockets, eyes downcast. "They gang up on me sometimes. Why can't Doppler be my bodyguard?"

"Unfortunately, Doppler is just a little squirt. You can tell the girls I'll take you all out for ice cream when you get back, but only if you get along."

"Okay." The dog was more excited than Jimmy when they reached the porch step. After a hurried discussion with his sisters, they headed off.

Allie stood in the doorway to watch the little boy and dog disappear down the road. Their laughs ringing in the air, the girls circled the pair on their matching bicycles.

Allie's laptop bleated with an urgency that sent her running to pick it up. She shifted the baby to her lap and squeezed into a chair at the kitchen table. When she clicked the incoming video call, her foster mom's face appeared on-screen.

"Hi mom." The baby giggled at the picture, and swatted the screen. Allie nudged it out of reach.

"Hi sweetie." Judy's gaze fixed on the baby. "What a cutie. Whose little one is this?" Her voice softened. "Oh, you're so cute. Yes, you are! Look at all that curly hair."

"This is Gina and Chris's baby, Mikey. Gina is working today and couldn't get a sitter. He is such a busy little boy. I'm exhausted."

"Hi darlin'. You're lookin' beautiful today." Her foster dad, a gentle man of few words, popped his head in to say hi and disappeared, probably headed out to tinker in the garage.

"When is Erin finished her training?" Although she spoke to Allie, her mom still made googly eyes at the baby. "Wow, she'll be a big shot FBI Special Agent, like on that TV show you used to watch. That must be so exciting."

"Soon, and then there's graduation." Allie tried to picture what Erin might be doing that very minute. Was she sitting in a classroom, driving at breakneck speeds, shooting her pistol, or doing something else?

Usually she felt more of a connection but today there was some sort of interference, like white noise, or the sound of water running from a tap. It was an irritating background hiss that she couldn't ignore. "Mom, do you believe in ghosts?"

"*Ghost* ghosts? Like in horror movies? No. Are the nightmares back?"

"Not nightmares." More like disturbing daydreams. Daydreams that turned her thoughts to Lily. Malevolent energy followed in the girl's wake, gleefully enveloping her. Lily's energy had wafted through Ciara's house in Winnipeg when they'd discovered the break-in.

The girl was gone but her words still echoed from the walls. 'I killed my mother'. Allie swallowed but her throat still felt dry. A Budweiser would quench this awful thirst.

Allie shook her head as if to expel the thought. Alcoholic beverages wreaked havoc on her intuition. That's the last thing she wanted. An iced green tea was more her style. What were they talking about? She'd asked about ghosts. "No. I don't believe in ghosts either, that's silly."

She looked up to her mom's furrowed brows. "But they're on your mind."

Allie plucked at the letter T on the keyboard. Something about that letter felt wrong. "There's something I still can't understand. When Lily stabbed me..."

Judy winced as if struck and shot a look to the baby, who discarded his toy and reached for the computer. Allie's mom hadn't been able or willing to say Lily's name since the stabbing. Maybe it was like saying the name of the devil for fear you'd invoke his presence. Allie chose her next words more carefully.

"Right after that, I told *the girl* that her mother had sent me. I have no idea why I said that. I've never even met her mom. In fact, she may not even be alive. That brings me back to the question of..."

"Ghosts." Allie's mom leaned in toward the camera. "Sweetheart, listen to me. You have a gift, intuition, whatever you want to call it. I don't know how it works any more than you do, but I do know that it helps you out, and it allows you to help others. What happened after you said those words to *that girl*?"

"She stopped hurting me, and she stopped fighting with Erin."

"Have you finally answered your own question?"

As if all the air in her lungs was stale and needed to be replaced,

Allie heaved a great sigh. That's all it was. A helpful little tip to get the situation under control. The only ghosts were in her imagination.

"Sweetie?"

Allie heard her mother's voice echo, as if through a long tunnel.

"Are you getting one of your headaches?" Her mom's face pinched with worry. "I thought you didn't get those any more. Not since, well, since that thing we talked about."

"It's not the same, but I do feel a bit weird." Lightheaded, Allie pressed her fingers to her forehead. Too late, she remembered her bandaged palm and dropped her hand into her lap. She hadn't wanted to discuss the lighter incident. Besides, the burn was nearly healed.

"What happened to your hand? Did you hurt yourself?"

"Nah, nothing to worry about."

Her mom eyed her shrewdly. "I suppose you'll tell me what you want to. Let me say this. Please take care of yourself, especially if you are taking care of little ones, and talk to Erin about whatever is going on. No secrets."

"I promise." But when would there be time?

The children burst through the door in a flurry of shouting, the girls following Jimmy and the dog. "I scream. You scream. We all scream for ice cream!"

Her mother burst out laughing. "That brings back memories."

Allie grinned and the baby clapped. "It sounds like our house about twenty years ago, doesn't it? I agreed to take Erin's sister's kids because she's been having a rough time with her chemo therapy. The poor woman needed a rest."

"That's my Allie. You were always great with children, whether or not you admitted it."

The kids entered the kitchen as one, Jimmy leaning on Allie's chair, and the twins peeping over her shoulders. The baby squealed with delight at all the excitement.

"Who are these beautiful children?" Allie's mom had certainly heard enough about these particular kids to be able to identify each one by name.

"I'm Sophie and this is—"

"I can say my own name!" The second twin bumped the first with her shoulder. "I'm Victoria, and I'm turning—"

"We're turning twelve in six months." Sophie bumped her back.

"We dressed up Wrong-Way Rachel, and renamed her Princess Lollipop."

"Oh my, the poor disabled cat." Judy shot Allie a look as if to say, "And you allowed this?"

"Don't worry, mom. Rachel only has three paws but she doesn't consider herself disabled. She loves every minute of dress-up time with these two. She'd make herself scarce if she didn't enjoy it as much as they do."

The girls giggled and nodded in agreement.

"And who is this handsome fellow holding Doppler?"

"He's Jimmy," the girls sang out together.

Ever precocious, Jimmy exhaled. "I'm Jimmy, and I'm going to go completely insane if I have to go to the park with my sisters again." He turned to Allie. "Can I wait on the front step with Doppler until you're ready?" She nodded, and he trudged out with the dog.

Victoria held out a small red folding knife. "Look what I got for camp this summer. It's the same as Auntie Allie's. My sister only cares about fashion, but I am going to have a summer of adventure."

"An adventure sounds good, but be careful with that knife." For the second time today, Allie's mom shot her daughter the dreaded frown of disapproval.

Victoria rolled her eyes. "Don't worry, I passed all the safety tests." She put it back in her pocket and counted on her fingers. "The one from my parents, the one from grandpa, and the hardest one from Auntie Erin. If I'm not responsible, it goes right back to mom until I'm thirty."

Judy stifled a laugh. "That's a lot of responsibility, just so you can cut your own marshmallow roasting stick."

"And I can build a lean-to like Auntie Allie showed me." She reached for the baby. "We need more practice babysitting. As soon as we're twelve, mom says we can make big money."

Allie waited until they went into the other room before she looked back at the computer screen.

"I can see your influence on the kids already. You really should consider motherhood. It's the most rewarding thing I've ever done." She gave Allie a wry grin. "And I've always wanted to be a grandmother."

"Mom! Have you forgotten?" Why would her mother taunt her like this? It was medically impossible. The night Lily had nearly killed her, she'd snuffed out any hope of carrying a child.

"No, I haven't forgotten." Her mother met her eyes. "There are many ways to be a parent. You are great with kids and you could offer so much to little ones."

Out of sight of the webcam, Allie traced the scar on her abdomen with her fingers.

"Maybe this is not the best time."

"No, it's not." How could she protect a child when she couldn't even keep herself safe? She examined the dust on the keyboard. The letters scrambled, and multicolored starbursts exploded behind her eyes. Oily smoke wound like a snake through the light, its black trail bleeding into the color. A dry lump lodged in her throat. *Scheisse.* What she wouldn't give for a Budweiser.

As hard as she could, she balled her hand into a fist, fingernails biting into her palms. *No. Not now.* She forced words past her lips. "I have to go."

"Right. You can't leave the kids waiting for ice cream." Her mother rang off.

Allie pushed the computer aside when the tabletop loomed in her vision. She closed her eyes in anticipation of her forehead colliding with polished wood.

"The twins already put the baby in the car. Are you coming, or…" Jimmy's concerned voice broke through the suffocating black clouds. "Auntie Allie?"

Doppler landed on her lap, licking her cheek in a frenzy of worry. A ray of light seared the mental fog, enough to allow her to open her eyes. She sucked in a lungful of pure air and the oily vapor dissipated.

"Are you okay?" He bent closer, his forehead puckered.

Doppler rubbed his muzzle under her chin and she stroked his back, feeling more herself with each touch. "It's okay, Chorizo." Her headache evaporated as quickly as it had assaulted her.

"Did you call him a Mexican sausage?" He gaped at Allie. "When Auntie Erin said that, you pinched her."

Sometimes Jimmy sounded more like a teenager than a seven-year-old, but she didn't want him to skip his entire childhood experience. She got to her feet and held out her arm. "Well, you'd better pinch me."

He brushed unruly hair from his eyes. "How about ice cream instead?"

"Sure."

"Can I bring my drone? I need to work on software compatibility with Uncle Thomas's new cell phone. We can fly it at the park on the way home." In his excitement, Jimmy rocked on his toes, like his auntie Erin sometimes did. He'd put in a year's hard work catching fishing bait to sell to Gina's Stop 'N Go, but the young entrepreneur's 'minnow money' was still a bit shy of his goal.

That's when Allie had suggested he ask Erin's brother to come on board as an investor, with flight privileges. She knew that Uncle Thomas, the self-professed computer nerd, couldn't resist opening his wallet for a new toy. Now the two of them were proud owners of a real-life aerial drone with a high resolution, onboard, gyro-stabilized video camera. They flew it every chance they got.

A mound of disorganized paperwork mocked her from the office desk. All this impromptu babysitting had cut into her work schedule. She hadn't planned to be gone that long, but the kids needed her and she needed them.

She flashed him a smile. Why not? The people in her life were more important. Like Jimmy. He was quirky, but also blessed with intellectual brilliance. Someday he might do great things. Who was she to stifle him? Ciara and Raphael could manage their Winnipeg office today.

She flung her bag over her shoulder and texted Erin on her way out to the Jeep. This was the first day they hadn't managed to connect, and it felt like a bad omen.

Erin's name popped up on caller ID before she could send it. "I was just thinking about you." They often called each other simultaneously, and it had long since become normal. "I wondered where you'd been hiding all day."

"I've been super busy." Erin paused to chomp down the rest of whatever she was eating. "Graduation is so close I can taste it." There was a crunching noise as she took another bite. "Everyone else is antsy too."

Allie looked at her watch. It had gotten much later than she'd planned. She should be feeding the kids dinner, not taking them for ice cream. She was a terrible auntie. She listened to Erin talk about her classes while she checked the clasp on Mikey's baby seat.

Sophie slid on her seatbelt, and beamed from her spot beside him. "I did it right, didn't I?"

"We," Victoria corrected from the front seat. "You meant to say *we*. I helped."

Jimmy sighed, and got into the back with Sophie and the baby. He delicately cradled the drone on his lap.

"Yes, it's right," Allie told her. She still had the phone pressed to her ear, but had missed some of the conversation. The acrid odor of oil filled her nostrils. One word had been unmistakable. "Lily? What about Lily?"

"Are you with the kids right now?" With this sudden turn of conversation, Erin's crunching noises had silenced.

"Yes," Allie said loudly. "I am taking the kids for ice cream."

Victoria led the others in the chant. "I scream, you scream…"

Erin's voice was serious. "Tell them I laughed my head off. I don't want to upset them, so I'll make this quick."

"She's laughing her head off." Allie stepped away from the Jeep and lowered her voice. "What's going on?"

"A few days ago, Lily crossed the border and might be in Montana."

"What? I thought you said…" Images of a yellow dotted line flashed past, an older man clutching his chest and falling onto a dirt road, tiny multicolored pills spilling onto a coffee table. A foul taste filled her mouth, and she leaned over to grab her knees.

"She escaped with a male. They are suspects in a carjacking, and also a robbery."

"A gun. She has a gun." The scar on Allie's abdomen burned in fear, and sweat beaded the base of her skull. From the corner of her eye, she saw Jimmy's head pop up in the back window. Summoning all her strength, she forced herself upright. Her stomach turned over once and quieted. She waggled her fingers at him, as if she'd only been bending to pick up something.

"Don't worry," Erin's words were calm but her voice tense. "They are headed west. The Bureau is on it. We'll catch her before you know it."

"No, she's coming back." Allie felt the oncoming storm in her bones. "What do you mean *we'll catch her?* Are you involved in the case?"

"I'm finished my training. All that's left is the actual graduation ceremony. They're letting me in on the hunt for Lily because I might have useful information. Strictly hands off, though. I get to tag along with two senior agents. I'll start with my real training agent when this is over."

"What about the ceremony? You earned it."

"You know where I'd rather be, Baby."

"Be safe, okay? Remember the hands off part." Allie hoped to hell there wouldn't be actual contact with Lily. Knowing that Erin would be associated with the case was bad enough.

"Hurry up, Auntie Allie!" Sophie had rolled down her window, and was now dangling her arms out in a display of impending tween drama. "We're *dying* for ice cream." She contorted, as if in the very throes of death.

"The kids. I have to go." Allie waved back in less dramatic fashion.

"Please," Erin blurted before she could disconnect. "Try to imagine where Lily might be headed. Your intuition usually kicks in if you think about something hard enough. Maybe even think about Derek. It might help us find his daughter."

Allie turned away from the kids and whispered. "Derek is still hiding. The police haven't been able to question him about that murder. Chris Zimmerman said the crime scene was horrible.

There was a tapping noise before Erin spoke. "Do you know if he did it? Where's he hiding?"

"You know I'm not a machine. I don't work like that. Intuition comes whenever it wants." Allie walked back and tossed her bag into the Jeep. "I'd like to help, but I've been really distracted." She stole a glance at the kids in the back seat. "I can't."

"I'm sorry. I had no right to ask. Not after…"

"Oh, Honey. It's okay. I'll help you any time I can, but I can't get my, what do you call it? My *mojo* back. The kids are waiting. I'll talk to you later."

"Auntie Allie? What's a mojo? Are you and Auntie Erin fighting?" Victoria's eleven-year old face suddenly looked too mature for her age.

"No, sweetie." She started the engine. "There's a lot of stuff going on right now. The world is not a perfect place, but we can try to make our little corner of it better." She smiled when Victoria exhaled in relief. "Let's go have some fun!"

"Yay!" In the back seat, the baby clapped his hands.

Allie drove past the houses and turned right onto the main

thoroughfare. A thread of memory tugged at her. Derek Peterson's flat green eyes when he nearly pummeled Erin to death on the river's edge. He was unpredictable, and dangerous. If she hadn't intervened...

She glanced over when sunlight flared off the window of a small car backed into an alley. Even squinting, it was impossible to see anything beyond the glare. *Drive. Keep driving.* She pressed her foot on the gas.

Inside the car, a man hunched in his seat.

CHAPTER ELEVEN

Derek slouched behind the wheel of his rental car when Allie's face turned toward him, and he stayed down until her Jeep was long gone. Had she recognized him? The manhunt for the killer of the victim in the motel was all over the news. He'd nearly run his car into the ditch when he'd heard his own name on the radio not five minutes ago. Was she reporting his location right now?

His stomach rumbled. He needed food and more beer, but the money was gone. The shakes would start soon if he didn't get a drink. The grocery store was always busy, so that was too risky. He kept off the main road and drove across town to Gina's Stop 'N Go, parking out of sight. What would happen if he sauntered through the door and picked up a case of beer? What if he bought a few of those big sandwiches too? The last time he was in there, he'd sworn Gina had a soft spot for him. Would she report him?

He shut off the engine and walked up beside the building. Maybe she wasn't even working today. That would make it simple. He could pull his hat down over his eyes and complete the entire transaction without being recognized. He bobbed his head around the corner and eyed the till. No one was there. Were they in the washroom? Could things be this easy?

He eased the door open, the little bell-on-a-wire tinkling softly. The store remained quiet. That was it, she must be in the washroom. He scurried to the closest fridge and grabbed a case of beer, allowing the door to thump shut in his haste. Gina's head popped up behind a shelf and he dropped into a crouch. His chest heaved and he could already feel the shakes starting. *Goddammit!*

He grabbed an armful of sandwiches from the deli cooler and crab-walked sideways toward the exit. Before he could reach for the handle, Gina loomed in front of him, hands on hips like a librarian about to scold him for an overdue book. The local radio station gave the fishing forecast on the overhead speakers. There was no doubt she'd heard the same report he had. The one that named him a 'person of interest' in the murder of Ethan Lewis.

Should he get up and walk right through her? It wouldn't be hard. He must outweigh her by at least eighty pounds. Yet, there was still that hesitation in the back of his mind. What if she fought? In high school she'd been the tough girl, fucking Erin Ericsson's self-appointed bodyguard. He narrowed his eyes as he remembered how many times she'd run interference between them. All he'd wanted to do was ask Erin out, maybe cop a feel of that developing female body beneath the bleachers, but after his first attempt, Gina had stepped in and he never got a second chance. *Damn her.*

"Hi Derek." One of Gina's hands left her hip and she turned her palm up.

Was she going to help him up or slap him silly? He rose to his feet and looked down at her. "I was just…"

"I see you're in a hurry. Would you like me to put that on your account and you can take care of it next time?" Her expression was innocuous, almost friendly, like she was having an everyday conversation with an everyday customer.

He stared at her but no words came. He was a dangerous felon for all she knew. She'd married a policeman, for frig's sake. What was she playing at? Gina's eyes crinkled at the corners. Was that concern? Worry? Was she afraid of him for a change? He took a step toward her and Gina stepped back.

"You're messing with me," he hissed through his teeth. "As soon as I walk out the door, there'll be four uniforms waiting to jump me." He dropped the armful of sandwiches and leapt forward to pin her against the shelf. "Who did you call? Did you call your husband? Does Z-man think he'll be the big hero if he arrests me again?"

"You're making a mistake." Gina stood stock still while Derek patted down her pockets with his free hand.

"Where's your phone?" He looked her up and down, considered shoving his fist into her shirt to check for it. Her eyes met his and then settled on his trembling hands. The stress was making it worse. Was that pity on her face? Pity for him? The pressure in his head increased. How *dare* she? She thought she was better than him, always had.

Before he knew it, his fingers closed around her windpipe. Soft skin crushed under his scraped knuckles, like velvet, like rose petals. Her hair smelled good. Shampoo with a hint of jasmine, or something. He squeezed, and was almost surprised when her face flushed red. Had he beaten and shot a man to death with these same hands? Oblivious to her fingernails digging into his arms, he bared his teeth like an animal. Like a monster. *Am I a monster?*

Sharp pain seared his right testicle and traveled up into his abdomen. He let go and reeled back, nearly dropping his beer. Nausea followed, and he bent double while saliva dripped from his mouth. Oh, God, had he really become a monster?

"You crazy son of a bitch!" Gina shook out the knuckles she'd jabbed into his groin.

"Z," he panted. "Is Z-man coming for me?"

"I didn't call anyone, you idiot." She massaged her throat and kicked the sandwiches toward him. "Chris knows where you're hiding. Where else were you gonna go? He'll come get you when he's ready. Now, take this crap and get the hell out."

"I-I'm sorry." Derek scooped up the sandwiches and limped toward the door.

"If you ever touch me again, I'll make sure you pee into a bag for the rest of your life."

The door clunked behind him when he fled back to his car. He'd made a colossal mistake. He threw the sandwiches on the seat and cracked open a beer. After the first one, his hands stopped shaking enough for him to get the shifter in gear. This wouldn't last long. He needed cash. Soon.

A few blocks away, he parked beside an abandoned garage. The lawyer owed him money and it was overdue. He reached under the seat for his cell phone, and left a terse voicemail message. A second beer in his hand, he leaned back in his seat to wait. Half an hour. The lawyer had thirty goddamn minutes to get here.

With each swallow, he felt more like himself. Gina was okay. He hadn't hurt her, not really. The lawyer would come with his money, and deal with the cops for him. It was all a big mistake that could be explained away. It *must* be a mistake, if Z-man knew where he was hiding out and hadn't yet arrested him. There wasn't any evidence, was there? He stared at his knuckles. Yeah, he was innocent. Innocent as a newborn babe.

"Shit!" He spilled a mouthful of precious amber liquid down his shirt when his phone rang. There were only a handful of people who knew this number, but caller ID was blocked. So, it wasn't the lawyer trying to cancel the meet. His curiosity overcame him and he touched the screen.

"Yeah?"

"Lieutenant?" Ernie's voice was hushed, as if he was hunkered in the back of the squad room and didn't want anyone else to hear.

"What's up, little buddy?" The relief from his shaking hands and pounding head was making Derek downright punchy.

"Have you heard the news?" Background voices cut out when the phone was muffled. "You should turn yourself in."

"Have they issued a warrant yet?" He drained the rest of his beer and twisted off another cap. Between swallows, he rested the cold bottle against his throbbing testicle. He'd deserved it. He could see that now. What was he thinking?

"Not yet," Ernie's voice dropped lower, "but Chief wants to talk. You need to come in now before this thing escalates."

"Is he there? He is, isn't he?" Derek smiled. "Well, you tell the chief I'm innocent. Unless he has enough evidence to arrest me, and I know he doesn't, he can kiss my hairy ass." He ended the call and tossed the phone on the seat.

The warmth of alcohol was replacing the searing pain in his groin when the lawyer's car pulled in beside him.

Richard skipped out the door and settled into Derek's passenger seat. "You're wanted for murder. I heard it on the radio."

"That's a fine way to greet me, you little shit, and you're wrong. They only want me for questioning. Ain't no warrant because I didn't do it."

Richard's self-satisfied grin faded. "They seem to think you did."

"It makes no sense! Why the hell would I kill a man I didn't even know was out of prison?" He pounded his fist on the dash of the rental car. "You'd better have a plan to get me out of this, Dick."

"They say you knew. They say you met with him that night." His lawyer slumped in the seat beside him. "They say he's the one who cut off your ear, back when you were—"

"Okay, if you're gonna bring that up, get it straight." Derek forced the words through clenched teeth. "He didn't *cut* off my ear. He *bit* it off. Like a goddamn rabid dog."

The lawyer's eyes bugged out, and he stretched his lips into a tight grimace. "And then they called you van G—"

"You weren't inside! You've got no right to say that." Derek leaned close enough for angry spittle to fleck the lawyer's cheek.

Grimace frozen on his face, the lawyer dared not make a move to wipe it.

"They're out to get me. I ain't going back to prison. Get your ass into the station, and fix this."

"We can talk about that in a minute." Richard slid an envelope onto the seat between them. "Here's your money." He flashed unnaturally white teeth that contrasted with artificially tanned skin.

Derek hated him for it. His nose was too straight and his hair was too black. Why didn't anyone look normal anymore? He riffled through the envelope, and held up three fingers. "I said three grand, Dick." He curled his lip. "Not two. Three."

Richard's cheeks reddened. "There is still the matter of my fee for your private investigator's license. I simply deducted the registration—"

"You don't deduct squat." He leaned over and exhaled beer-soaked breath. "I'm a desperate criminal, remember? I'm likely to lose my cool and murder you right here."

"Whoa, whoa, here's the rest." The lawyer retrieved a roll of twenties and dropped it onto the seat. He pulled out a second roll to place beside the first. "This is an extra thousand. A total of four. And I'll agree to represent you at trial on that murder charge."

"Ain't gonna be no trial."

"What do you say we resolve this with a little exchange? I've been thinking about your offer."

"What are you talking about?" Derek frowned.

"Well, you offered to take care of my business partner." His eyes darted to the alley and back. "You know, rough him up some."

"Don't tell me, you've changed your mind, and now you want me to break both of his arms for diddling your wife?"

"Not exactly. I'd like you to take care of my *wife*, permanently."

Derek stared at him. He set down his bottle, curled his fingers tight, and split open his barely healed knuckles on Richard's face. The first punch flattened his nose. The second smashed the lawyer's mouth and sent him backwards. He leaned across and pulled the door latch. With his boot, he shoved the man out onto the gravel in a humiliated heap.

"I ain't no killer for hire, and I don't hurt women." He swallowed the rough lump in his craw. He was not a monster. No, he wasn't. "Don't ever contact me again." He pulled the door shut and spun his tires, leaving the man to spit blood through broken teeth.

Derek slammed the gas pedal to the floor and hit the main road at highway speed. It occurred to him that if a patrol car spotted him, it would all be over. He swore through his clenched jaw and slowed the car. The lawyer had him all wrong. No matter how angry he'd been at his ex-wife, he'd never lifted a hand to her. That thing with Gina hadn't really happened. It was a hallucination or something. That's not the kind of man he was.

Really, was he sure about that? Was he the reason his daughter was bad? Was it genetic? Had Tiffany given Lily the nightmares she drew on the closet wall? Had she really run off and left their daughter? Left him? Maybe it was all his fault. He was poison in their lives. Now, Lily was in a Canadian juvenile detention center, and Tiffany was gone. Had they failed so miserably as parents that they'd destroyed their kid?

CHAPTER TWELVE

In my dream, I shove my mother into the deep end of the bog. She's always telling me what to do. *Shut up. Shut up!* I hit her with my stick, and mud fills her open mouth as she's sucked under. A pocket of air burps to the surface, and then smoothes over as if she had never been.

I squat alone on the little trail, her abandoned purse halfway between me and the spot where she disappeared from my life. The sun moves in the sky and the shadow by the rock inches toward me. Flies buzz around my head. Somewhere a crow calls.

Inside, I expect to feel agony, sadness, all those emotions they talk about in the movies but there's nothing, not a damn thing except a burning desire to know what's in her purse. Finally, I get up to fetch it, take what I want and fill it with rocks. I throw it in after her. She's never coming back.

Worry I'll be discovered, and relief that she's gone, flutter together in my chest. I smoke all her cigarettes until my head pounds. It's time to go. As I turn my back, a skeletal hand darts from the ooze. Bony fingers reach for me, gouge bloody trails in my skin. My mother's face emerges, mouth open in a ghostly wail.

"Mommy! Mommy!" I shove T's arm off my bare chest and sit up.

He groans, squints at me and rubs his eyes.

It's dark. Long seconds pass before I remember where I am, somewhere in Montana, or is it Idaho? In the old house where we are hiding out from the cops.

My mother's screams still echo in my ears, even through my cupped hands. She screams louder, and louder. I'm going insane.

I rake the last few pills off the coffee table and shove them in my mouth. I don't care what color they are, as long as they make the noise stop.

T reaches over and slides a bottle toward me. "Nightmare, snuggle-bunny?"

"I don't dream." I snatch it up, and down the pills with a few swallows of warm beer left over from last night. "And I don't get fucking nightmares. That's for pussies." I wrap my shirt around myself and lean back. I'll feel better soon.

"Whatever you say, but yelling 'Mommy' in your sleep sure sounds like a nightmare." He's ready for it and deflects my backhand before it connects.

When I've finished what's left in the bottoms of all the abandoned beer bottles on the coffee table, my headache eases. "We're out of pills and we're out of beer. It's time to go."

"Okay." He gets to his feet and pulls his sweaty T-shirt on, adjusts his stained ball cap, and tucks his dark hair behind his ears. "Let's see if there's anything here we missed first. We were pretty wasted the last time we searched." He tosses a crocheted doily at me and it makes a spiderweb across my face.

I hate those dainty little things. It reminds me of churchlady's house back in Morley Falls. Everything so neat, and tidy, and old. It was all old.

He disappears into the back of the house and I hear the toilet flush. Then he whoops like he's scored a touchdown. "We forgot to check the bottom drawer in here." He comes out with a handful of prescription bottles. "Look at all the goodies I scored."

I check the labels. "Oxy-something. You smeared it and I can't read the rest."

He laughs with glee. "Don't worry bunny rabbit, anything that starts with Oxy is bound to be good." He pops open the bottle and puts a tiny white pill on his tongue. "What else do we have?"

"There are red capsules, yellow ones and pink ones too." I dump them all out of their bottles and mix them up in my hand.

"That one looks good." T reaches for a shiny red capsule. "I'll have it for dessert."

I snatch it away at the last second, and he looks like I kicked his puppy. "Loser. You're so slow." The pills I already swallowed burn my stomach, and all the straight lines of the room bend into waves. Memories of the skeleton ghost in my dream flutter.

"Give me those." He chases me around the coffee table.

With one hand holding my T-shirt in front of me, I keep the pills clenched tight in my other fist. His eyes flit to the revolver and back. I stop dead. "You wouldn't."

"I'm smarter than that." He snatches my shirt from my fingers and runs. I am after him like a panther, ready to rip him to shreds, but my legs don't cooperate. Walls fold around me like wet cardboard.

By the time I get to the kitchen, T has my shirt in the sink and is standing by an electrical switch on the wall. "Give me those pills or say goodbye to your shirt."

"Kiss my ass. I hate that shirt."

He flips the switch, and a god awful noise emanates from the garbage disposal unit beneath the sink. "You sure?" A wicked smile twitches at the corner of his baby mustache when he turns on the water tap and pushes my T-shirt into the drain.

I narrow my eyes and turn on my heel. "You're a pig. You always take too many. I'll hold the pills." I jam my fist into my pocket and walk out, naked from the waist up, to the sound of T laughing and my shirt being torn to shreds.

In the living room, I pull out my lighter and hold it to a goddamn crocheted doily. Flames devour the lacy edges. I toss it on the couch when it singes my fingers. It smolders out. I light another, and another, until they're all a heap of charred thread. The pills are no longer making me dizzy. Now I feel like I am standing a foot above the floor, and my fingertips buzz with energy. Maybe I've finally transformed into a superior being.

I toss my head back and laugh, but no sound escapes. Instead mud erupts from my guts and splashes on the pink carpet. My mother's skull rises to mock me with its black stare. She's coming for me. Head first, I dive in to gather her bones in my arms. I kick to the surface and stack them like cord wood on the shore. I must burn them. Burn her. I have to get her before she gets me.

"Lily! What are you doing?" T's big hands shake my shoulders and I realize he's standing over me, brows furrowed over dark eyes. "Are you tripping?"

"I have to burn her bones." I shake my head to clear my vision. Someone's smashed the legs off the coffee table and I'm twisted in the throw blanket from the back of the sofa. My fingers are squeezed tight around my lighter. "I want to burn this place down."

"Is this about the lady from church? Are you thinking about how you killed her?" His breath comes, quick and shallow, and he shoves a hand sideways into his jeans pocket. "Tell me about it again."

"Churchlady? Oh, her. I actually didn't know it would happen like that." My head is filled with images of my mother rising out of the mud, and it's hard to wrap my head around what he's asking. "I don't want to talk about churchlady."

"Please, sugar. Please? Tell me how you blew the back of her house clean off. Did you see her explode? Tell me what the fire smelled like. When did you know you'd killed her? Tell me how it felt. Do it for me."

I've told him before, and I tell him again, in a monotone. He thinks that was the first time I'd ever killed anyone, but it's not. My mother was first, but I'm not talking about that. If I say the words out loud, she'll hear. And she'll claw me into the muck with her.

When I'm finished describing how churchlady's blackened shoes stood empty on the top porch step, he drops to his knees beside me. He peels off his T-shirt and slides it over my naked shoulders. It hangs on me like a trash bag. "Sexy," he murmurs. He fusses with the oversize neck so it doesn't slide off my shoulder, and looks down at my hands. "Here, let me help."

I relax my fist, and let him take the lighter from my stiff fingers. Solemn as the god he wants to be, he holds it out in front of his bare chest and ignites the corner of the paper take-out bag. Flames leap upward when he holds it to the drapes, and smoke roils like dragon's breath across the ceiling. The fire alarm shrieks.

T yanks me to my feet and presses the lighter back into my hands. "Your turn."

I light the rest of the wrappers, one by one, and toss the fireballs. My mother fades with each smoky breath I inhale. I'm done. "Let's go."

"Just a sec." He disappears into the bedroom and emerges, pulling on a western shirt that must be a hundred years old.

I cover my mouth before I laugh in his face. "You look like a gay cowboy."

"You know I make this look good." He snaps the pearl button on the breast pocket and stuffs the gun into the back of his jeans. "Let's go get something to eat, sweet cheeks."

When we drive away from the house, an orange glow behind the curtains bids us goodbye. Fire is my friend.

We drive until early afternoon and swap license plates, but we both know we need a new car soon. T has been begging for hours. It makes no difference because I won't give him any more drugs until we stop for the night. He's a useless moron when he's high, and he chopped up my favorite shirt in the goddamn garbage disposal. His smells like a billy goat, so I'm not sure I can forgive him for it. He's all smug in his gay cowboy shirt, driving like a boss, and I'm here in his sweaty, smelly shirt that's falling off my shoulders.

We do a gas and dash somewhere near Yellowstone Park, and T even scores us some food before we make a run for it. He's more controlled, less of a maniac when he's not high.

"Blowing shit up is more fun than burning shit down," he says out of the blue.

"What are you talking about?" I lick the last of my lunch off my fingers and toss the wrapper out the window.

"Remember how it felt when that lady's house blew up in a big fireball? I know how to do that, on purpose. It's way more fun to blow shit up than to play with matches."

"Shut up." What right does he have to criticize my love of fire? "Asshole."

"Come on, sugar." He tilts his head at me. "Don't be like that. I'm only suggesting that you'd enjoy explosive devices. I used to make bombs with my buddies. It's fun."

"I don't think it's my thing." I imagine my lighter heating up in my pocket, burning a hole through my thigh in retaliation. The vision of churchlady's house returns, the explosion and the concussive force of the blast knocking me on my ass, the wonder, the sheer awe of such power. My heart beat fast enough to tear through my chest. "Maybe. I'm just saying maybe."

His little mustache twists, but he's smart enough to play it cool. "Awesome," he whispers. "We are gonna have so much fun together."

I lean back in my seat and pull the huge T-shirt up over my head.

He can drive for a while longer.

Movement in my pocket wakes me and I instinctively lash out. We're stopped on the side of the road and T withdraws his hand to pop something into his mouth.

"You shit!" I kick him away. "I told you, no more until tonight."

"Only a couple, sugar." He sticks out his tongue to show me that he finally got one of the bright red gel capsules. The dessert he wanted so badly. Beside it is a small yellow tablet, and he swallows quick before I can stop him.

"Idiot."

He flashes a row of white teeth and slides back behind the wheel. "Showtime. We need gas and there's a little place up ahead. I doubt there are security cameras."

"Whatever." If he does something stupid, I'll put my knife in his throat and leave him behind. I don't need his shit. I cross my arms, turn my face to the window, and ignore him until we get there.

He pulls in front of the gas pump and gets out to fill up. "Stay out of sight, sweet thing."

I scrunch in my seat. By now, there could be descriptions of us everywhere. I imagine wanted posters on every fence post, like in the old west. In the picture, I'm leaning against the front bumper with the revolver in one hand and my knife in the other, a sneer on my lips. I wish it were true. It could be true if we had a camera.

When T goes in for food, I follow. He shoots me a look and shrugs when the guy behind the counter ignores me. While he picks stuff off the shelves, I check out the cell phones. I've never had one, but kids in school were married to theirs, might as well have been, because they took them everywhere. They'd crowd around each other's tiny screens, whisper and laugh. No one ever asked me to look at their phone. Maybe it had something to do with the fact that they were scared shitless of me. Well, fuck 'em. Now I'm going to get my own.

"Would you like to look at this one?" The man behind the counter has magically appeared, and can't take his eyes off the way T's big shirt hangs open at my neck. I'm pretty sure he can see right down to my belly button.

"Yeah."

He takes one out of the box and turns it on. It lights up with rows of little square pictures when he hands it to me. I have no idea what to do but the kids at school poked at theirs, and wiped those little pictures around, so I do too.

"Nice display, isn't it? It works on GSM, HSPA and LTE. It's got quad core processors and a sixteen megapixel camera."

None of that makes sense except the word camera. "Does it take good pictures?"

"For sure. One of the best out there. Optical zoom, LED flash, and high definition video." He touches one of the square pictures and I see my dirty shoes on the screen. I hold my hand in front of the little glass dot on the back, and my ragged fingernails appear. I'll get T to take a picture of me, one they can use for my wanted poster.

The man looks at my shoes again, and I see judgment crinkle his eyes. "Then there's this one over here. It's a little cheaper and—"

"I like this one." I pick up the box it came in and turn to T. "I'm getting this."

"Great, if you'll come to the counter," the man says, "we can start the paperwork to activate it." He looks sideways at T, who is shoveling candy from the bulk bin directly into his mouth. "Sir, that's not allowed."

T ignores him and pops open the beer he took from the cooler. He drains half in a couple of swallows. "You want one?" he asks me.

"Grab a case and let's go." I walk to the door but the man blocks me with his body.

"I'll have to ask you to—"

I take out my knife and flash it in his face. "I'm leaving, loser."

He grabs a three foot length of pipe from behind the counter and holds it like a baseball bat. "I don't know what you kids are up to," he growls, "but it ends here."

"We'll take what we want," T snarls. "Get out of my way." He snatches the revolver from the small of his back and points it at the man's chest.

"That's probably not even real. You're only a couple of hoodlums. I'm calling the cops and you'll learn your lesson." He reaches for the phone.

T shoves him backward and the man brings up his pipe, clipping him on the side of the head. Blood streams down his temple. He wipes it and stares at the red on his hand. Anger flashes in his eyes. He points the gun at the man's face. Seconds tick by, but T doesn't move. His finger trembles on the trigger.

"T, you're such a pussy." If I had the gun, I'd have shot that shirt-peeping bastard in the face by now. "Do it."

"No." The man's flabby cheeks flush pink. "Drop it and walk away. They'll be easier on you if you do." His voice rises so high he sounds like a woman. It's funny and I snort through my nose.

T's trigger finger tenses. "I'll do it. I swear to God, I'll—"

The man swings his pipe again, and there's a ping when it bounces off T's kneecap.

T squawks and squeezes the trigger. *BANG!* The man goes down.

Goddamn it. He finally did it. T shot that guy. I didn't think he would. Blood gushes through the man's shirt, already spilling onto the white tile. I squat beside him and watch his eyelids flutter, excitement bubbling in my belly so hard I want to shout, to scream at the top of my lungs, to dance in a circle like a wild savage.

Instead, I freeze in awe when the blood spreads into a pattern across the floor, like butterfly wings, like spilled juice. I poke him in the ribs with my blade but he doesn't make a sound. He's a deader, for sure.

I tuck my knife back into my pocket and look back up at T. He's still standing there, gun held out in front of him, frozen like a hulking statue in a gay cowboy shirt. That's when I spot the glass eye of a security camera mounted on the wall. How did I not see it before? It's staring straight at me.

I tear the gun from T's hands and he unfreezes. He crumples to the ground, holding his knee. My ears are gonna bleed with the way he whimpers like a baby. It's annoying. I prod him with the toe of my shoe.

"Ow! That's cruel."

That makes me smile. "Maybe. Get up. We gotta go." I point to the camera on the wall, but T curls into a ball beside the dead guy, whose blood is still oozing through his shirt.

What the hell, they've already got me, so I might as well enjoy my moment of fame. I raise my new phone and touch the square picture, point it at the pair of losers and do what the man did. I poke the dot and the screen flashes. The picture stays for a moment and then slides right, ready for the next. This is the coolest thing ever. I take a couple more and go to the door.

"I need a doctor," T groans like a pussy.

"I'm leaving. You can lay there with the dead guy, or you can get your ass in the car." I pick up the case of beer and walk out.

By the time I get behind the wheel, T is staggering out the door. Blood has matted his hair and he's putting all his weight on one leg. He collapses into the back seat and stretches out, chest heaving with the effort.

I hand him a beer. "Here put this on it. It's cold."

"Thank you," he says, like a child.

"And maybe you'll stop your whining." I put the car into gear and hit the gas. They'll be coming. As soon as the next customer walks through that door, the troopers will be on our tail. We need to switch cars, but there's no time, and I'm not carrying that jackass anywhere.

T begs until I give him more of the little white pills, the ones he calls Oxy. They're his favorite, and the only way to shut him up. When they kick in, he conks out. I keep driving until daylight's gone and the gas tank is nearly empty. Now I'm getting tired, but there's no good place to pull off for sleep. Besides, that's a sure way to get arrested, right?

Finally, his clothes rustle and his head pops up in my rear view mirror. "I gotta take a whiz." Even in the dark, his eyes are bloodshot.

"Can't you hold it?" I don't tell him I already stopped twice to pee while he was sleeping and didn't bother to wake him.

"Hell, no. I really gotta go. I can't make it all the way to California without taking a leak." He snickers and I know he's not feeling much pain right now. Whatever is in Oxy, he loves it.

"I told you, I don't want to go to California."

"Sure you do. We'll live on the beach, and surf, and make babies."

"I don't fucking want to live on a beach!"

He stops like I slapped him. "But, I thought—"

"I *never* wanted to go to California. Fuck California! I told you, I want to go home."

"I'm sorry, sugar. I didn't realize you seriously wanted to go to Minnesota."

"Yeah, I'm serious." I am rip-out-your-throat serious.

"Okay. We'll talk about it. Right after you stop and let me take a piss."

"Fine. At the next turn— holy shit!" I was so distracted by T's California delusion that I never saw it coming, until red and blue lights blaze into my eyes from all the mirrors at once. That trooper is right on my ass. I grip the steering wheel with both hands. This is it. Do we run or fight?

"Should I shoot him?" T yells from the back seat. "Should we take his gun? Hey, let's steal his car." He sounds high and I'm not sure I can trust him.

"Hand me the gun. I wanna do it." I ease off on the gas pedal and T lurches forward. He's wasted. He can barely sit up on his own. I steer to the right and the trooper slows too. "Give me the gun, goddammit!

T drops it over the seat. I fumble for it in the dark and wrap my fingers around the grip. The weight of it feels good in my hand. I'll shoot that guy in the face and he won't even know what hit him. What does it feel like to shoot someone? I'm pretty sure I'm gonna like it.

The cruiser's lights blind me, his bumper close enough to kiss mine. I slow to a stop, but my mind is miles ahead. The anticipation of the biggest event in my life is more of a rush than any of those pills in my pocket. As soon as that cop walks up, I'll blow him away.

CHAPTER THIRTEEN

Newly minted FBI Special Agent Erin Ericsson nodded her head at the images on her training agent's cell phone. Pictures from the gas station's security camera were still flooding in, but Erin didn't need to see any more to be able to identify Lily Schmidt. A year-and-a-half older than the last time she'd seen her, but the girl had stared straight into the camera and there was no doubt.

She'd never seen the male suspect before, the tall young man with the gun who'd walked out with a bad limp. She handed the cell phone back to Special Agent Shirley Lockwood.

Erin had met Shirley for the first time yesterday morning at eight o'clock sharp in an FBI Academy conference room. While Lockwood and the Academy Director had discussed the logistics of her being brought in on the task force, she'd fidgeted at the other end of the table.

It was highly unusual to allow a trainee to exit early, he'd said, even this close to graduation. But she had a connection, and valuable insight to offer on an ongoing investigation, Lockwood had countered. The verbal ping pong went back and forth until Erin's head throbbed.

Her instructors had been consulted, and signed off on all training requirements, all but the dreaded law course for which she'd written her last exam an hour ago. She willed her leg to cease its incessant thumping under the table while they waited for the results.

The Director leafed through the instructor reports, summarizing the highlights. "Exemplary, outstanding, good, good, excellent driving skills, honors in firearms and fitness." He looked down the table at Erin. "I see that you completed the Yellow Brick Road more than once. Your instructor noted that you did it 'for fun'. I'm not sure if I'm impressed, or alarmed that you seemed to enjoy our grueling obstacle course."

Erin's face flushed.

Lockwood guffawed.

The Director shook his head. "You're one to laugh, Shirley, you over-achiever. How many bricks have you earned now? Yellow, blue, green?"

"Green?" she sputtered. "I can't smoke that many cigars!" They laughed like high school friends.

Erin traced the outline of the table edge, back and forth, again and again, until she realized what she was doing and stopped that too. She looked at the clock. It hadn't moved more than two tick points from the last time she'd checked. When the desk phone finally jangled, her pulse thudded in her ears.

"Director Simms." He listened for a moment before plunking it back into its cradle. "Very well."

Erin shot to her feet so fast that her chair rocked back, dangerously close to overturning. "Yes, sir?"

"Congratulations, Special Agent Ericsson. Although I regret that you will have to miss your official graduation ceremony, I wish you every success in your future with the Bureau." He reached out for Erin's sweaty hand, and she wiped it on her pants before they shook.

"That's good news." Lockwood rose to her feet. "Pick up your firearm and get your things in order, Ericsson. We've got a flight to catch in an hour, and a long trip ahead." She held the door open for Erin. "The clock's ticking."

Erin sprinted for her room, stopping long enough to hug Davis in the dorm stairwell.

"Don't worry, hummingbird, we'll keep in touch." He lifted her off the ground and squeezed the breath from her lungs. "Sorry you'll miss the graduation party, but we're all jealous that you get to be the first one in the field." He rubbed a misty eye. "Thanks for helping me pass firearms, and remember to be safe out there."

"I have to pack!" She kissed his cheek and wiggled free, sprinting up the six flights of stairs to her room. She threw her belongings into a suitcase without folding them, which irked her immensely, and sat on it to get the zipper closed. After one last check for forgotten toiletries, she raced to pick up her Glock 40 on the way out. Even with her haste, they missed their flight to Salt Lake and were rescheduled to the next one, with a four hour stop in Dallas.

Erin could still hear Lockwood's exasperation with the airline booking agent ringing in her ears. 'Dallas! If I wanted to go to gaul darn Dallas, I would have booked tickets to Dallas. I need to get to Salt Lake, pronto!'

They'd bided their time at Dallas airport with Erin fidgeting uncontrollably, and Lockwood stonily silent. Erin opened her bag and made sure she hadn't forgotten anything. Toothbrush, check. Toothpaste, check. Underwear, check. Had she remembered the toothbrush? She started again. The third time she checked for her toothbrush, she realized she was being watched.

Lockwood exhaled loudly. "You're driving me batty, with your packing and unpacking. Why don't you go find us some coffee and I'll babysit your luggage?"

"Uh, okay." That's what Erin needed, a brisk walk. A run would be better but she could imagine the commotion she'd cause if she sprinted through the airport. Maybe she could find something to clean her fingernails.

She power-walked from one end of the airport to the other. *Focus on the present. Don't worry about the past, nor the future. Focus on the job at hand.* Her dad's words resonated in her mind. He was a smart man, always saying what she'd needed to hear.

In the restroom, she washed her hands, and then she washed them again. She straightened her hair and made sure the little spikes stuck upright, evenly arranged, but seemingly random.

She returned to Lockwood in a calmer state, carrying two hot coffees. When they finally arrived in Salt Lake, there was barely time for a short nap before their morning meeting. Erin was bone-tired and starving.

Special Agent Javier Gonzales, who was joining them on the investigation, smiled when he let them into a conference room. Erin beamed back, her day brightening considerably when she spied a box of pastries and a pot of coffee on the desk. She didn't even care if it was that watery swill from the grocery store. There was coffee and food. She could have kissed his sun-bronzed face.

A few hours later, they'd signed out a Bureau car and Gonzales drove them north to the Idaho-Utah border, where the State Troopers were planning a takedown.

Agent Lockwood jotted notes on a yellow legal pad, and turned to a middle-aged state trooper with stripes on his sleeve. "You understand that this is an officer safety issue. It's not about jurisdiction, or whose pecker is biggest." She smiled and crow's feet radiated from the corners of her eyes. Each syllable that followed was carefully enunciated. "Your man is about to get himself into an untenable position with two armed felons. I'm respectfully requesting that you direct him to stand down and allow the suspect vehicle to come to us. We're better prepared at this location."

The trooper's jacket flapped and he held onto his hat when he tilted his head toward her. The wind tore the words from his mouth as soon as he uttered them.

Erin turned away, unable to continue her eavesdropping. She picked up the computer tablet from the hood of the State Highway Patrol car, and rotated the map of Utah on the screen. "Where was the car spotted?" she shouted above the gale.

Beside her, Agent Gonzales followed the network of highway lines and pointed to a spot north of Ogden. "Right here." That was only a few miles from their current road block. He leaned in and traced the line to a dot further north in Idaho. "This is the gas station they hit. The owner played dead until the suspects left, and then managed to call 911."

"Corporal Porter. Stand down! Stand down!" The trooper shouted into his portable radio. The wind swept the hat from his head, but he made no move to chase it when it bounced across the asphalt. "Kyle, do not engage that vehicle."

He stomped his boot at the garbled reply, and repeated his message before calling out to a young trooper. "What's the ETA on our suspects?"

"Ten minutes!" the trooper shouted above the wind. He dashed across the road and deployed the Stop Stick, a device designed to puncture tires and bring suspect vehicles to a halt.

"Ten minutes?" Agent Lockwood shouldered her way between Erin and Agent Gonzales. "If that's how much time we've got before the party starts, that's time enough to fill you two in." She held her pad of paper close to her ample chest and peered down through a pair of bifocals.

Erin and Gonzales exchanged a grin. Fighting a losing battle with the gray streaks in her auburn hair, Lockwood was old school. Old, old school. Months from retirement, she hearkened to the days where phones had dials and records were made on paper, not tapped into magical glowing boxes.

Agent Lockwood peered through the bottom half of the lenses at her handwritten notes. "Lily Anne Schmidt, fifteen years old, NCIC says she was serving a youth sentence for assault causing bodily harm up in Cana—"

"Should have been one count of murder and one of attempted murder. I'm certain she was the one who killed that girl's father and Allie nearly died too, but they plea bargained—" Erin stopped mid-sentence when she caught her training agent's frown.

"Yes, Agent Ericsson. We've all heard about what happened to your wife."

Erin's mouth twitched. "She's not technically my wife."

"Uh, huh. I guess that depends on your definition of *wife*." She exhaled loudly. "Now, can I carry on before two bad little kids drive right past our road block while we're standing here arguing semantics?"

Erin looked at her shoes. "My apologies, ma'am."

Lockwood squinted back down at her papers. "The young man's name is Trenton Leslie Madison, age seventeen." She twisted her mouth. "Geez, with two girlie-sounding names, it's no wonder that boy goes by T. Numerous convictions for fraud, false pretenses, and oh lookie here, he's a sex offender. Likes pre-teen girls. Well, that explains why he's on the run with your little friend. She looks young enough to be in elementary school."

Erin raised her eyebrows.

"You wanna say something enlightening before we run outta time?"

"Uh, before she was caught the last time, Lily was with a girl. I sort of assumed..." She cleared her throat. "I was wondering what the power balance is between these two suspects. In my experience, Lily likes to be in charge, to call the shots, so to speak. She's comfortable in the woods and prefers rural settings. With this older boy and his revolver, I wonder if the power balance has shifted. He's nearly a man. Perhaps he's in charge. If so, her actions may be unpredictable and it's anyone's guess where they are ultimately headed."

"Good point. I guess you won't be any help on this case after all. Might as well pack your PJs and go home."

Erin's jaw dropped and she shot a sideways look at Gonzales, who was studiously examining his fingernails.

"Oh, lighten up Ericsson. I'm makin' a funny." Lockwood handed her cell phone to Erin. "I know the gas station pictures are on there, but I can't for the life of me figure out where they went. Why does the Bureau keep making us do so many dang upgrades? I just got the last phone figured out and now I have to learn a whole new one. I'm putting you in charge of organizing the data our agents at the scene are sending over."

Erin took the phone and forced a smile, as if she knew Agent Lockwood was kidding the whole time. She thumbed through the images, and made a new folder to store the files from this case. Living with a tech savvy girlfriend had taught her a thing or two about digital organization.

"How much time have we got left, sir?" Lockwood shouted to the trooper, and nodded when he held up five fingers. She turned back to Erin and Agent Gonzales. "His boys are going to come in from the north, in case the kids spot us and double back. Let's go over the route to see if we can figure out where they're headed." She circled an entry on her notepad and drew a rudimentary map of the northern U.S.

"We got an illegal border crossing here, a string of vehicle thefts across these three states, and the carjacking here. That's when they accelerated and stabbed the elderly female. The male victim suffered a heart attack two miles down the road when he went for help. That's our first casualty. Then they graduated from a knife to a gun when they pulled the truck stop robbery near Billings."

Gonzales nodded. "We're working on a probable connection to a residential break-in and subsequent arson in the general vicinity of that same truck stop, so it might be where they holed up. Those two idiots actually held up the same truck stop twice."

"I guess they liked the food," Lockwood snorted, "or they're stupid."

"Stupid and high on drugs," he agreed. "Witnesses say they were irrational, out of control. Video from the most recent crime backs that up. It sure seems like they're on something."

Lockwood nodded. "The residential break-in and fire. That's probably why they dropped off the radar for a couple of days. They lie low to recharge their batteries, and torch it when they're done. The next time they rob a gas station, they're bolder. They try their hand at murder, but don't quite succeed. You can bet your next paycheck that they'll do it again. Am I missing anything?"

Erin clenched her fist until her fingernails bit into her skin. "Lily is like a ghost. One second she's there, but if you blink, she's gone. She's been driving since she could reach the pedals and stealing cars almost as long. She likes fire. It's probable that she's the one who instigated the arson. She's impulsive and doesn't care who she hurts, as long as she gets what she wants." The memory of Lily's cool green eyes boring into hers sent a shiver up her spine. "And the boy's injured. It didn't look like he could walk far on that leg."

"Noted." Agent Lockwood turned and peered down the road at a set of oncoming headlights. "If there's going to be a foot chase, I call dibs on the gimpy one."

Erin's heart sped up. She retrieved a standard issue shotgun from the FBI vehicle, and hunkered behind the engine block of a marked car beside the young trooper who'd deployed the stop stick. He edged over to allow her room to chamber a cartridge. She sighted down the barrel and waited, her breath steady and even. Wind howled across the road and treetops scraped jagged fingers against the sky. Fine hairs on the back of her neck pulled taut.

The approaching headlights were nearly upon them when the trooper in charge called out. "It's Kyle!"

Erin raised her barrel to the sky while the incoming squad car eased behind the highway patrol vehicles lining the pavement. When he was safely out of the way, she sighted down the road again. And waited. And waited.

"Where in tarnation did they go?" Agent Lockwood shouted.

The trooper was already on his radio, calling back to the chase vehicles positioned to the north. "They didn't turn around. No one's come back the way they came. They've vanished. Boys, let's get out there and search every inch of this highway. We'll have our men come down from the north to squeeze them in the middle. Those rabbits have gone to ground and we need to flush them out." He motioned to Agent Lockwood who snatched up her notepad and leapt into the passenger seat of his car. "I want check-ins every five minutes. Nobody approaches that car on his own," he hollered out the window as they drove off, followed by a trail of highway patrol cars.

Gonzales shrugged at Erin. "I guess it's you and me, kid. I'm driving."

Erin looked at the 870 Remington in her hands. "Then I guess I'll, uh, I'll call shotgun."

He cackled and got behind the wheel of their unmarked car.

CHAPTER FOURTEEN

"Shut up! I should have left you back there with the dead guy." My head will explode if T whines one more time.

"But it hurts a lot. Look how swollen it is." He pulls up his pant leg to show me his knee. It's purple and twice the size it used to be. "Come on, Lily. Gimme another Oxy."

That's it, he needs to shut up. I dig into my pocket for another pill and toss it on the floor where he scrabbles for it like a starving dog. The beer ran out long ago, so he's got to dry swallow it, but he manages to choke it down. Soon, he sighs and leans his head against the seat, his long legs twisted sideways. With his blood-crusted hair and sweaty face, he looks like shit.

I guess today might not have been one of his better days. He almost pissed his pants when he thought that cop was pulling us over. I, on the other hand, was kind of looking forward to it. It was such a huge disappointment when he suddenly turned off his lights and blasted past. As soon as he was gone, T threatened to take a leak on the floor unless I pulled over right then and there.

I was so angry about losing my chance to shoot the cop that I cranked the wheel and bumped a half mile across a farmer's field before I let him out. Good thing too. We'd never have seen this truck behind the Quonset otherwise. How often do you find keys in the ignition and a full tank of gas? Sometimes I'm lucky.

I crank down the window and hang out my elbow, trying every damn back road in the state to figure out which one will link up with the highway. Finally, there's a paved road with an actual yellow line painted down the middle. This one will do. The sun is coming up in my eyes and my stomach is rumbling again, but it feels damn good to be headed east. Home is east. The sign for Rock Springs flashes past. We're in Wyoming.

"Tell me about Minnesota, sugar." T's eyes are closed and his words tumble out all fuzzy, like he's got a mouth full of cotton. "Can we surf?" He pulls his hat down to shield his face from the morning light.

"It's perfect. There's a house, and a shed, and a dock to the river. I can take the boat all the way downstream to my secret place. It used to be my grandfather's, but it's mine now."

"Sorry to hear your grandpa died."

"He's not dead. Last I heard he's still breathing, but he's messed up."

"So, how is the place yours?" The bastard tilts the brim of his hat up to squint at me.

"Shut up, T. I said it's mine." I could punch him in the sore knee right now if I could reach that far.

"You've been gone a while. What if your grandpa sold his place?"

That possibility had never crossed my mind. Why does T have to continually piss me off? I slam my fist into the steering wheel until my knuckles sting. If someone new is at my bog, they'll be sorry.

"Are you even welcome at home? What aren't you telling me?" He's wide awake now and straightens up in his seat.

Scheisse! Shut up. I fish around in my pocket until I find a pill and flash him my happy smile. "Here, you need one of these."

He raises an eyebrow when he takes it. "Somebody's keeping secrets."

"We need beer." I really do need a Budweiser. I like the little white pills too, but I hate waking up with T's sweaty hands all over me. Beer is better.

"Why won't you tell me?" He pokes me in the shoulder with his finger. "Don't keep secrets."

"Secrets?" If the gun wasn't tucked in the back of his pants right now, I'd be tempted to shoot him in his lying face. "Who's keeping secrets? You're the guy who won't even say why he was in juvy! I don't believe the bullshit you made up."

He narrows his eyes, black with anger, good ol' boy grin fading. "I'll tell you if you tell me."

"You first."

He bites his bottom lip for a moment, and I wonder if he too wants to shoot me in the face. "I was in for using credit cards that weren't mine, a lot of credit cards, and a school fundraiser I took cash from."

"What else?" There is no way that is the secret he was protecting. There's more.

"I wrote checks on an account that wasn't mine. It was my neighbor's. That old lady practically gave them to me, leaving them lying around like that."

"That's not everything. I won't tell you shit if you don't tell me."

He takes the time to bend the brim on his hat until it's the right curve. "A kid said I, uh, messed with her." His eyes are on his shoes when he says it.

I cover my mouth so I don't laugh. T's a skinner. In juvy, child molesters like him were fair game for anyone who wanted to pound on somebody. Even the staff, who were supposed to protect everyone, turned a blind eye when it happened. T was the guy at the very bottom of the juvy ladder. "Holy shit. No wonder you were hiding out in the library. Did you kill her?"

"No! I never hurt her. Never, never. I loved her. Besides, she was eight, going on eighteen, and she was asking for it. You should have seen the outfits she wore. She came on to *me*."

"You and I both know that's bullshit. She probably hated you the whole time."

"No." The hamster wheel turns in his brain. "Maybe. See this?" He touches the bridge of his crooked nose. "My sister broke it when she found out. *She* hates me for sure. Wasn't no family loyalty there. She turned me over to the pigs faster than I could pack my shit and get out. Said I can never see her or her kid again." He looked up from his shoes. "Now you hate me too, don't you?"

"Why? I don't give a shit who you screw. Do whatever you want, but not to me. I don't like to be touched." At first the pills were fun, but I hated the way they made me feel afterward. I was weak, and I despised waking up with his hands on me.

"Aw, come on," he pleads. "I knew, I fuckin' knew this was gonna happen." He hammers his fist onto his swollen knee and yelps in pain.

Why do people hurt themselves when what they really want to do is hurt someone else? I wish, someday, someone would explain that to me.

"Come on, sugar. I'll be so gentle." His eyebrows tilt, begging me to trust him.

I shake my head. My own tricks are not gonna work for you, loser. "No way. You know what'll happen if you try it."

"You gotta understand, a man's got *needs*." Is that a tear rolling down his cheek? Unbelievable.

"I don't care. Find someone else." Oh my God, he's being such a dramatic pussy, I can't believe it.

"Lily, please."

"Fuck, I'll help you find someone else, if you keep your paws off me." I can't believe those words came out of my mouth. When the hell have I *ever* offered to help anyone? Well, maybe once. I remember the freckled girl who had a crush on me in Winnipeg. Innocent, smart Nina, who was almost perfect. Then she wasn't. I got easy time in juvy, and she got sent to Lakewood.

"Really? You'd do that for me?" He couldn't be grinning any wider. "How did you know it's my birthday?"

"Bullshit."

"It's true. Today I turned eighteen."

"Really? You're an adult?" I kind of believe him. He looks twenty-four. "You better get to work on that mustache. You've got a long way to go until you're a man." I punch him in the ribs.

He takes it without flinching and looks me square in the eye. "What are you giving me for my birthday? Will you help me find someone we can party with?

"Yeah, sure. Why not?" This is a new twist for me. Maybe it would be fun. T is more exciting than Nina ever was. She was such a stick in the mud, but he's a rush to be around when he has a gun in his hand. That dead guy we left at the gas station is proof. If T gets this one thing he wants, will he help me do what I want?

"Tell me your secret." T leans forward. He doesn't want to miss a single word I say.

"Let me hold the gun first."

He doesn't hesitate to hand it over, and I grip it tight. It feels like a living thing against my palm. Not a friend like my knife. Something else. An ally?

"Now tell me." T squeezes his hand into his pocket and closes his eyes.

"No." Not for one second did I intend to tell him a damn thing. I'll never tell him about the witch in Morley Falls who saw inside my head the first time we met. Even with my knife in her guts, she wouldn't die. If I kill her and her cop girlfriend, my mother will stay in her grave and I'll finally be free. Free in my bog. *My* bog.

My stomach growls like it's eating itself from the inside out. "I'm starving. I want a cheeseburger, and we're outta beer again."

CHAPTER FIFTEEN

Perched on the desk, Wrong-Way Rachel grumbled when Allie pushed her chair away. The cat swished her tail and stretched out across the keyboard, the glow of the computer monitor backlighting her gray fur like a halo.

At some point, when she was configuring a client's network connection, the sky had grown dark. Allie hadn't thought to turn the lights on until now. She got up and hit the wall switch, blinking in the sudden glare.

Shadows retreated, but she could still feel them, like insects crawling on her skin, like tar bubbling on the surface of a road patch in blistering heat. Lily was coming. She knew it as surely as she knew the sun would rise tomorrow. Cells vibrated in her body and she could not sit still. A veritable tidal wave of darkness was headed straight for Morley Falls. It threatened to drown her, and those to whom she was closest. Could Erin find Lily and stop the wave before it arrived?

Was the alarm set? She'd checked it an hour ago, but had she turned it on, or off? Doppler got up from his bed and paced her to the front porch. The security system was so old, she didn't even know if it worked any more. What if she was setting it every night and it was useless?

She unlocked the knob, pulled the door open and counted the warning beeps. It usually reached ten or eleven by the time she punched in her code, even with an armload of groceries. Sixteen, seventeen... The beeps were closer together now. Would it go off or mock her with its silence?

Doppler's tail stuck straight out behind him, and his hair raised on end, when the siren abruptly wailed. Like an old police car from the movies, it was much louder than she'd ever guessed. She jabbed at the numbers, got it wrong in her haste, and tried again. The red light turned to green and the horn silenced. Her ears rang like they had after her first rock concert.

"I'm so sorry! That must have hurt your ears." Doppler put his paws on her knee, wanting to be picked up. She scooped him into her arms and snuggled him to her chest. Wait until Erin saw what she'd been letting him get away with.

With two fingers, she opened the blinds and peeked out the window at porch lights turning on halfway down the street. Inquisitive neighbors wanted to know what the ruckus was about. She hoped no one called it in. It would be embarrassing to have the police swarm the house with guns drawn. Officer Chris Zimmerman might be the only one who would understand, and forgive her for testing the alarm so late at night.

Suddenly she was starving. It was as if her stomach was eating itself from the inside out. She desperately wanted a cheeseburger. She snatched her bag and car keys, and headed out to the Jeep. Nothing was open this time of night. Nothing but Gina's Stop 'N Go. She loaded the dog onto the passenger seat and backed out the driveway.

As if she'd been waiting, Gina opened the door when Allie arrived. "I was about to lock up. What are you doing here so late?" She looked over Allie's shoulder to the dog standing on the driver's seat, paws on the wheel to watch them. "You run out of dog food?" She glanced at her watch. "Come on in, girl."

Allie hesitated in the doorway.

"There's no closing time for you." Gina ushered her in and shut the door. "We can catch up on gossip. Chris is home with Li'l Z tonight. Omigosh, I can't believe I called my son that! Those guys at the station are incorrigible. They even bought Mikey a little police vest that says Li'l Z across the back. I didn't name him after my father so everyone could call him some rapper name."

She stopped and reached out for Allie's hand. "Are you okay? You're so pale, you almost look Caucasian." Her smile faded. "Seriously, are you coming down with something? Would you like to sit down?"

"Do you have any cheeseburgers? I really need a cheeseburger." Allie could think of nothing else. The desire was so great, it was all consuming. "And a Budweiser."

"A cheeseburger? You, Alyssa Brody, want a hunk of fried cow? You *are* sick. When did you start eating beef? Not that there's anything wrong with beef, but—"

"And a beer. I need a beer." Allie stared past Gina at the rows of shiny cans glittering in the fridge.

One hand on her hip, Gina positioned herself between Allie and the coolers. "You don't drink, remember? Bad things happen, you lose your freaking mind and stuff. We've talked about it over chamomile tea, like a million times. What's going on? Do I need to call an exorcist or something?"

"What?" Oily black shadows swirled in her mind, and then vaporized. "I don't... I don't know why that came out of my mouth. Burgers are disgusting. And if I was ever stupid enough to drink alcohol again, it wouldn't be beer."

"It would be that blueberry wine Erin's mom makes," Gina finished. "That stuff's yummy." Her mouth smiled, but her eyes were still worried. "Seriously, do you want me to call someone? Your mom? Erin?"

Allie shook her head. "Erin's in the field."

"I haven't seen you this upset since you came back from Winnipeg." Gina tilted her head. "Is that what this is about? Has something happened?"

"Lily's escaped. She's coming."

"Holy hell! So, that's where your hot girlfriend is. I wondered what happened to her graduation. I thought maybe she had to do some remedial..." She waggled her hand.

"Erin and her training agents tracked Lily west, but they lost her. I think that's because she's not going west. She's coming here."

"That's bad news. Let's hope they catch her quick." Gina rubbed a red mark on her throat. "Derek's going to have a total meltdown when he finds out."

A vision of large hands around Gina's neck surfaced in Allie's mind, the man bending double and cupping his crotch. "Did you tell Chris what Derek did to you today?"

"How can you know that?" Gina frowned. "I wish you'd called

me earlier and given me a little heads up on that."

"I didn't know it until now. I looked at that display and imagined the two of you struggling in front of it."

Gina straightened a package on the shelf. "Yup, you guessed it. This is where it happened. Don't tell Chris. Derek didn't mean it, and believe me, he's sorry. He'll be crying for days, every time he pees." She shrugged at Allie. "You see all this, and you don't realize when you're channeling a beer guzzling, burger-eating carnivore?"

"Channeling? I'm not—"

"Girl, you can say you're a good guesser, or you have intuition, or whatever works for your denial system, but my gypsy ancestors called it being psychic. You're psychic."

"No. I'm..." Allie sighed. "I have a weird ability. I don't want a label. I can't do party tricks. I can't solve crimes. I can't even get it to work when I want."

"Don't worry, Chris didn't need you to tell him that there weren't enough grounds to arrest Derek, and frankly I'm not convinced he's the one who murdered that guy. I've seen him at his best and worst. He's a pathetic jerk, but I don't want to believe he's a stone cold killer." She distanced herself from the offending shelf. "Even so, the dumb ass should check himself into detox before he really does kill someone."

"I should go home. Maybe I've been working too much. All I really need is a little milk for my morning latte." Allie plucked a carton from the cooler.

Gina waved her money away. "Don't think of it. I'm coming over first thing in the morning to drink it anyhow. You're going to make me a fancy coffee, and we'll talk about what a great night's sleep you got. Mikey can pull every damn thing from *your* cupboards for a change, and we can talk about how smart he's getting."

"Maybe between the two of us, we can keep track of him." Where were her keys? Had she left them in the ignition? She had not been herself when she'd arrived.

"Hah, he takes after his dad," Gina snorted. "We can also talk about Erin's little niece. Not the twin with the fancy dresses, the one who wears the army boots."

"That's Victoria!"

"Go figure. She's what? Eleven? Too young for sneaking around with boys. Her young fella comes in and buys the candy, but I see her out there behind the trees. I don't want to be the one to tell her mom. That's your job, okay?"

"So that explains why she takes off alone on her bicycle every once in a while. A boy. I'll talk to her about sneaking around." Allie opened the door and turned back to Gina. "You had gypsy ancestors?"

"No, not really, but it's a good story, eh? Now, get in your Jeep, and call your parents in Toronto before you even turn the engine on. You need a mom hug or something." Gina closed the door and twisted the deadbolt. "See you tomorrow." She stayed behind the glass until Allie showed her the phone in her hand.

Doppler perked his ears up when her mom answered the phone on the second ring. "Hi sweetie. It's late. Rough night? Need to talk?" The dog wiggled onto her lap. What would Erin say about all the bad habits he was learning in her absence? The last vestiges of shadow smoke wafted away. Allie put the call on speaker before she drove away.

CHAPTER SIXTEEN

Derek Peterson pulled the collar of his windbreaker up over his ears. He backed his shoulders against the concrete bridge supports under the lip of the deck above. Two feet from where he stood, fat droplets of rain bounced off the pavement. His shoes were soaked, and his pants were wet to his knees from slogging through the swamp to get here.

Ernie had picked this location. It had been their meeting place when he was still on the job. Two patrol cars could fit end-to-end under the bridge, one to keep watch and write reports, the other to catch some shut eye, although it always seemed to be Derek's turn to nap.

This place was easy to access by car, but he hadn't wanted to risk being spotted crossing town in his rental. It had not been as easy to get here on foot in the pouring rain. He was soaked to the skin and his pants chafed at the crotch. With trembling fingers, he teased the sodden fabric away from his tender right testicle.

He should have known better than to put his hands on Gina Braun. She was a firecracker, always had been. It was the way she'd looked at him, a mix of pity and disbelief, that made him finally see himself through her eyes. He was a pathetic drunk, a goddamn has-been, a fucking loser.

Derek had been waiting half an hour when he spotted Officer Mark Jenssen approach in his marked police cruiser. Better known as Ernie, the other half of the department's Bert and Ernie Muppet joke, he rolled through water puddles and parked in his usual spot.

Derek opened the passenger door, and adjusted his pants before he squeezed in beside the bracket of the Remington 870. "How's it feel to be nice and dry when I'm out here like a wet muskrat?" He rested one hand on the shotgun's pistol grip, and jammed the other in his jacket pocket. Ernie had probably already noticed that he had the shakes, but at least this way they wouldn't have to talk about it. He'd run out of whiskey hours ago and he badly needed a drink.

"Sorry about the weather, Lieutenant. I ordered up sunshine for this morning, but I guess I didn't pay my weather bill on time." Ernie snickered.

"Well, I'm not in handcuffs, so I guess that bastard Z-man still doesn't have enough evidence to get a warrant."

"Aw come on. Z's a good guy. He's doing his job. You might be surprised that he is the one guy, besides me, who might actually think you're innocent."

"You're pullin' my leg." The way Derek saw it, Z-man had always been the first in line to try to take him down. Erin had caught him the last time, but it had been Z-man who'd made the arrest official.

"It's true." Ernie handed Derek a plain envelope. "This is Bert's Ident report. The victim, Ethan Lewis, was killed by two bullets to the chest. The lone assailant beat him in the face with a blunt instrument ante mortem."

"Beat, and then shot." Derek's fingers squeezed the handgrip tighter. His knuckles were scabbed over but still looked like hell. "Wait a minute. You said blunt instrument, not bare knuckles."

"Yeah," Ernie nodded. "That's what Bert figured. He said there was some sort of rounded shape to it, like a steel pipe."

"Or a police-issue expandable baton." Derek felt the finger of blame point directly at him again.

"Uh, possibly."

"Shit. Mine was at home last I saw it."

"Great, we'll contact your ex-wife."

Derek kneaded his forehead with dirty fingers. "She sold the place right after she divorced me. Sent me a letter to tell me she threw out everything I owned. It's gone. There's no way I can prove I don't still have it."

"And there's the issue of your prison association."

"Fuck, that's bad news." Derek put his head in his hands. "It's a frame-up. It's gotta be. I didn't. I couldn't have. I can't remember."

"That's bad news indeed." The in-car laptop blipped and Ernie punched the keyboard. "I think it might be a good idea to stay out of sight a while longer. Z-man's not ready to take you in, but—"

"He couldn't catch me if he tried. That straight arrow couldn't do covert ops if his life depended on it. The problem is that he's a linear thinker. Point A to point B. I'm smarter than him."

"Like I said, right now you're only wanted for questioning. You're right, Z-man goes by the book. He's not coming after you, but there are half a dozen others who might be tempted, warrant or not."

"I can't go back to jail. I've got a life to build. Has anything surfaced on Tiffany? Any word at all?" Derek knew he sounded desperate, but he didn't care.

"Nada. Nothing since you said you last saw her. She dropped off the radar, went off the grid. You know, there's a possibility that she's not hiding at all." Ernie glanced at him sideways. "In most missing persons cases, this means they met with foul play. Have you considered that?"

"No way. She was a saint. She didn't have an enemy in the world."

Ernie paused. "Have you talked to Armand? A guy like that would notice a filly missing from his stable."

"She wasn't like that. She was a good person. A good mother."

Ernie held up his palms. "I'm not saying she wasn't, but you should consider the possibility that her pimp might know something."

"She didn't have no pimp, and that's the end of it." Derek glared at him, seriously considering ending their partnership here and now.

"I see you're in a bad way, and I'm not passing any judgment here, but as one friend to another, is there anything I can do for you?"

Derek thumped his soggy shoe on the floor mat. Water squished out the sides. "Yeah, I need a favor, buddy." The shakes were reaching his legs now, and he didn't know how much longer he could hold out without a drink. He took a couple of bills from his wallet, unable to meet Ernie's eye. "I'd be in your debt if you'd pick me up a two-four from the Stop 'N Go. I'd go in myself, but with all the *trouble...*"

Ernie looked at the twenties and pursed his mouth. He shot a glance over his shoulder and back at Derek. "It's not what I had in mind. If you let me take you in, I promise to keep it away from the press. There's a nice detox—"

Derek swore his blood pressure rose ten points. "I don't need detox. I need a goddamn case of beer," he hissed.

"I'd help you out if it wasn't for this call that just came in, Lieutenant. I really should… Aw come on, you want me to buy beer when I'm in uniform?"

"Tell her you're planning an after-work party for someone's retirement. What's so hard about it?" Derek pulled out ten more bills and slid them across the seat. "For your trouble, and for the Ident report. I sincerely appreciate all you do for me."

Ernie exhaled, and his hand darted out for the cash. "I guess I can think up something. I'll be right back."

Derek stayed out of sight under the bridge until Ernie returned. He leaned against the concrete to keep his knees from shaking when he saw the car round the corner on its way back.

Ernie rolled down the window and handed out the case. On top of it was a plastic bag that smelled divine. "Gina laughed in my face when I told her about the retirement party. She sent this bag for you. There's fried chicken, a couple of hot dogs and I think she put in a pint of milk." A grin slid onto his lips. "She said to tell you you're a dumb ass, and she hopes your balls get better soon." He rolled up his window and drove off.

Derek ripped open the top of the case and tugged a bottle through the hole. He poured half a beer down his throat without swallowing, and let out a belch. The rain had stopped, and when the sun came out, he convinced himself that everything would turn out fine. He'd prove his innocence, stay out of jail, and find Tiffany if it was the last thing he did.

He drank another beer before he looked in the bag Gina sent. The steaming, foil-wrapped packages smelled good. He ate a piece of chicken between swallows of beer. After he'd thrown three or four empties into the ditch, he was feeling himself again.

He glanced down the sidewalk and spotted Armand's low-rider Chevy parked on the street. That meth-head pimp had some explaining to do. He left what remained of his two-four on the sidewalk, strutted up to the front door and knocked on the faded wood with his scabby knuckles. Not a single floorboard creaked in response.

What was he thinking? It was too early in the morning for drug-dealing pimps. They were creatures of the night, vampires. He booted the flimsy door open and let himself in.

The living room was a mess of stained furniture and drug paraphernalia. Foil wrappers, dusty plastic and discarded clothing littered the floor. He stepped carefully around the trash. A used needle would penetrate his shoes faster than he could say communicable disease.

He found the bedroom and stepped into the darkness. It was true, unkempt humans were the foulest smelling creatures on the planet. A Confederate flag thrown over the curtain rod blocked any possibility of light, or fresh air, from entering. If he had another choice he'd back out right now, but this might be his last hope of finding Tiffany. He flipped the light switch on and prodded the twisted lump of blankets on the bed.

Not one, but two naked figures emerged. Probably younger than she looked, the female pulled the sheet up over sagging breasts. Her mascara-smeared eyes flared wide when she focused on the stranger in the doorway. She took the sheet with her when she scooted off to the washroom.

Derek kicked the edge of the bed and kept his distance. "Get the fuck up, Armand." Druggies were unpredictable. You never knew if they would come up swinging, or if they would whine like little pussies. He'd been popped in the face more than once when he was still on the job.

"Angie? Where you gone, baby?" Armand sat up, and tossed his long braid over his shoulder. Save for his face, his entire body from the waist up, was covered in tattoos. Skinny and long-limbed, his leathery skin stretched tight to his bones like a rattler. He froze when he spotted Derek. "What's goin' on? Is it a raid?" He slid one hand slowly under his pillow.

"Not today, dirtbag." Derek grabbed him by the ankles, and hauled him off the bed before he could retrieve whatever weapon he was going for. Armand landed in a serpentine knot on the soiled carpet. He knelt on him, one knee pressing into the back of his skull.

"Ain't got no cash," Armand grunted. "And my delivery doesn't come in until tomorrow."

"That's not what I'm after." He let pressure off so Armand could talk without grunting. "Tell me about Tiffany."

"Are you the guy on the news? The one wanted for murder? Are you gonna kill me?"

"Like I said, not today, dirtbag. And I didn't kill anyone. Today, we're only gonna talk."

"Like we're only talking here now?" Armand twisted to glare at him. "If you say so."

"Tell me about Tiffany Schmidt." Derek kneeled on his head until there was a subtle pop, and the drug dealer groaned. "You were her dealer. A few years back."

"Ohhh, *Tiff*. I haven't seen her since she stopped using. She told me she was getting clean. Going to marry a cop, or some damn thing." Armand's foot twitched. "My whole body's going numb, man. Come on, let me up. I won't do nothin' but sit here."

Derek let him go and stood.

Armand curled into fetal position. Was he waiting to pounce, or was he really hurting? "Was that you she was talking about?" he whispered. "I thought it was her fantasy."

The washroom door opened briefly and closed again. Armand's girlfriend wasn't dumb enough to try calling the police. She'd stay there and wait it out, as long as it took.

"Wasn't no fantasy," Derek muttered. "You swear to God you don't know where she is?"

"I promise, I ain't seen her. Nobody has. But that was a long time ago."

"If I find out you had anything to do with her disappearance, I'll come back and strangle you in your sleep." He picked his way through the rubble in the living room and walked out the front door. His two-four was right where he'd left it. Z-man wasn't going to catch him. No one was. He picked up the case and trudged back to the swamp.

CHAPTER SEVENTEEN

"Over there." Erin pointed to a set of tire marks that veered off the road a couple of miles north of the roadblock they'd recently dismantled. "They might have gone cross-country. That's the only explanation for why we haven't located the car anywhere in the area." In the last four hours, they'd been back and forth on this road a half dozen times, but this was the first time she'd spotted the tracks. Early dawn's glow had made it easier to see.

Gonzales slowed. "Where? I can't see a thing."

She pointed the LED spotlight. Faint tracks led down through the dried-out ditch and up onto the other side. She traced the path through the weeds and grimaced. The underside of a vehicle had laid bare a patch of dirt and rocks harsh enough to tear loose a car's oil pan. It had bottomed out, but had still made it through.

Gonzales sucked air through his teeth and regarded the marks for a moment. "I guess they've already smoothed it out for us." He hopped out, retrieved a traffic flare from the trunk, spiked it into the asphalt, and gave Erin a wink when he jumped back in. "If they got through, we can too." Eyes blazing with determination, he turned the wheel and hit the gas.

She grabbed the door handle when they plummeted to the bottom of the ditch, and the undercarriage squealed in protest. A large rock spewed sideways, and tires spun gravel behind them. They found traction and vaulted up the incline.

He laughed when they topped the rise and leveled out. "I love Chevys."

They jounced across the bumpy field and Erin's teeth rattled against each other, her body slamming back and forth against her seatbelt. "Ho-ly cr-cr-crap! S-slow down!"

"Most fun I've had in ages!" Gonzales' delighted grin lit up his face. "Why don't you notify Lockwood of our location? Suspects might still be out here somewhere. Look, there's an outbuilding."

She tried to text the coordinates, but touching the right spots on her phone's screen was impossible when she was being continually jarred.

"Why don't you phone her? Tell her to watch for the flare." He shook his head. "She doesn't know what to do with texts and it'll take her forever to reply."

Erin steadied her hand long enough to hit Lockwood's contact icon and put the call on speaker.

"Whaddya got?" Agent Lockwood was all business, pleasantries were a waste of valuable time.

"We f-found ti-tire t-tracks. No-orth of th-the—" Erin scowled at Gonzales. "S-slow d-own!"

"What in tarnation is wrong with you?" Lockwood's voice boomed over the tinny speaker. "You find a bouncy castle or something? Dang it, what's going on?"

Gonzales shrugged sheepishly and slowed enough for Erin to catch her breath.

"My apologies, ma'am. We've spotted recent tire tracks approximately two miles north of the road block location. We're following them west across a field. Nothing yet, but we wanted to keep you apprised of the possibility that this is the route they took."

"You find any other indicators of our suspect, or are you going on pure gut instinct, Ericsson?"

"Uh, a little of both?" The line was silent. Lockwood needed more. "Well, given the timing of their disappearance, coupled with the possible escape routes, and the areas that have been covered so far, this is most likely."

"What else?" The old crocodile was not making this easy.

"Umm, judging from an approximation of the track width, the vehicle we're following is slightly smaller than our Chevy. The marks we were able to see, when it disturbed the soil, indicate a shorter wheelbase, and corresponding turning radius, which is also consistent with the suspect vehicle."

"Anything else?" Lockwood was persistent. No stone unturned, literally.

"These tracks veered off the main road and hit the ditch at a fairly high rate of speed, considering the rough terrain. Someone was in a hurry, or they made an impulsive decision, or both. This fits our situation, and it fits Lily. She doesn't seem to be much of a planner, ma'am." Erin felt as if she'd finished an impromptu exam, and she probably had.

"Very well, exercise caution, and I'm talking to you too, Gonzales. If you spot anything, wait for backup. I don't want to attend either of your funerals."

A moment later, they approached the Quonset building Gonzales had spotted in the distance. "Something's on fire." He pointed to a fine trail of dark smoke curling skyward.

Abandoned behind the structure was the car they'd been searching for, smoke trickling through the rear window molding. Erin called it in, and backed off to a safe vantage point.

Minutes later, the sun breached the horizon and a white 4x4 truck with a reinforced push bumper poked its way across the field. It parked beside them and Lockwood spilled out the passenger door. "Dang, Marty! You get the economy shocks on this truck? That ride rearranged my giblets."

The trooper raised his eyebrows in genuine concern. "Awful sorry, Shirley. I took it as easy as I could."

Out of her sight line, Gonzales waggled his eyebrows at Erin. "Shirley," he whispered. "No one calls her by her first name. No one."

Lockwood laughed and slammed the door behind her. Gonzales rolled down his window when she approached.

"Ericsson, how about you and me go have a look-see? The forensics people are on the way, so keep your paws off anything you don't absolutely have to touch. Gonzales and my new friend Marty can provide backup.

Gonzales shot Erin another covert expression of disbelief. He mouthed the word, "Marty."

Erin approached on foot, shotgun to her shoulder. One side of the Quonset had collapsed, its dilapidated door hanging sideways. Lockwood trotted over, and peeped through when Erin shone her light inside. It was empty.

When Lockwood opened the driver's door of the car, blue smoke billowed out. She ducked away from the dark cloud. "Idiots tried to torch the evidence but didn't make sure there was enough air for it to catch. Thank the Lord no one's in there." She pulled the trunk release so Gonzales could check the back.

"Marty, you got a—?" She stepped back when the trooper aimed his fire extinguisher through the door to blanket the smoldering seat. "Of course you do." She smiled at him and he blushed, running a nervous hand through his thinning hair.

Hidden behind the raised trunk, Gonzales waggled his eyebrows at Erin again. Erin frowned back. What was this? Grade five?

He slammed the trunk down with gloved hands, and opened the rear door. "Trash, fast food containers," he called out, "a lot of empty beer bottles, and pills spilled under the seat. Some might be prescription narcotics." He cocked his head. "Not sure what the others are."

Lockwood shielded her eyes from the morning sun. "There appears to be blood in the back. The boy, Trenton something or other, was struck by the gas station owner. It's probably his. Looks like you're right, Ericsson. If the boy's in the back seat, she's up front, and the power balance has shifted."

She squatted to examine the exit tracks leading away from the scene, and the trooper followed her sight line. "Marty, would you be so kind as to have your office check ownership of this property, and get us a description of the vehicle that might have been here? I'd bet breakfast that our fugitives traded this little junker in for a pickup with a key left in the ignition." She stood. "It's been four hours. They could be halfway to Vegas by now."

"What if they turned around?" Erin couldn't imagine what Lily would do in the Nevada desert. Her roots were in the swamp.

"Why in the world would you think that?" Lockwood used the toe of her shoe to nudge an empty beer can in the grass. Its faded condition implied it had pre-dated this event. "Their route has been consistent. They're headed southwest, maybe Vegas, maybe even as far as the west coast."

"They may not be headed southwest any more," Erin said. "If Lily's in control now, she may have changed direction."

"You figure she doubled back?" Lockwood's keen attention was unnerving.

"It's a possibility." Erin turned at the squeak of shocks. A tow truck navigated the ruts in the field, and a sport utility vehicle marked *Ident Unit* followed in its wake.

Lockwood spoke to the forensic tech for a moment while he took photos and made a cursory check of the vehicle.

Marty cleared his throat. "When we're done here, Shirley, I can recommend a fine spot for debriefing."

"Does this spot serve bacon?" A dazzling smile lit up her face and took years off her age.

"It surely does." The trooper gallantly held open his passenger door, and she stepped in. "Patriot, ten miles back, just off the main highway," he hollered, before he hopped in the driver's seat.

Gonzales raised an eyebrow to Erin but this time he mouthed *bacon*. "Let's go," he said.

Through the steamed window glass, Patriot Diner's outdoor sign was lit up in neon letters, and it was indeed an appropriate spot for the group of empty-handed Bureau agents to meet with local authorities. The aroma alone made her mouth water after the long night of beating every bush between Ogden and the Idaho border.

Erin excused herself to make a call when the conversation became circular. They couldn't understand how the criminal duo had eluded The Bureau, as well as local law enforcement from the north. Erin knew the answer. No one was at fault; Lily was a force of nature.

She pressed her ear to her cell phone and turned away from the group seated at the table. "How's the weather out there?"

"Raining like the dickens," Z-man said.

She imagined water running down the windshield of his cruiser as they spoke, and it made her homesick. "You think the rain's going to hurt the rhubarb?"

"Rhubarb. Ha! Why did you really call, munchkin? You miss me?"

"Of course I miss you, and Gina, and Li'l Z." She examined the dirt under her fingernails. It was impossible to concentrate with that staring back. The germs alone…

She headed for the checkout to search for a toothpick. Allie would say her OCD was getting out of hand, and she should learn to let some things slide. After a day like this, anyone would understand that Erin needed her control back.

"How is your training officer? Learning a lot?" Zimmerman

suddenly sounded less like a friend, and more like a mentor.

"I have two, so I'm the annoying third wheel. Gonzales knows his stuff."

At the table, Gonzales pointed to something on his computer tablet and the others leaned in. Lockwood put on her glasses and frowned at the screen.

"And there's a crocodile named Shirley Lockwood." Erin smirked when Lockwood shoved the computer tablet aside and unfolded a huge map. "I've never met anyone in this field so resistant to technology. She's a hard ass, but maybe I've spent too many years working on my own."

"Ha, ha. That was you a few years ago before you met Allie. You couldn't even tie your own virtual laces." Zimmerman tapped on a keyboard. "Lockwood. Shirley Lockwood. I've heard of her." He tapped some more. "Yup, she was the agent involved in that case with the girl held captive for a decade, followed the case long after everyone else gave up, and was the one to finally pull the kid out of that basement herself."

"I don't recall hearing about that." Erin's estimation of Lockwood rose a notch.

"It was a long time ago. In the mid-eighties."

"No wonder. I was a baby then." She'd still been playing with colored blocks.

"Remember the kidnapping of that family in Colorado?"

"Three police officers were killed, and a bunch wounded in the standoff, but not one Bureau agent." Erin had been in university when the media followed that case for the entire week. The world cheered when the family was pulled unharmed from a madman's doomsday bunker. Then they mourned the fallen officers, and cursed the criminal who finally gave himself up to a female agent. She stole a glance at the authoritative woman, stabbing at a map with her index finger. "That was her too?"

"Yup," Zimmerman said. "She was involved in a lot of other high profile cases. She's determined, and has a reputation for following her instincts, no matter what anyone else says. Sound like someone you know? Here's a hint, look in the mirror, girl. I'd consider you lucky to be learning from her."

Lecture completed, his voice softened. "So, how's the search for Lily going?" He'd heard, of course he'd heard. Z-man had contacts everywhere.

This was not something Erin wanted her trainers to know she was discussing outside their ranks. On her way out to the lobby, she plucked a toothpick from a little bowl beside the cashier. "We lost her in Utah," she whispered. "We were so close, and then she disappeared." She ripped open the plastic wrap, and held the phone with her shoulder so she could scrape out the guck under her thumbnail. Satisfied, she started on the next finger. She'd finish, get a new toothpick and start all over. It was not something she could control when she was stressed. If she'd had time for a run, it might have helped.

"The guys at the station have been following her crime spree across three states, since she and that boy escaped. It's like our own super bowl, with crews betting against each other on how long it takes the FBI to catch them. Wait until someone leaks it to the media."

Erin groaned. "I can see the headlines now. Raging Ranger and FBI trainers on the trail of poor misunderstood teenagers."

"Nobody calls you that around here anymore, not in front of me anyway. If you ask me, the guys are actually kind of proud of you. Especially Bert and Ernie."

"Is Bert enjoying Ident? Word is he aced his course. He's a natural." Erin kept any hint of jealousy out of her voice. She'd been gunning for that job before her career took a right turn to the FBI Academy.

"Ernie is walking by my office now." His voice suddenly sounded far away. "You wanna say hi, Muppet Man?"

"Oh, I assumed you were in your car." Erin's homesick romantic view of Morley Falls PD shuffled to a different backdrop. She heard a faint "hey kid" from Ernie in the distance.

"Nah, no more night patrols. I'm the boss man now," Zimmerman said. "I get to sit inside, read reports and drink coffee," he said in a monotone. "Big fun."

"Allie thinks we missed Lily because she doubled back," Erin blurted, unable to contain it any longer. "She's headed to Morley Falls. If it's true, I'm worried about Allie, I'm worried about my family, I'm worried about *your* family."

"Allie said that? Lily is coming here?" There was a pause and Zimmerman's voice muffled as he held his hand over the receiver.

"Can I help you with anything else, Ernie?" His voice came back on the line. "That boy is either lazy tonight, or I'd swear he was hanging around to listen in."

"Wasn't Derek his training officer? That kind of bond runs deep." A hum of activity inside the restaurant signaled that the impromptu meeting had ended. She hoped the twenty she'd left on the table had been enough to cover her share. Things were more expensive away from Morley Falls. "Are they still in touch?"

"You're right. That sneaky little Muppet is probably phoning Derek to tell him right now. If this doesn't coax him out of his hidey-hole in the swamp, I don't know what will." His chair squeaked. "I'll buy Ernie breakfast if he gets that drunk in here for an interview about our murder."

She imagined him leaning back in the sergeant's executive chair, with his humongous feet splayed in front of him. "How many critters did the department let you move into your office?" She'd wager half his lizard collection had been set up under a heat lamp on the big bookcase.

"You psychic or something?" He laughed, a pleasantly deep rumble that she missed terribly. "You guessed right. My best boys Merlin and Picasso are here." His voice took on an indulgent tone, the same one he used on his toddler son. "The new guys are at home under lock and key from Mikey who wants to be their best friend."

"I can't remember," Erin quipped. "Is Merlin the hamster and Picasso the python—?"

"Merlin is my spotted gecko, and…" Zimmerman huffed. "Don't you ever tire of that joke?"

"You fall for it every time, buddy." Erin laughed. It was good to talk to her best friend.

"Seriously, when you convince your hotshot FBI trainers that Lily is headed back here, I'll be happy to coordinate the setup of a temporary field office in our boardroom. No one uses that damn place anyway. I'd love to meet the legendary Agent Lockwood, and of course everyone misses your shining face."

"Thanks, Z." In the meantime, she knew Zimmerman would stay on top of their search for Lily and her accomplice. "Give Gina a hug from me."

"Give it to her yourself when you get here."

"Can you do me a favor and keep an eye on Allie for me? She

sounded jumpy the last time we spoke and I'm sure she's concerned about Lily too."

"Yeah, Gina said she seemed out of sorts when she came in to the Stop 'N Go the other night," he said. "But don't worry, we're staying close."

Bills paid, Lockwood entered the lobby as Erin was finishing her call. "Thanks for breakfast, Ericsson," she quipped as she marched past Erin. "Gonzales will fill you in on what you missed."

"You're welcome... thank you... no problem... I'm sorry?" Erin's tongue tangled in the multi responses, far too many of them apologetic. What was it about Lockwood that made her nervous? No, not nervous. Intimidated. Lockwood was perceptive, direct, unapologetic, and so competent that she was weak in comparison. Like a bare-naked baby in a thicket of brambles. In fact, it reminded her of Auntie Vicky.

She smiled. She'd cut her teeth on her boisterous aunt's bear-fighting stories, some of which might even be true. It was hard to tell, because there were always subtle changes in the way she told them. The only parts of the story that remained unchanged were that, as a young girl, she had indeed chased off a bear and saved her little sister, Erin's mom.

She may or may not have had a butter knife, or a hatchet, or a stick, and may or may not have screamed loud enough to split the heavens open and bring down Zeus the God of Thunder to help her.

When Erin was little, she remembered hiding under the table, wide-eyed and trembling in fear, during the telling of that story. It felt a little like that now, and she hoped that she would grow to like Lockwood a fraction as much as she had grown to love her strong, crazy, Auntie Vicky.

"Are you coming, Ericsson?" Gonzales tilted his head, and handed her a handful of plastic-wrapped toothpicks. "Here's a few more for the road." He held the door open.

"I know the fingernail thing is—" She was acutely aware of the heat rising in her cheeks. How long had he been watching her? Would this go in his report? Would she destroy her career before it began?

"My brother does the same thing, only with him it's hand washing." Gonzales shrugged. "It's a disorder and he can't stop, even when his skin bleeds. It messes him up so bad he can't hold a job.

Yours seems more like a nervous habit. We've all got our kryptonite. You, me, Lockwood."

"What's her kryptonite?"

In the parking lot, the senior agent looked annoyed to be kept waiting, a frown creasing her brow deeper than ever.

"That's for her to tell you, or you to figure out on your own." He tossed her the keys. "Time to face your fear, grasshopper. I'll hop in the back."

CHAPTER EIGHTEEN

"Hello? Lieutenant?"

Derek hit the speaker icon and rested his cell phone on the rental car's hood. "What's up Ernie?" He leaned against the fender and crossed his arms. It felt like old times, shooting the breeze with a work buddy. Back then, he'd been drinking coffee, not beer. "Is Z-man coming for me today?"

With a flick of his wrist, he tossed the bottle into the weeds where it smashed against the last one. He regarded the now-empty case. Once again, he was running too close to the edge and would have to do something about this situation soon. Would it be such a bad thing if he turned himself in and went to a nice detox country club?

Ernie was out of breath and excited about something. "I have news for you, boss. I just found out and wanted to let you know right away."

"Well, spit it out, boy." *Why all the mystery?*

"Z-man's not coming for you, but I overheard him talking to Erin Ericsson on the phone."

"Don't tell me she's coming to try to catch me. Seems a bit below her high falutin' new job to be poaching on local turf." When goddamn Ericsson had left for Quantico, he thought he'd finally be rid of her, but she kept popping back up. Would she never leave him alone?

"She's not coming to arrest you, boss. She's after your daughter."

"Lily? But she's in Canada, isn't she?" Derek sat up. "Isn't she?" Allowing himself to be trapped in detox became a sudden impossibility. His daughter needed him.

"She escaped almost a week ago—"

"And you didn't think it was important enough to tell me?" Like acid, Derek's anger funneled from his gut to his throat. "Why the fuck not?"

"Uh, it seemed she was headed south, nowhere near here. You have a lot on your plate and I didn't want to worry you."

"She's my daughter!" Sour vomit filled his mouth and he bent to retch. Were his hands shaking? Already? "I oughta bloody your nose for that," he sputtered. "We're buddies ain't we?"

"I'm sorry, Lieu, I should have."

"What else do you know that you are holding back to protect my delicate sensitivities?" Derek balled his scabby hand into a fist and pounded the hood of the car.

Regret washed over him as soon as the cell phone bounced onto the gravel. He leaned over, picked it up and glared at the new crack in the screen. It would have felt a lot better had that been Ernie's face, or Ericsson's. No doubt about it, that bitch had a vendetta against his family. If she was coming back, there'd be hell to pay.

Ernie couldn't have missed the thunder on the connection. He chose his words carefully. "After everything that... happened here, there's the question of why Lily would even *want* to come back."

"To see me, of course. I'm her goddamn father. Why else?"

"Um, no one told her you got out early. She might think you're in prison."

"Hunh." Hadn't they told her a damn thing about what had happened to him? Why hadn't they let her write?

"Perhaps there's something else. Something she needs to take care of. A secret."

"No, I would've known. She didn't hide anything from me." As the words spilled from Derek's mouth, he knew they weren't true. Everything Lily said or did was a lie. Had Tiffany told the girl where she was going? Was she keeping a secret for her mother?

"Uh, there's a little more." Ernie hesitated so long he wondered if he'd lost the signal. "She escaped with another inmate, a seventeen year old boy. The two of them are suspects in a number of serious crimes across three states. That's why the FBI is involved."

The phone shook in Derek's hands and he placed it back on the hood. "It's not my kid. It's the boy. If he hurts her, I'll kill him."

"Don't talk like that, Lieutenant. You're already in enough trouble."

"Swear you won't hold nothin' back from now on. She's my daughter. Promise me."

"Yeah, boss. I'll call as soon as I hear anything."

"Phones don't work so well where I'm staying." Nothing worked in the swamp now. Not phones, not electricity, not anything. He was tired of warm beer, and sandwich meat that smelled like it was going south. "You keep tryin', you hear?"

Derek touched the screen to end the call. *Goddamn Ernie.* These days a man couldn't even trust someone he'd trained himself. He left the car and walked the three blocks to Armand's house. Armand the pimp. Armand the drug dealer. Armand the guy who might know a little something about what went on in the underbelly of Morley Falls.

The broken front door hung ajar, and he shoved it open with the flat of his hand. Angie squeaked and made a dash for the bathroom, but this time he blocked her escape route. He pointed to a spot on the sofa next to Armand, who was snorting something off the coffee table. Meth? Stolen prescription medication? Who cared anyway? This was no official visit. Angie sat rigid and stone-faced while her boyfriend finished.

Finally, Armand's head flopped against the sofa cushion, scraggly hair over his glazed eyes. They popped wide open at the sight of the burly ex-policeman, and the drug dealer sat up. "Why are you back, pig? I told you, I don't know nothin' about why Tiff left you." His high gave him false courage.

Angie fidgeted and scratched an invisible spot on her arm. Her eyes darted to Armand and back.

Derek wanted to punch him right in his druggie mouth, but first he needed to make him talk. "Who killed that guy in the motel?" He reached over and took a handful of Angie's hair. Her breath quickened, but she didn't make a sound.

"Hey, you leave her be," Armand protested, rising to his feet. "She's a good earner. I won't have you messin' with business."

"Tell me who killed Badger in that motel. You know, don't you?" He twisted the handful and elicited a squawk from Angie. It had the desired effect.

Armand sank back to the sofa. "Sorry, baby, I wanna protect you, but this guy," he glanced up, "this guy is outta control."

He twisted a little more and Angie kicked Armand in the shin. "Tell him!"

"I don't know his name. Word on the street was Badger used him to get meth into the prison. He might work there. That's all I know!"

Derek released Angie's hair and picked up a bottle of Jack Daniel's from the table. There were still two inches of precious liquid in the bottom. He'd take this for his trouble.

Angie slapped the drug dealer's face. "Why you let him treat me like that?" She smoothed her rumpled hair and shot Derek a dark look.

He watched her skinny butt pump under her skin-tight skirt until she slammed the bedroom door. Angie a good earner? Her johns must be too wasted to see straight. Tiffany was not like her at all. She was too good for this life. No wonder she had run away.

"Call me if you hear anything." Derek flicked his P.I. business card so it sailed to the floor.

He left Armand to enjoy his buzz and scratched his unshaven chin as he strolled to the sidewalk. Badger had been smuggling drugs into Stillwater Prison. That explained a lot, like why a weasel like him always had a big fella watching his back, and why he wouldn't let things go. Who was his smuggling partner, someone outside, or in?

He walked back to his car, drove to the end of the road, and parked in his usual treed spot. The rain had stopped and the short walk back to Gunther Schmidt's property was much more pleasant than when he'd left in the downpour.

Everything was as he'd left it, the shed with its cell-like hidden room, the musty bed he'd hauled up, and the fridge he avoided because it was starting to smell.

He took the last swallow and set the whiskey bottle he'd liberated from Armand's house on the work bench. When the fridge stink got worse, he'd have to consider moving on. Besides, when Erin got here, she'd know right where to find him. Hell, if Gina had been telling the truth, Zimmerman already figured it out.

The swamp simmered in the heat that followed the downpour. Each organism had a life of its own and the bog kept secrets he could only imagine. He watched from the doorway and considered his options. If he turned himself in, he'd be back in prison before nightfall. That wasn't gonna happen. He had to find Badger's partner, the real killer, and help his daughter.

He shut the door to keep out the mosquitoes and walked to the bog. At the far end, marked by the blackened spires of burnt trees, stood the remains of the Johnson house.

When he'd been called to investigate that fire, it had sure seemed like an accident, the misadventure of an addle-brained old woman living by herself in the middle of nowhere. He should have spent more time poking around the ashes instead of swapping jokes with Ernie out on the main road.

Pant legs tucked into his socks, he followed the overgrown trail to the property. There was a gap in the fence, the gate long since missing, and he slipped through. Now abandoned, the cinderblock foundation and brick chimney stood amidst charred wood. Voracious weeds and poplar seedlings had taken over. Separating the yard from the bog was a white picket fence, rotten from neglect.

When Erin had seen him in prison, she'd said Lily had been watching Mrs. Johnson's house. She had blamed his daughter for the fire, but could he believe it?

He walked the path from the driveway, and imagined the structure when he'd last seen it standing. A well-kept bungalow, it was the sort of place you'd expect a particular old woman to tend. He circled the foundation and returned to the trail.

If he'd been the one watching, where would he have stood? He sidled along the fence, side-stepped and peered through a bare spot in the bushes. There was a clear view of the back steps. A few years ago, this opening would have been a few inches lower, the right height for an eleven year-old kid. Maybe so, but that didn't mean it was Lily. He squatted. This location offered complete concealment. Still…

His alcohol-deprived body rebelled and his trembling knees gave way when he tried to stand. He grabbed the fence for support but the boards came loose under his hands. "Damn!" He crashed to his ass in the wet grass and curled into a ball.

Five minutes, maybe fifteen, he stared at the bottom of the fence. Wedged between the boards, where the wind had blown it, were the remnants of a faded cigarette package. Marlboro was Tiffany's brand. The brand Lily liked to steal from her purse.

Tiffany Schmidt was a town girl. She liked nice things and she liked nice shoes. She wouldn't be caught dead out here, smoking goddamn cigarettes in a mosquito-infested swamp. Sure, there might be a few others in this piss pot town who smoked the same brand, but this was one more coincidence in a veritable heap. A prosecutor might say this kind of evidence was merely circumstantial, but this particular heap was beginning to look pretty convincing. Erin might be right about Lily watching Dolores Johnson's house. His head spun. *Could it all be true?*

He forced himself to his feet and brushed twigs from his pants. Now he was soaked to the knees and feeling the chill. Or was that the shakes coming for him again?

Somehow, he made it back around the bog. Since it had been drained, there were fewer mosquitoes than usual, but blackflies had chewed the backs of his ears raw, and his fingers were bloody from scratching. He pulled his shirt over his nose and mouth to keep them out. What was worse? Hordes of mosquitoes or clouds of blackflies? Both could drive a man insane if he didn't have decent shelter, or DEET insect repellant.

He quickened his pace, eager to get into the shed. The vestiges of sunlight slanted through the trees when he reached the excavator, and a glint caught his eye. Half the water in this end of the bog was gone but the recent rains had refilled the hole in the middle. Already the bog was reclaiming itself.

Water sloshed over the toes of his shoes when he edged out on the wooden plank. It wouldn't take but a minute to rinse the blood off his hands, and he could get a better look at whatever it was shining in the mud.

He shuffled out, one foot after the other until he reached the end, still yards from the sunken excavator. Most of the forward track was underground, the glass windows of the cab peeping out. How the hell had the operator gotten out? Maybe that glint was something he'd lost, maybe something worthwhile.

He squatted, and leaned toward it as far as his trembling legs would allow. The object that had caught the light was there, just out of reach. It was a rusty metal, horseshoe-shaped buckle of some sort, attached to a leather band, from a bag, or... a purse?

He lost his balance and toppled into the mud, elbows splayed like a newborn fawn. It was denser than he feared but he managed to get most of his weight back onto the plank and haul his upper body out. He rolled to his back, chest heaving. The blackflies would soon be coming with a vengeance but he didn't give a shit.

The last time Derek had seen Tiffany, she'd talked him out of a fifty dollar bill. She'd smiled at him and tucked it into her purse with her Marlboros. The diamond ring he'd given her flashed on her finger when she'd snapped the buckle. The little horseshoe-shaped buckle on its leather strap.

CHAPTER NINETEEN

"What the hell is this?" How friggin' hard was it for T to do what I told him? I click out of the video app and put down my new cell phone. *Get me a cheeseburger and fries* I'd said, right before he hobbled on his sore knee into that goddamn green and yellow restaurant.

"It's a runza. They said it's really good. Everybody loves them here in Nebraska." T squeezes two sodas into the cup holders.

"A fucking what?" I pick up my phone and zoom in on the greasy package he's holding. Just looking at it makes me wanna barf.

"A runza. A stuffed sandwich with beef, cabbage and onions."

This is not what I asked for, and he knows it. He unwraps the white paper, takes a big bite, and smiles like an idiot for the camera. I do a close-up of the bloody scab twisting the hair on the side of his head. That completes the disgusting picture.

"Didn't they have cheeseburgers?"

"Yeah, but everyone in the lineup was getting these. They said they are way better." He takes another bite and offers me a french fry.

"What the hell is that?" In the package, god awful onion rings sit side-by-side with the fries. "They got your order wrong."

"This is what I asked for. They call them frings. Half fries and half rings, get it?" He pulls a second package out of the bag. "Look, there's one for you too."

I bat them away. "That's messed up. You can't do that to fries." I swear to God I wanna poke out my own eye right now. Who does he think he is? "Go back and get me what I want."

He shoots his hand into his pocket and shows me a jumble of coins. "This is all that's left. I spent the rest." He holds the runza out like I'm a baby that needs to be fed. "It's tasty. Try a bite."

"I'm not eating that." I throw the thing out the window and pull away from the restaurant.

Fuck him. Fuck all of this. It's always been this way. If I want something, I have to get it myself. Two blocks away is a drug store with a faded blue sign. I tuck my phone into my pocket and leave the truck running, with T still sitting there eating his fucking frings.

Inside the doors, I stalk past the pimply checkout guy to the back and jump the counter. A little man in a white lab coat stares at me with his mouth open when I shove my knife against his ribs.

"Give me the cash." I need money for beer. Beer and a real cheeseburger. I consider T, who hasn't had any drugs for a while. He'll be whining soon, and I'll need to shut him up. "And gimme all your Oxy."

The color drains from his cheeks. "I can't. It's in the safe. There's a time release."

I press the knife through his coat until he winces from the pressure. "You better do it. Now."

He opens the cash register and forks over all the money. "Here, but I can't—"

"Do it or die." I stuff the bills in my pockets. No way is T getting any of this.

His mouth turns down and his eyelids flicker. Is he gonna pass out right here? He whimpers and a yellow puddle forms on the tile between his shoes.

Scheisse! I don't want his piss on me. Knife out, I jump out of the way. There are so many bottles of drugs on the shelf. What is the big deal? I point to the closest package. "What about that one? It says Oxy right on it."

"That's Oxytocin. It's not—"

"Give it to me." I point to another. "And that one. It says Oxy-something too." What a liar. There is plenty of Oxy on the shelf. That was bullshit about it being in the safe. "Give it all to me or I'll cut out your gizzard."

He shovels the row of bottles into a bag.

I let him go. "If you call the cops, I'll find you and slit your throat."

"Dad?" The pimple-faced checkout guy has come to see what's happening. "Is everything okay?" He stares at the piss between his pussy father's feet for a moment before he brings his eyes up to mine. He can't be much older than me, and his pupils are pinpricks of fear. Will he wet his pants too? I show him my knife and try to push past him, but he stands his ground.

"Move, or I'll shove this in your guts." Why doesn't he step aside? Is he stupid?

"No. Give that back."

Is he kidding me? He's a kitten facing off with a panther and I have no time for this. "Fine, have it your way."

There's a subtle pop when I drive the knife through his white shirt and pull it out. He doesn't go down like I expected. He hunches his back and clutches at the red spot spreading through the fabric.

"No." The man in the white coat groans but his feet don't move. He's paralyzed, glued to that tile.

I can't take my eyes off the stain bleeding into the boy's shirt. It's hypnotizing. Irresistible.

I shove the drugs into the front of my pants and fumble for my phone. This is a moment to remember. My heart skips a beat when the video of his bloody shirt comes on-screen in brilliant color. I pan from the shirt to the man with the puddle of piss at his feet. I can't wait to watch it over, and over.

On the display, the pimply boy slowly reaches for the phone on the counter. *Don't do that.* I step in to stab him again and my knife flashes in the corner of the image. This video will be amazing.

Before I can plunge the knife into his throat, the man in the white coat jumps me like a big hairy ape, an ape that smells of piss and fear. How did he manage to unglue himself from the floor? I'm faster, but he must outweigh me by a hundred pounds, and he catches me off guard. I've totally underestimated him.

We crumple together, and the knife flies from my hand as my skull collides with hard tile. Right now, all I can think about is my need to get the hell out. Psychedelic colors explode in my head. Somewhere a man must be breaking concrete with a jackhammer.

Through the noise, a male voice shouts. The kid I stabbed is calling the cops. With my last ounce of strength, I wriggle free and stagger for the door.

Away from the building, it seems the sidewalk is crooked and I have trouble steering my feet to the truck. I take the long way around a lamp post and adjust my balance to make it to the passenger side. "T! Let's Go."

His eyes widen when he sees me coming. "What did you do?" he says through a mouthful of something disgusting.

"Move over. Drive!" As soon as he slides over, I tumble into his spot. Sirens are coming. He hits the gas and we peel away before they get closer.

We're on the highway, heading out of town, and T hasn't asked me a single question until now. "What did you do?"

There is so much noise in my head and I can barely hear him over the little workers hammering between my ears. Everything is off, like a video out of sync with its audio track.

"Are you hurt? You have blood on your phone." His voice has that weird edge of concern that my grandfather's had when I hurt myself.

Scheisse! My phone. My amazing video. What if it's smashed? I can't bring myself to check it.

"Looks like the blood's not yours." T tugs the little white bag I had forgotten about from my clenched fingers. "What's this?"

Drugs. This is why I went to see the pharmacist in the white coat. I stabbed his son before he jumped me and slammed my head into the floor. "I got you a present," I mumble. "All the Oxy you want."

He peeks inside and his dark eyes burn. "Did you kill someone for this?"

"Maybe." How I wish I had. I can't believe that I lost my knife, but somehow managed to hold onto the damn plastic bag. My priorities are messed up.

"Ooh, look at all the pharmaceuticals." The truck swerves across the center line and back. T's smile is like Christmas morning. "Take the wheel, honeybun." He dives into the bag and shovels through the contents with his hands.

I can't see straight, let alone steer from way over here. The truck swerves again, but T keeps his foot planted on the gas pedal and I have no choice but to try to keep the wheels between the yellow line and the white one.

"Pull over *dummkopf.* You'll put us in the ditch," I yell on sheer instinct. Man, how many times did my grandfather say those exact words? When my head clears, we're cockeyed on the shoulder, wheels threatening to dip into the grassy ravine.

In my hand, I release the death grip on my phone and realize that it works, and the video is still running. I point it at T, who now has the bottles and boxes lined up in order of size. He picks up the first one and squints to read the tiny print on the vial. "I've never seen Oxy come in liquid. It says Oxytocin, IV infusion, single dose injection."

"Are you gonna do it right now? Why don't you wait until we get where we're going? My head hurts. I need you to drive."

He points to his knee as if I'm stupid. "I can't drive with all this pain."

I shut off the camera. My head is banging like a kid with a tambourine, but I don't whine like a pussy. "Fuck, whatever. Do what you gotta do, and let's get back on the road. We could be home by tomorrow."

"I don't know how to take this kind. It's not in a pill and I can't smoke it either. You're supposed to use a needle."

"So drink it. Pop a hole in the top and suck it down." Seriously, if he can't figure this out, he has no business getting high.

He grins and jabs his pinkie nail through the foil. "Bottoms up." Head tilted back, he lets it drain down his throat. "Ugh! That tastes nasty. Gimme the rest of your soda."

"Drink your own." I turn my back to him and clutch mine to my chest. He's not getting any.

I fall asleep to his grumbling and the sound of the truck's tires on pavement.

When I wake up, we're stopped, T's gone and the headlights illuminate a gravel road. The jackhammers in my head are quiet, but my neck is as stiff as a rusty hinge.

Grunting bear noises carry through the open window. My gaze travels from the revolver on the seat, to a shadow squatting outside the circle of light, and settles on the keys dangling from the ignition. It's an invitation, an escape from this sniveling loser who has become a sore in my ass.

It's his fault I'm hungry right now. If he hadn't spent all the money, I wouldn't have had to rob that drug store. Now my neck hurts and that's his fault too. I should slide over right now, turn the key and drive. Or should I pick up the gun and get rid of him for good? I haven't yet decided when the moose noises stop and T is at my door.

"Will you drive?" His face is pale, eyes sunken like he's got the flu. "My guts are on fire and I could shit two quarts through the eye of a needle. This is the third time I've had to stop."

I've already slept through two opportunities to ditch him. "Are you already coming down?" Those drugs wore off fast. Good thing I got a whole bag.

"Coming down from what? I never got high." He opens the door and folds himself onto the seat like a stiff-legged spider.

"Maybe you didn't take enough. You said that bottle was single dose. You're a pretty big guy."

"Nothing happened, so I drank the other three." He points at four empty vials on the floor. "That Oxy didn't work. All it did was give me wicked stomach cramps and the shits from hell. Do you have any idea how hard it is to squat with a bum knee?"

If he wants sympathy, he's out of luck. "That's what you get for the stupid runzer. Karma's a bitch." My rumbling stomach agrees with me.

"It's called a runza, and you'd know how good it was if you'd tried it." He uncurls his body a little and picks up one of the remaining bottles from the drug store. This one is labeled Oxybutynin. "I don't like that liquid stuff but these are different. They'll work." He shakes out an innocent-looking blue pill and holds it up to the interior light.

The other blue pills he got from the dealer at the truck stop gave me a happy rush the first time I took one. Or were they pink? I didn't even care when he touched me. What if I could feel like that again? What if my neck stopped hurting? "I'll take one if you do."

"These are tiny. One won't get you high." He's got that look in his eye. The look that makes me wish I hadn't lost my knife.

What if I could feel like that again, without waking up to T's hands groping my crotch? "Okay, I'll take a bunch if you do."

His teeth glitter in the dash lights. "You're on." He pours out a handful of pills.

"Only if I get to hold the gun."

"Aw, I won't do nothing to you. I'm too sick to think about that." He looks whipped, but I hold out my hand anyway. Who knows how he'll be in ten minutes, and if there's one thing I've learned by now, it's what he's like when he's high.

I stare him straight in the eye so he knows I mean business.

Finally, he hands over the gun and I thumb the latch to pop open the cylinder. I give it a spin, because they always do that in the movies, look down the barrel, and then check how many bullets are left.

My grandfather never let me touch his guns, but T has explained the basics. From this angle, I can see that four of the bullets are spent, because dimples mar the centers. Two shiny primers remain. Like little buttons, each nestles in the unspent cartridges, waiting for me to pull the trigger. When I do, the firing pin will hit the primer, which will explode and ignite the gunpowder. *Fire in the hole*, T says. The bullet has one escape route, right out the barrel.

I want to be the one to fire these last two rounds. I want to shoot someone so bad it makes me sweat. What would it feel like to point this gun at T's face, and fire? Would it look amazing? Would it be an explosion of blood and brains?

T knows a lot about explosives. If a bullet can make a small explosion, a bomb can make a big one. He says I'd love setting them off. Maybe I would. That's one reason to keep him around.

I rotate the cylinder, so the next bullet up will be a live one, and snap it closed. With the gun in one hand, I down half a dozen of the Oxybutynin pills and start the truck. My neck will feel better in a few minutes and we'll be in Minnesota by morning. After I take care of a few things, everything will be perfect. "T, how do you make a bomb?"

"Ungh, you want to make sexy talk right now? My guts are burning like I swallowed snake venom."

"Do you ever think about anything besides your dick?"

He shifts his weight and curls tighter. "Well, right now all I can think about is how bad my guts hurt and trying not to puke. I couldn't get it up if I wanted to."

"Good. Tell me about bombs."

He frowns and exhales. "It'll take my mind off how bad I feel until the new stuff kicks in."

"How do you build one? How do you set it off?" All the explosion scenes, from every movie I've ever seen, play in my mind. My return to Morley Falls will be epic.

"All you need is a chunk of metal pipe, threaded at both ends. Drill a hole in one end, fill it with gunpowder, attach a fuse, and screw on the other cap. When you light it, run like hell, and ba-boom!"

"Can we make one?" Excitement wriggles in the area where my heart is supposed to be. I want to make something go ba-boom. "Where do we get the pipe?"

"That's easy. Any hardware store will have it."

"Can we use the powder from our bullets?" I grip the revolver tighter. I don't want to sacrifice the remaining bullets, but if it's the only way…

"Not enough. We'll have to get more from a gun shop."

I can imagine robbing a survival store with our little pea shooter. They'll blow us away with fifty assault rifles before we make it in the door. This is starting to sound stupid. "What about a fuse? Where do we get that?"

"You can buy electrical detonators for toy rockets in a hobby shop."

"Are you making this shit up on purpose? That sounds impossible."

He shrugs. "A shoelace might work."

"Have you actually made one?" I used to believe T's stories but, after I found out he's a low-life skinner, I'm not so sure. Everyone knows you can't trust a pedophile.

"Swear on a stack of bibles, me and my buddy used to make them all the time." He crosses his heart. "Three Finger Jamie blew off his thumb, pointer finger and the tip of his nose. His face healed up okay but he wouldn't build them with me any more after that." He laughs. "It was his own fault. He knew he was supposed to brush the gunpowder off the threads before he screwed on the cap."

"Ba-boom?"

He laughs. "Ba-frickin'-boom, girl." The way his eyes catch fire, even when he's sick, convinces me that blowing shit up might be worth the effort.

Without warning, my stomach lurches and a vile taste fills my mouth.

Judging from the sweat on his upper lip, T's feeling the same way. "Pull over!"

By morning, we're both done puking and we've thrown the rest of the pills out the rear slider into the box of the truck. Obviously they are poisoned or something. Pharmacies must have sneaky ways to make sure you don't steal their shit. The way banks put exploding dye packs into bags of money for robbers, pharmacies must put poison into their drugs. Fuckers. The next guy in a white coat I see will pay for this.

Hours ago, we buried the farm truck to its axles in the river and stole another. This one is newer and smells flowery. T says it reminds him of a girl he knew once, but won't tell me about.

I can smell the change in the air too. It's richer, more full of oxygen or something, definitely better. I spent some of the cash from the drug store and T has been sleeping on and off since we finished that six pack of beer. His bladder should wake him in time to get his first glimpse of Morley Falls.

I nudge him with my foot until he rubs his eyes. The town's welcome sign, complete with a happy fisherman, flashes past. I'm back. My gut instinct is to drive straight home, but what if T is right? What if my grandfather sold it? What if someone new is sitting out there, looking at my bog?

I don't have the heart to go there yet. Instead, I beeline for the far side of town, where the nicer people live, the ones who mow their lawns, fix their fences, and don't holler at their kids in the street.

There's the cop's house, exactly as I remember. How many nights did I crouch behind the hedge to watch through the windows? I flicked my lighter until I scraped the flint wheel smooth, imagining all the ways to burn it down. When I got close, that damn blind dog barked. I had no desire to find out how sharp those teeth were. Even scared dogs can bite. And the cat, the goddamn cat, always watching me out the window.

Today, there is no truck in the driveway and the hedge is overgrown. Officer Ericsson likes everything ship-shape. She'd never leave it like that. Maybe she's not here, hasn't been for a while. What will I do if she's moved away?

A red Jeep pulls in front of the house and a woman steps out. It's the cop's girlfriend, the one I knifed in the belly, the witch who said my dead mother sent her. I slouch when she looks straight at the truck and tilts her head. She hurries to get something out of the back, and peers over her shoulder as she heads for the house.

All those days in juvy, reliving that night, I'd imagined her stooped, broken, blood-stained from the inside out. She's absolutely fine, healthy even. Angry blood sizzles in my veins. How is this possible?

"You're sexy when you growl. You know her, don't you?" T is watching me the way he did when we first met in the library, like he wanted to peek into my brain, like he was excited by the possibilities.

"I shoved my knife into her liver."

"She lived, and you got three years in juvy anyway. That's a travesty."

I pull the gun from my waistband and wrap my fist around the handgrip until the color is squeezed from my knuckles. I'll run across the road right now and shoot her in the face. Twenty seconds, tops, and it'll be all over.

Solemn as a priest during confession, T shakes his head and points at a cop car crossing the side street. "Patience, bunny rabbit."

I don't want to wait. I want Ericsson to come home and find her girlfriend's guts splattered across the porch. But Ericsson's not here. Hasn't been for a while. I don't want to wait, but T's right. This time I must succeed. I put the truck into gear. I won't burn that house down. With T's help, I'll blow it to hell.

T smiles at me and I want to smile back. I let him lean against me a little. I want to imagine that I like him, that he is more than a tool I used to get back here.

"Let's get more beer. Then I'll show you our new home." I hope T is wrong. That the bog is still mine.

T has sleepy eyes, like I imagine people have when they're in love. "I'm hungry, honeybun. Where's the closest restaurant?"

I laugh, not because he's funny, but because there are only a few restaurants in this town and none are open at this time of the morning. If you're lucky, you can get a bagel at the Angler's Coffee Stop, but it's really just a trailer parked in an empty lot.

I take a left toward the place where the Stop 'N Go used to be. From the time I was nine or ten, I'd sneak in for beer, and my favorite pizza sandwiches. That was before I burned it down. I hit the brakes in the middle of the road when I see what has replaced the building's blackened carcass. "Holy shit!"

The whole store has been rebuilt twice its original size, with flashy gas pumps outside and a new light-up sign shaped like a fish. It's way brighter than the old one. The name's different too. Now, Gina's name is right up top.

They should have called it *Nosy Gina's Stop 'N Go*, because she was always up in my business. As if I needed to call the Kids Help Phone to talk about my problems.

I dig a wad of bills out of my pocket and shove them at T. "Go buy beer and get us food. No goddamn shit I never heard of this time."

"You're not coming in?" He snatches up that cash faster than my mother took money from the strangers who left her bedroom.

"Naw." I turn my camera on and point it at the store. "Bitch in there knows me."

He goes in, and I film him robot-walking on his wonky knee. "And get smokes!" I yell out the window. "Marlboros." I wish I could add the soundtrack from Terminator. This movie is gonna be award-winning.

CHAPTER TWENTY

Allie put on the kettle and found Erin's favorite mug, the one with the hand-painted flower and perfectly shaped handle. She tugged the sleeves of Erin's FBI sweatshirt up to her elbows and rested them on the table. She was tired. Even with the dog and cat both snuggled up to her, she hadn't been able to sleep. Between alternate bouts of stomach aches and phantom dizziness, she'd drifted from nightmare to nightmare. A knife, blood seeping through snow-white cloth, over and over in video replay. She'd woken up once to check if little blue pills tumbled together in her palm. The dream had been so real.

Lily was close. This connection to her sickened Allie, the constant barrage of psychedelic colors, raw emotion and disjointed thoughts. The girl's mind was altered. The girl was drinking, or on drugs, or mentally ill. Maybe all three. It made no sense.

If she could focus and figure out Lily's plan, or her location, it might help. The hard part was that Lily seemed to have no plan. Each day, each action, seemed to be decided in that moment. The one thing she was sure of was that Lily was coming, and they were all in danger.

Finally, Allie had gotten out of bed and watched a classic movie on TV. Katharine Hepburn dressed as a man in 1935's Sylvia Scarlett did the trick and she fell asleep for two glorious hours on the sofa.

"I missed you a lot, Auntie Allie." Erin's nephew Jimmy came though the door and, as usual, headed straight for the dog's special cupboard. "You're the only one who understands me when I talk about my drone." He rolled his eyes. "Mom doesn't even know what

GPS is."

The dog nipped the treat from his fingers before he had a chance to react. He frowned at the domineering Chihuahua. "Doppler, you're being a naughty boy. When did you start doing that?"

Allie had been letting Doppler get away with a great deal of questionable behavior in Erin's absence. It was giving him big dog attitude. Nipping a little boy's fingers was unquestionably over the line. She turned to intervene but stopped when she saw Jimmy's determined face.

After a series of hand signals, the dog sat and waited patiently for his treat. He got a belly rub for his obedience. "I think he's bored, Auntie Allie. He needs more kid time. Can I take him home this weekend?"

She raised her eyebrows. Doppler was keeping her anchored right now. "Not today, but you can walk him if you'd like."

Jimmy's older sister, Victoria, joined them in the kitchen. "Can we have pancakes?"

Her twin, Sophie, with Wrong-Way Rachel draped over her shoulder, wasn't far behind. "Mmm, pancakes. Kitty loves pancakes, don't you kitty?" The cat, a string of fake pearls dangling from her neck, stretched out a lazy paw to poke at the beads. Her purring could probably be heard on the moon.

"Didn't your mother feed you this morning?" Allie knew what the kids were up to. They'd pretended to eat breakfast at home so they could save room for another one here.

"We're absolutely *starving* for pancakes." Victoria batted her eyelashes. It might have worked if she'd been five years younger, maybe it still did.

"Are you hungry too, Jimmy?" Allie put her hands on her hips.

"Actually, I am, and I really do enjoy your pancakes. They are nice and fluffy. Not at all like the hard ones mom makes." He wrinkled his nose.

"I'm sure she wouldn't appreciate your honesty the way I do. Okay, kids. I'll make pancakes—" Allie was drowned out by cheering from all three. Not to be outdone, Doppler hopped on his hind legs. "On one condition, that you give me two whole hours to work. No interruptions, unless the house is on fire, or there's an alien invasion."

"Aliens." Jimmy chuckled. "We promise."

Allie watched her spoon go round and round in the bowl while she mixed the batter. The swirls divided and blended, almost forming discrete shapes before they were gone again. Lily. The boy.

Doppler's paws on her knee snapped her away from the thought as it was materializing. She leaned down to pat him. "Hey Chorizo. You need to go out?"

Jimmy waggled his finger at her. "We really should talk about why you and Auntie Erin keep calling him a sausage. You're going to hurt his feelings."

Allie laughed. "I would think a dog might be pleased about that."

He frowned with one eyebrow and went to find the leash. "I'll take him. I don't want to delay your special pancakes."

A prickle of fear sent a shiver along her spine. "Around the block. No farther." She turned on the griddle and finished mixing the batter. There was nothing special about her pancakes, nothing more special than the box they came in. Kids thought things tasted better at someone else's house, and truth be told, she liked cooking for them. Maybe they'd roll hot dogs in dough and make pigs-in-a-blanket for lunch. This home was becoming more and more like the one she'd grown up in, and she was surprised that having children around made her so happy.

The kids ate every pancake Allie made, except for one snuck under the table to the dog. She left them playing a board game and settled into her office chair for the promised two hours of uninterrupted work time. She smiled. She couldn't love those kids more if they'd been hers by blood. Even the opinionated cat had decided they were worth it.

She initiated a video call and Ciara's face appeared on the central monitor. The others continued to refresh a variety of network statistics and logs, the numbers scrolling by at dizzying speed.

"Hi boss." Ciara's bare feet on the desk took up the left third of the image. Today she wore her famous Batgirl shorty pajamas, even though it was well past the time when other professionals at least wore pants. Her long hair was dyed a combination of blue and purple, but she still managed to look like a runway model on her break. In the background, her business and life partner, Raphael, thoughtfully tapped on a computer keyboard.

"How are things with the Vista Project?" Allie turned her head to the first monitor to check the stats. "It appears up and running, and no major issues with implementation. Any more hassle at the GSM base station?"

"Are you talking about Mr. Franklin? That old raisin wouldn't let Dale and Sammy onto the roof to access the antenna. We pay for that office. He knows the owner signed that agreement months ago. I had to go visit him myself and eat a half dozen of his stale biscuits before he agreed to hold up his end of the bargain."

Allie laughed. She could imagine Ciara towering over the little old man in her fierce leather boots and candy skull T-shirt. "He's probably a lonely building manager, waiting for a young girl to eat cookies with."

Raphael's grinning face popped up. "He'll have to fight me for you."

Ciara held up both hands in surrender. "Mixed martial artist versus old wrinkled man. No contest." She turned back to the screen. "Seriously Allie. Everything here is running tickety-boo. No issues right now. Nearly everyone working on this project is local, so that makes our client very, very happy. They're so happy that they want to see what it would take to provide free internet to a school up north."

"Really?" She'd never gotten the impression that the backers of the Vista Project would be interested in philanthropy. It was all about money. Money and power.

"And computers. Those kids all share a couple of old dinosaurs and a dial-up connection."

"It would make a difference to their education to have better access." Allie had seen news coverage of the conditions some children in Northern Manitoba lived in. This could be a life changer. "You tell them we'll halve our fees for it. They know they'd recoup their cost in new projects with all that positive PR."

"I'm going to get them thinking about building a new school gym for next year's project." She wiggled her toes on the desk, giving Allie an up-close view.

"You know you have carte blanche to do whatever you think is best. You and Raphael are pretty much running the entire company now. I'm only an advisor."

"Pshaw, you're the brains of the operation." Ciara blew her a kiss. "Gotta go, *boss*." She stressed the last word. "Meeting with Vista soon."

"You might want to get dressed first." Allie was still smiling when she disconnected. Ciara had been her friend since their university days, and theirs was a bond that she trusted.

She finished her work and was done in an hour and a half, thirty minutes earlier than she'd told the kids. The house was eerily quiet, only Wrong-Way Rachel lounged on the back of the sofa, her long fluffy tail swishing as she watched something out the window. The prickle of fear crept further up Allie's spine to lodge at the base of her skull. She hurried out the front door.

Sophie and Jimmy sat on the step with Doppler between them. All three had the same hangdog expression.

Allie's heart stalled. "Where's Victoria?"

"She took off on her bike. Again." Sophie shrugged.

"It's your fault she ran away," Jimmy groaned. "Why do you two always have to argue? It's stunting my growth."

"Don't blame me. She's the one with the secret boyfriend."

The boyfriend part was not news to Allie. This must be who Gina had been talking about. The boy who bought Victoria candy.

"Is too your fault. You called her mean names." Jimmy waggled his shoulders like a street girl with attitude. "Floozy, floozy, floozy!"

"Grandpa says it. It can't be that bad." Sophie twirled the skipping rope around her wrist, her eyes bright with tears. "What if she never comes back?"

"Where did she go? Who is this boy?" When the kids shrugged, Allie ran to the house for her keys. The sun dipped behind a cloud, and she shivered in its shadow. Lily was out there.

She had opened the door to load the kids into the Jeep when Victoria rounded the corner. Sandaled feet pumped the pedals as she lazily wove her way down the street. Her purple bike helmet popped up when she recognized them in the driveway, and she straightened her trajectory.

"Are you going for ice cream *without me?*" Victoria's eyes widened in confusion until she looked at Allie and dipped her head. "Oh, you were coming to look for me."

"I was worried to death." Sophie reached out to her sister. "I'm sorry I called you a floozy."

Victoria brushed off her hand. "So much drama. You were annoying, and I needed a break. I rode my bike around the block." She peeked sideways at Allie. "I didn't go any further. I promised I wouldn't."

Jimmy shook his head in disbelief. "You were gone an awfully long time."

"I rode in circles over by the McTavish's until I was ready to come back. I'm sorry if I worried Miss Drama Princess."

"I think you can agree that it was unfair to punish everyone to antagonize your sister." Allie laid a hand on Victoria's shoulder. "We were worried that something might have happened to you."

Victoria rolled her bicycle to the yard and returned with her head down. "I'm really sorry, Auntie Allie. I would never do anything on purpose to make you feel bad."

"I know you wouldn't, sweetie, but you should consider everyone else's feelings too."

A black and white police SUV turned onto the road, curtailing the rest of Allie's lecture.

"It's big Z!" Jimmy hopped up from the step and met Chris Zimmerman at the curb. The dog leaped inside as soon as the door opened.

"Whoa! Doggie germs." The lanky policeman froze while Doppler licked his chin. "Will someone please detach this mammal?"

"You crack me up, bro." Jimmy folded the excited Chihuahua into his arms and put him on the ground. "He's not dangerous."

Zimmerman stepped out and brushed tiny hairs from his pants. "Remember that best man thing you did for me?"

Jimmy nodded. "Best day of your life, you said." The two had looked handsome in their matching suits.

"That comes with a lifetime agreement to rescue me from all fur-bearing creatures." His face was serious, but his eyes sparkled with mischief. "It was in your contract, dude. Didn't you read it?"

Jimmy chucked his arm and then dutifully pulled the dog away from Z's uniform trousers.

Zimmerman nodded. "That's what I'm talking about." He turned to the girls, who gaped up at him as if he were a true life giant. "Yes, before you say it, the weather is fine up here, and you two are looking remarkably intelligent today."

"We *look* intelligent?" Sophie and Victoria exchanged a puzzled glance.

"It's not about the package, girls. It's what's inside the package. If I complimented you on your beautiful eyes and great hair every time

I saw you, you'd think that was all that was important. Gina says that would be a disservice to all women, and you better believe I listen to my wife." He grinned, and the girls blushed as he succeeded in complimenting their looks after all.

"Kids, would you get started on making the pigs-in-a-blanket? Everything you need is in the kitchen, and I'll be in to supervise in a minute." They trooped into the house and she called after them. "Don't forget to wash your hands!"

"You're like the child whisperer," Zimmerman quipped. "They listen to everything you say."

"Bribery helps." Pancakes at least.

"Ha! I'll remember that. At a year old, Mikey is already sassing me. His favorite is *Da-Da. No.*"

"How's the new babysitter?"

"Good, Gina has time to work and I have time to sleep on night shift, but that's not why I'm here." He looked over his shoulder at the closed kitchen window. "Have you, you know, *seen* anything lately? I understand Derek is hiding out at Gunther's old place, I'm sure the mosquitoes will drive him out of there soon enough, but do you have any idea where Lily is?"

The scar on Allie's abdomen throbbed at the mere mention of her name. She cupped her hand over it until warmth radiated through the fabric. "She's not alone."

"Yeah. Intel says she's still with a boy from juvy. He's a piece of work. Has a long record for—"

"Stop! I don't want to hear it." Images rushed into her mind faster than she could block them. They spilled like muddy water into a pool of sadness. The sadness of a mother for the tarnished innocence of a little girl. She closed her eyes and focused until the images fled.

"All I want to know is where they might be. When they get near…"

"Lily's already here."

"Where?" His eyebrows shot up. "They must have driven non-stop from the last sighting in Nebraska."

"I'm not sure, but it feels like the temperature dropped ten degrees since this morning."

He looked up at the clear sky. "Maybe a storm's coming."

"Yes, I'd say. I'm keeping the kids close." If she wore a sweater, she'd pull it tight to keep out the chills. "Erin will be here this evening. Are you going to be on the task force too?"

"You bet your metaphysical tuchus. I spent all morning setting up the board room for them." He rested his oversize hand on Allie's shoulder. "I'm not far away. You call me if you see, or feel, anything out of the ordinary."

A whiff of oily smoke diverted Allie's attention and she bolted toward the house. "I need to check the kids."

"See you later, supermom." Zimmerman saluted and walked back to his car.

She ran to the kitchen where Jimmy stood at the counter, dusted with flour to his elbows. The dog jumped on her the moment she entered the room. "Down, Doppler! What's got into you?"

"How many cups are in a pint?" Sophie squinted at an open page in the *Northern Heritage* cookbook Allie hadn't even remembered they owned, although the cover looked vaguely familiar. It had become a spacer for the bottom of the dog treat cupboard. "You don't have any buttermilk, or baking soda."

"What are you doing?"

"We're making the dough for pigs-in-a-blanket, like you said." Jimmy brushed flour from his hands and it drifted to the floor like snow.

"There's a mix in the cupboard. See?" Allie reached in for the blue and white box. She was suddenly cold again. "Where's your sister?"

"There was no buttermilk, so we were going to make some, but you had no vinegar either. We called Gina, and she said we could get the stuff we needed on your account."

"Where's your sister?" Allie asked again, but she knew the answer.

"Uh, she rode her bike to the store." Jimmy shifted his weight from one foot to the other.

"Oh, no!" The fear lodged in her spine split into shards and Doppler skittered around her legs. He whined, wanting to be picked up. Smoke whirled around her and she wondered if the kids could sense it too, or if they were frightened by her reaction.

Sophie put down the cookbook, eyes glistening. "It's only a few blocks away. I said we should wait, but she wanted to make you really happy, by making lunch all by ourselves, to make up for before."

Allie grabbed her phone and called the Stop 'N Go, trying to keep the panic from her voice after she had to wait three rings. "Is Victoria there?" she blurted before Gina had a chance to finish her phone spiel.

"She called, but I haven't seen—"

Allie disconnected and shepherded the kids to the driveway. "We have to go. Hurry."

Tears streaked Sophie's face when Allie loaded them all into the back seat of the Jeep, barely giving them time to secure their safety belts before she squealed off.

As if she peered through an enhancing filter, colors leaped out at Allie, more vivid than true. She followed them until they funneled into one dark spot on the side of the road, a black hole that consumed all light. They were not two blocks from the store when she slammed on the brakes. This was the place.

Sophie's tears became hiccups and Jimmy's cheeks blanched. He wrapped his arms around the dog. "What's wrong? Tell us what's happening."

"Stay here," Allie commanded and jumped out. Ahead, Gina hurried to meet her, a mama bear out to protect her young. Allie hadn't even had to tell her what was going on. Her mother's intuition must have sent her into action. Heaven forbid anything ever happen to her own child.

"I locked the store. Is Victoria missing?" Gina was breathless from the two block dash in her flip flops.

"Will you watch the kids?"

Gina nodded. "I got this." She pulled out her cell phone and waved reassuringly to the kids, who hugged the dog between them.

Allie signaled them to stay put, and bolted into the tall grass. A small track, narrow enough for a bicycle, or one person on foot, led down the ditch and up the other side. This area was uncultivated, too rough for housing development. Here, the brush tangled thick and wild among rocky outcroppings.

"Victoria!" she yelled. Something had happened. Something awful. Did she imagine that Lily's oily smoke trail still wafted through the air, clinging to delicate branches like tree sap? Had Lily really been here, or was she chasing shadows and memories?

She pushed her way through the undergrowth and doubled back along the fence line. Oblong shapes in the flattened grass betrayed where deer bedded down in the afternoons, but there was no sign of Victoria.

She suddenly felt foolish. She was being hysterical. Maybe this was nothing. Victoria might have snuck out with her mystery boyfriend. She should call the neighbors. Maybe Victoria hadn't gone anywhere at all. Maybe she was simply riding circles by the McTavish's again. She might be on her way home right now, wondering why they'd gone out and left her. The cold fist in her gut convinced her that her intuition was on target. Victoria had been taken.

The crashing of large booted feet made her blood freeze. Someone was coming up behind her full-tilt.

"Allie! Victoria!" Z-man's voice sounded marginally less panicked than she felt.

"Chris!" she called back.

"Gina phoned me, said Victoria's missing." He swatted branches away from his face and forced his size fourteen boots through a dense thicket of northern bayberry to reach her. "I was on my way back to your house and saw your Jeep. Talk to me."

"She went to the store and didn't get there. Something has happened. I think…" She couldn't say the words but Zimmerman's face told her she didn't have to.

He radioed the station and relayed the information. "You go that way and I'll follow the fence." He headed off, sweeping his feet across the grass like a berry picker.

Allie went the way he'd pointed and was surprised when Doppler bounded through the brambles. He must have escaped through an open window. She scooped him up and pulled a prickle from his ear. "Help me," she whispered.

A warm tingle coursed through her body and charged her nerve endings. She turned to an overcrowded thicket she was certain she'd already checked. Poking toward her like an accusing finger was a purple handlebar. Victoria's bicycle.

CHAPTER TWENTY-ONE

When T got back from the Stop 'N Go, we dove into the food he'd brought. Goddamn, I was happy to see those pizza sandwiches. They were as good as I remembered, and I made him drive so I could give them my full attention. A tourist in my own town, I couldn't get enough of the Morley Falls experience.

I was still licking sauce from my fingers, and thinking about lighting up a cigarette, when we saw her, the kid on the bike, riding like she was in a hurry to get somewhere. She looked familiar, but so does everybody in a small town. Dressed in checkered cargo shorts and tank top, she was younger than me, not yet at puberty. Her long hair spun the light into gold.

T's head snapped around when we passed her, a wolf who's caught a scent. "Ahhh. Who's that pretty young thing?"

"You gotta get your eyeballs checked. That's a little kid on a bike." I glanced sideways at him and back at the kid. Suddenly, I got it. I slid my phone from my pocket, turned on the camera and pointed it at T's face.

"She's the one." A corner of his baby mustache lifted. "If you won't let me have you, let me have her."

"Sure," I said, and swiveled to record the girl. "And then we'll build a bomb."

It started as a lazy thought, and I never believed he'd actually do it, but he smoothed his hair and spun the truck around so fast I spilled beer on my shirt. I've seen him in action before, sweet-talking the old lady to take us across the border, but not like this. He was all glittery teeth and handsome charm.

The kid bought it, and I could tell she honestly wanted to help him with whatever urgent problem he was making up. He pointed into the bush but she spotted the camera phone in my hand. That was the moment she backed away. By then, it was too late. T struck like a cobra and grabbed her by the throat.

You can always count on farm trucks to carry duct tape, a coil of rope or a string of barbed wire. I tossed over the roll of tape I found under the seat, and he got that kid under control in seconds. By the time I'd hidden her bike in the bush, he had her wrapped into a neat little package between his knees.

I climbed into the driver's seat and cracked open another beer. "What are we gonna do now?"

T still had his glittery smile on, and directed it at me. "Find someplace to play with her." He reached down and stroked the girl's blonde hair.

That was twenty minutes and a loud argument ago. He is pissing me off with all his big ideas. "You got her. Why can't you do what you want and get over it? Stop wasting time."

"But honeybun, it's gotta be done right. Everything has an order, or it's a waste." T is still petting the squirming lump on the floor, but his snake charmer smile fades. "We're gonna party and I want it to be good. We need something for her, and for us. Where can we score around here? "

"I dunno."

"Weed, hash, hell, I'd do a line of coke right now if we had any." He sounds like I used to when I wanted candy, or cigarettes. "What about meth? You ever tried meth? It's mind-blowing. You must know someone who sells."

"Maybe." There was a guy, said he was my mother's special friend, who used to give her stuff. I might remember where he lived. I can't believe I'm doing this for T when I have more important shit to do, better shit, but I want to use him for my revenge.

I drive back and forth on both sides of the railroad tracks, and I still can't figure out which house it was. My mother used to make me wait by a white fence at the curb while she went inside. There is no fence now. Finally, one place tweaks a memory and I pull over.

T's face lights up. "This is it?" He plunks his big feet on top of the squirming package.

I nod and step out of the truck. My mother always used the back door, so I head around and come face to face with a woman who's leaving. She's as surprised to see me as I am her, and her too-tight face stretches when her eyebrows shoot up. Her skin is dry like old paper and she has that look, the look of all the people I remember from this place. Here, but somehow not present.

"Armand's not looking for new girls." She adjusts the oversize bag on her shoulder and looks me up and down with interest. "You're familiar."

"I'm no fucking whore." I brush past her. "Where is he?"

"Who's there?" Armand is in the doorway and he's exactly as I remember, a skinny loser covered in tattoos. With a flick of his hand, he dismisses the woman and she struts off with a clip clop of shiny heels.

"I need drugs. What do you have?"

He laughs and holds the door open. "The narcs are hiring a bit young these days, aren't they?"

The revolver sags in the back of my pants under the tail of my shirt, but I'm reminded that there are only a couple of bullets left, one for the cop and one for the witch. Will he give me what I want if I wave the gun at him? Will he call my bluff and make me waste my ammo?

I reach into my pocket and show him what's left of the money from the drug store. "What can I get for this?"

Armand looks at the crumpled bills and leans his bony shoulder against the door frame. "You're no narc. Who sent you? Boyfriend?"

"He couldn't come. He's... busy. He wants meth."

"Meth?" He laughs again, and I remember how much I hate him. "Well, that's in short supply today, but I can sell you Oxy. One of those will put you in the mood for all sorts of things."

My guts still haven't totally recovered from the last batch of poisoned Oxy. How can I tell if these are the same? "Uh, do you have anything else?"

"You want a high, or a nice mellow low?"

"Something for..." It probably wouldn't bother him, but I decide against telling him about the package T is guarding outside. "We want to party."

His jaw muscles flex and release. "Girl I know has a kid with ADD. I've got some Adderall from her. Good stuff, straight from the drug store. Take it with a few beers to keep you partying all day."

I hand over the wad of cash. "You don't have to stick a needle in my vein do you?" I'll be damned if I let Armand do to me what he did to my mother. I saw a helluva lot more than that when I used to peek through his open curtains.

"Nope, just a pill even a baby can swallow." He goes inside, comes back with a prescription bottle, and hands it over. When our eyes meet, he tilts his head and his eyebrows furrow. "Do I know you? You look like... nah, that was a long time ago." I can feel his eyes bore into my back long after I walk away. *Fucker.* I should come back and burn his house down.

"Amphetamines are da bomb," T says and grabs the bottle out of my hand as soon as I show it to him. He pops the cap right away and downs a pill with a gulp of beer. "Take one. I want you to party with us, love bunny."

No way. I'll wait a few minutes to see what happens to him before I swallow anything that would give him two girls for the price of one. Not gonna happen. I don't give a shit what else he does, but I'll cut off his fingers before I let him touch me again.

Turns out I didn't need to worry. I'm swerving around a rock in the donkey trail when T slides his ass out onto the window frame. He's all but forgotten his precious prisoner, and thumps his big hands on the roof in a crazy drumbeat. "This is amazing! Oh, you're about to run over a crocodile!"

"You're a lunatic." A loud screech tells me the crocodile was another rock, and I've trashed the undercarriage. I was watching him and missed it. Before we're high centered, I hit the gas and manage to skid over.

"Go faster. Faster!" All I can see are his long legs and smelly shoes on the seat. "Are we there? Are we there?" He giggles. "Mommy, are we there yet?"

"If I had a kid like you, I'd drown it." I pull over and reach for the bottle. I want what he took.

"Hey, why'd we stop?"

I pop a pill in my mouth and swallow hard.

He climbs back in, folds himself onto his seat, and seems almost surprised at the package on the floor. "How's my girl?" With thumb and forefinger, he pries the duct tape from her mouth and waggles his fingers at me in a give-it-here gesture. I drop a pill into his hand.

He shoves it between her lips and grins at me. "See? Like candy."

When she spits it in his face, I almost pee myself with laughter. She got him good. I instantly like her a little bit. This might be an interesting experience. We kidnapped her. We're kidnappers. I like the sound of the word, and roll it around in my mind. It's scary and dangerous.

T's ears are red when he takes a second pill from me. This time, he holds her head, shoves the pill in, and pinches her nose until she gulps for air. "Swallow," he orders and she does. Her mouth is empty when she opens it again. "Good girl."

With gentle fingers, he strokes her head. When she pulls away, he holds her still with a rough hand on her throat. I can tell he likes them feisty, by the way he has his other hand on his crotch.

"My aunt will come for me. She'll hunt you—"

He covers her mouth. "Shh."

The ADD pill is kicking in for me and what she said is all messed up in my head. Her clear blue eyes and blonde hair are so familiar. "Who's coming?"

"Auntie Erin will make you pay for this." The kid struggles to sit up. "She's an FBI—" The rest of her threat is muffled by the duct tape T presses back over her lips.

FBI? Fucking Officer Ericsson isn't in Morley Falls any more. Not in the squishiest part of my brain did I ever imagine that she wouldn't be here when I got back. I want to scream.

"Lily, You hear that? FBI, seriously." T's pupils are so huge they're freaky. His chest pounds like his heart will split his ribcage, and his stare is intense.

Suddenly, it occurs to me. When my ex-friend Nina found out that her dad did nasty things to her little sister, she completely melted down, so much that she actually helped me kill him. I'm not stupid. That was the day I learned that the worst thing in the world you can do to someone is to give their kid to a skinner.

Who needs a bomb? Fuck bombs. I have the niece of Officer Erin Ericsson, and T is my perfect weapon. When she finds out, she'll come. This will be the best revenge ever. I turn on the camera and bare my teeth at the lens. T and me, together, we have never been so fucking powerful.

"Bitch. You know who I'm talking to. You and your witch girlfriend. Look what I have." I pan over to the kid, her little stare like an angry hamster, harmless. "Come and get her, if you can. What's that you say? Oh, too bad. You're late. And she's already his." I move the camera from the kid to the sweaty, dark-haired man-boy who grins back at me.

"Who are you talking to?" Between T's high, and his lack of brain cells, he's utterly confused. He's having more and more difficulty controlling his captive. Either she's getting stronger or he's losing it.

"Unfinished business." He had his secrets and this one's mine.

"Where are we going?"

I drive to the end of the dirt road, and T is singing the theme song to a cartoon when we lurch to a stop at the boat launch. Ahead of us, the road simply dips into the river, but I'm not going that way. I turn the wheel and ram the front bumper into the trees, gunning the engine until the tires spin rooster tails.

T can't get out his door, so we drag the kid through my side. Like a sack of corn off the back of a farmer's wagon, he dumps her on the ground and we break off branches to camouflage the truck. It's impossible to spot from the road, even the ruts from the spinning tires are hidden in the tall grass.

"Let's go." I tuck the gun in my pants, carry the beer, and leave the sobbing kid to T. He hefts her, trussed hand and foot, over his shoulder. Standing at the riverbank, his face pales. "I'm not such a good swimmer, and with her…"

"No, stupid." What a moron. I point to the trail along the river. I haven't been here in so long that only the occasional deer has kept it from becoming completely overgrown. "It's not far, a few miles." I can't wait to get there.

As soon as I'm in the woods, my panther feet find their way beneath me, and I settle into a trot. The beer bottles jingle in their cardboard case.

Behind me, crashing noises tell me that T is not having such an easy time. I'll wait for him but my heart's racing. The only thing on my mind is how bad I want to get there.

The pile of snapped twigs I've arranged on a fallen log has grown into a horrible mound of broken angles by the time T stumbles into me. Sweat runs down his neck and soaks his shirt.

"I heard something. Someone's back there." He drops his package and looks back down the trail. The kid doesn't make a sound. She's tougher than he is. "My leg is killing me. Why didn't you get more

Oxy?" He sits beside me.

"Did you forget the shits you got last time? Nasty."

"Oh, yeah." He eases his leg up on the log and rubs his knee. "This girl is heavier than she looks."

"Is she dead? How many pills did you give her?"

"Just the one." He glares at me, but I don't care enough to laugh at him again. "She spit the first one out, remember?"

"Uh, huh. Can she even breathe? You might have already killed her."

He forgets about his knee and leans down to rip the tape off her mouth. The kid is silent as death. He hurries to untie her. "Shit, no, no, no!"

"She looks croaked." She's not, but this is too much fun to give it away so soon. Her eyelids flickered a moment ago. She's playing possum, and she's good at it. I turn the camera back on and wait.

He checks her wrist for a pulse and looks at me. He checks again. "I can't feel anything!" He's in the wrong spot, so of course he missed it, and he's freaking out. This movie will be so awesome to watch tomorrow. I zoom in on the kid's face and there it is. One nostril flares and her eyelid twitches again. This kid is making my day.

On his feet, T spins around. "We gotta get out of here. Which way did we come?"

"You sure you don't want to hide the body before the flies find it?" A hand on my gut to hold the laughter in, I clutch my beer to keep from spilling. T is pathetic.

"She isn't, really." He bends to examine her face. "Is she?" Chalky residue dribbles down her chin. Ha, she cheeked the pill.

I kick the kid in the ribs. "Show's over. Get up."

With a move fast enough to make Bruce Willis proud, the kid head butts T in the face and leaps to her feet. He goes down, spider legs thrashing in the brambles. A spray of red bursts from his nose, and I make sure I get a close-up. This will be the best movie ever.

The girl bounds, not back the way we came, but further into the woods. Willow branches whip into place behind her. It's as if she knows where she's going, and she just might. A lot of town people come here to pick blueberries along the power lines. Some of them even follow it back home. She's already proven she's not stupid. But she has made one huge mistake.

T is pissed. I've never seen him angrier. With giant leaps, the city boy with the bloody nose stomps through the trees, not bothering to protect his bare skin from sharp branches. The kid squeals like a snared rabbit when he catches her, and he twists her arm.

"Nice try, kid." A fat tear rolls down her cheek when I taunt her with the camera.

He ties her hands together and prods her to walk on her own, in front where he can keep an eye on her. He wipes his nose on his shirt and pops two more ADD pills with a beer. He's already taken at least three I've seen, and maybe another I haven't.

"We're getting close." Quivers of excitement vibrate up my spine. It's going to be a good night, and I'll drink beer while I record T's little party. Wait until Officer, no, *FBI Agent* Ericsson sees the video.

CHAPTER TWENTY-TWO

"There!" Erin pointed to flashing lights on the desolate stretch of highway, and Gonzales pulled in by the Minnesota State Patrol car parked behind the tow truck. Hooked to the iron jaws of the wrecker was a mud splattered half ton matching the one Lily and Trenton had stolen.

"Good work, Ericsson," Lockwood piped up from the back seat. "Exactly where you thought it would be. We're closing in."

When Erin and Agent Gonzales got out, she stayed put, her stony gaze fixed on the screen of her laptop computer. Ever organized, she had a lot of information to sort through before they arrived in Morley Falls in a few hours.

A young trooper and a ruddy-faced tow truck driver with hands as big as baseball mitts hurried to greet them.

"Afternoon." The trooper snapped his shoulders back as if under inspection. It wasn't every day the FBI came to inquire about the recovery of a stolen vehicle. Now covered by a thick layer of river mud, his boots had probably been spit polished this morning. "Dispatch called to say we weren't to touch a thing until you folks arrived, but—"

"My apologies sir, ma'am," the tow driver gallantly interrupted. "I already hooked 'er up and hauled 'er out by the time Robbie passed that on to me." He nudged the trooper with his elbow. In this part of the state, the two were probably blood-related somewhere down the line. "I promise I didn't touch nothin' inside 'cept the steerin' wheel, if that's any help. I noticed there sure are a lotta empties and garbage.

Pills too, handfuls of 'em under the seat—"

"Charlie, please." Robbie the trooper interrupted what sounded like a fairly complete search of the truck's interior.

Gonzales grinned, and pointed at the trail of mud from the river to their present location. "You spot anything down there when you were hooking on?"

Encouraged, Charlie gave them a full report of the tracks leading down to the river before he'd ground the evidence into oblivion with the dual rear wheels of his Ford Super Duty. He reached into his pocket, and pulled out a handful of prescription bottles. The name of the pharmacy in Lincoln Nebraska clinched the link.

"I wonder why in hell they wanted these." He put his big finger on the vial labeled Oxybutynin. My wife's sister takes these pills for her, uh, so she doesn't have to go to the ladies room so often."

"They're for urinary incontinence?" Gonzales held out his hand for the bottle.

"When she first started taking them, she got the upchucks and the runs. That was not pleasant to hear about over Sunday dinner." The big, ruddy-faced man grimaced.

Erin examined the label on the other bottle. "This empty one is Oxytocin. Might be a hormone or something. I don't think it will get them high."

The trooper cocked his head. "Why did they steal hormones and drugs that stop you from peeing yourself?" He flinched at the unanticipated hand on his shoulder.

With a plastic bag opened wide, Lockwood stepped between them. "Because they're idiots. Kind of like law enforcement agents examining fresh evidence with their bare hands." Erin and Gonzales sheepishly dropped their bottles inside. "Oxycontin is a common drug of abuse. I bet these particular idiots couldn't tell the difference."

"For what they did to that good old truck, I hope they're suffering worse than my wife's sister."

Erin grinned. "We can only hope." She painstakingly recorded the details of each medication's name, dosage, prescribing doctor, and pharmacy before she caught Gonzales watching her.

He snapped a few pictures of the bottles with his camera. "It's not necessary to handwrite every single thing. We have the photos."

Erin's cheeks warmed. She was doing it again. Fretting about unnecessary details when she needed to stay in the moment, to see the big picture. Why was it such a challenge? Was she trying too hard to impress Lockwood, who was paying absolutely no attention anyways? *Get a hold of yourself, girl.* She wrote down the essentials and tucked her notebook away.

They made a cursory check of the recovered vehicle before the Forensics crew arrived in the Ident van.

Relaxed, Gonzales clicked a few more photos. He turned and tossed her the car keys. "We are on your home turf. Take us to meet this Z-man with whom I've been liaising." He winked. "He said his wife made cookies."

Lockwood settled herself in the back seat and opened her laptop. "Did you say cookies?"

Erin had reached highway speed when her phone rang. She fumbled in her pocket and handed it to Gonzales.

He hesitated, finger poised above the screen. "There's a list of missed calls from someone named *My Hot Girlfriend.*"

"Ugh, it's a joke. A guy in training did that," she huffed in frustration. "Answer it."

He poked at the icon and held the phone to his ear. "Special Agent Erin Ericsson can't take your call right now." He shot a helpless look at Erin and cupped his hand over his other ear, as if that would help him hear over the wind howling through the open window. "Pardon me? I can't…"

Erin thumbed the automatic window button, and the howling retreated outside the glass. She mouthed *speaker* and he touched the display. Allie's words were still unintelligible, but it was clear she was panicked. Not just panicked, her nieces would say 'totally freaking out'.

"What's all the hubbub?" Lockwood grumbled.

"Baby, slow down. I can't understand—"

"Victoria! She's been taken!" Allie shouted, finally coming through loud and clear.

"What? Who took her? How?" In Erin's gut, she already knew it had to be Lily.

"It was *her,*" she sobbed. "We're looking everywhere. We found Victoria's bike in the woods."

"Did you call it in? Does my sister know?" There was a digital squeal on the line. "They'll find her."

Erin glanced over at Gonzales, who shrugged. "My niece", she whispered. His mouth opened in a silent O.

"Gaul darn son of a biscuit!" In the rear, Lockwood stomped the floor.

"I should have kept a better eye on her. I should have known." Allie's voice cracked. Could she hold it together? If there was ever a time they needed her gift, it was now.

"I'm coming as fast as I can." Erin stepped on the gas, and flicked the concealed emergency flashers. "Is Z-man there with you? Can I talk to him?"

"This is a nightmare." Zimmerman's deep voice rumbled over the speaker without a trace of his usual humor. "You *know* we have every car out looking. Damn, the whole town's looking. Even guys on their days off are coming in. We're doing everything."

"Do you have any leads at all?" She white-knuckled the steering wheel and willed the car faster.

"Gina said a tall young man came in for beer earlier. He's not from around here, and she half-wondered how legit his ID was. I guess now she wished she'd checked it more closely."

Lockwood snapped down the lid of her computer. "Aw, H.E. double hockey sticks."

"Our male suspect, Trenton Leslie Madison, is six foot three inches. Dark shoulder length hair—"

"Yeah, I read that on the alert. This sure sounds like it might be your boy. No sightings of Lily, but Gina got the impression there might have been someone waiting."

She didn't need to point out what was on Trenton Madison's record of conviction. They'd both tear that boy to pieces if he laid a finger on her niece.

"Help Allie calm down. She knows what to do."

He grunted in response. He knew exactly what she meant.

"We'll see you soon." Erin clenched her jaw and forced the car to its limits.

"Pedal to the metal, Ericsson." Lockwood tightened her seat belt. "Can't you move this tin-can-on-wheels any faster?"

Two hours later, they skidded to a stop in front of Morley Falls Police Headquarters, a squat brick building built in the seventies. The cracked steps were badly in need of repair, and Erin took them two at a time.

They were greeted by Deputy Chief Williams when she flung open the doors. He'd been the Chief's stodgy right-hand man for over a decade, and some said he was actually the one in charge.

"Good to have you back, Erin, but not under these circumstances." Williams was pale, concern furrowing his brow as only a father's can. He briefly shook with Gonzales, and then cupped both of his hands around Lockwood's. "Special Agent Lockwood, I'm very pleased to make your acquaintance."

"You've got a kid missing. Let's get moving." She squeezed back, locking eyes like a boxer feeling out the competition before a match. Williams released first, and directed them to the department's dated boardroom.

Zimmerman had told Erin that he was preparing the conference room, but she was still surprised when she entered. The walls, usually decorated with suspect photos and flowcharts of current investigations, were bare. Today, the wooden table shone with new wax and the overflowing boxes of files were stacked neatly in a corner. Bright blue Ethernet cables snaked from the outlet on the wall, ready to connect them to the internet. The white board was scrubbed clean for the first time ever.

Williams poured three glasses of ice water, and motioned for them to sit. Erin's adrenaline screamed in her veins. She ignored his direction and paced to the back of the room.

He tipped his head in acknowledgement. This was not the first time he'd seen Erin too keyed up to keep still. "It appears the situation has escalated with the kidnapping of an eleven year old female."

"My niece, Victoria," Erin interjected.

"Of course." He referred to the clipboard he'd brought, "Victoria Cook disappeared on Willow Street three hours ago. She left 29 Poplar Court—"

"My house." Erin knew this. What did it matter? Lily and the boy had taken her niece. They needed to be out looking, not sitting here rehashing the agonizing details of the abduction.

"—at approximately eleven-forty this morning and went missing shortly thereafter, wearing a blue T-shirt and tan shorts. There were scuff marks in the gravel, possible signs of a struggle near the location where her bicycle was found."

"What have you got to tie this missing child to Schmidt and Madison?" Lockwood scribbled notes on her legal pad.

The taste of metal filled Erin's mouth. She'd almost forgotten that Lily shared her last name with Gina's godfather. The gruff but kindly man had survived her poison, but would forever require a home care assistant. The kid didn't deserve his good name.

"Shortly before the incident, we have a witness who spotted a male matching the suspect's description at the convenience store two blocks from the scene." Williams read off his paper.

"Oh, for Pete's sake!" Erin shouted. "Lily is here. Z-man's wife, Gina, saw Trenton in the store and Lily was probably right outside. They're on some goddamn crime spree across half a dozen states and now they've abducted Victoria. It's her twisted payback. I need to see Allie and we need to get out there!"

"Still a hot head," Williams muttered.

If he spoke those two words, if he said *Raging Ranger*, Erin didn't care how many stars were on his lapel, she'd leap over the table and shake some sense into him. This was her sister's little girl! She'd felt protective of her from the first moment she'd seen the squirming newborn twins in her sister's arms.

Lockwood slammed her hand on the table. "There is a missing child we're dealing with here! It's no time for petty grievances."

Williams flinched as if slapped. The hard glint in her eye set him back in his seat with flushed cheeks.

Gonzales nodded almost imperceptibly. Lockwood's kryptonite. This was it. Somewhere in her background was a case that had gotten under her skin. A case with a child and an awful conclusion that still haunted her. She would not allow it to happen again. Erin saw her resolve and was reassured.

Lockwood took a deep breath, but when she spoke her words had a steel edge, as if one misspoken comment would get him cuffed alongside the ear. "Our objectives seem to have converged, Deputy Chief. I believe that if we work together to catch these two, Erin's niece can return home unharmed." She stretched out the final word.

"Certainly." Williams kept his face neutral, although his body language said he'd rather bolt out the door and lick his wounds. "I apologize for that remark, Erin," he muttered, and pushed his clipboard aside. "But I can assure you—"

Lockwood put down her pen and turned to Erin. "You know this

Schmidt kid. You knew she was coming here. You have good instincts and I'm encouraging you to trust your gut. Where would she take your niece?"

"Gunther's old place. The river," she blurted.

Lockwood nodded. "Family? Friend? Is that where she was living?"

"Yes, with her grandfather, but I doubt she'd try to contact him after what happened."

The senior agent waggled her hand, as if to say that was a story for another time.

"Her father is Derek Peterson," Erin offered.

"Is that *the guy*?" Lockwood made a notation. There had been no secrets about her involvement in the case that had brought months of negative media attention to the doorstep of Morley Falls PD. To her credit, Lockwood had not batted an eye.

Williams cleared his throat. "Mr. Peterson may be connected to a local murder. We haven't yet been able to locate him for an interview."

"I see the kid has predictable genes." Gonzales offered his first verbal input of the meeting. Lockwood's frown made it clear that smart ass comments were inappropriate. He flushed and examined his hands.

"Uh, uh." Erin shook her head. "Derek's always been protective of kids. I'm certain he wouldn't be part of kidnapping one."

"So, the two suspects are virtually untethered by local connections. That might make it easier, or harder, to find them, depending on how you look at it."

Thunder sounded down the hall, and huge galloping feet signaled that Zimmerman's arrival was imminent. Red-faced, he burst through the door, flung his arms around Erin and lifted her to her toes. "I heard you arrived! I can't believe what's happened."

"I'm so glad to see you, Z." Relief unleashed the emotion she'd been struggling so hard to keep at bay, and she choked back a sob. He held her until she got control.

"We'll find her." He turned to the others at the table and cocked a thumb at Gonzales. "I brought you cookies from my wife, as promised. They're in the car."

Gonzales rubbed his hands together. "It's great to finally meet you, too."

Zimmerman gave them the shortened version of their efforts so far. "Our guys are doing a grid search of the entire town, Fire is headed to the river with their boat, and paramedics are combing the streets too. Your parents are organizing dozens of volunteers at the church. Your sister Liz is having chemo over in Duluth today and she's beside herself. Her husband is on his way to get her." He clenched his fists. "I told them I'd bring their daughter back if it's the last thing I do."

Tremors threatened Erin's jaw and she clamped down hard. "How's Allie?"

"She's got a loaf of banana bread for you from your mom, because you're always hungry, and is waiting for you in the coffee room - with the dog."

"Go," Lockwood told her. "We'll grind through the formalities with the Deputy Chief."

CHAPTER TWENTY-THREE

Allie wasn't sure if she felt better or worse after seeing Erin. Their brief time together hadn't been enough to quell the horrible guilt in the pit of her stomach. She didn't want to go home and hope for some sort of inspiration, some intuitive clue she could call Erin with. And she wouldn't sit on her comfy couch and wait for news. Erin's mom was organizing a hundred volunteers. She could probably use the help, and they'd all be calmer if they were kept busy.

She buzzed through the house and gathered sleeping bags, flashlights, and insect repellant. "Come on kids. We are going to grandma's."

"I'm bringing this." Jimmy scooped up his aerial drone and tucked it under his arm.

Red-faced from crying, Sophie stared round-eyed back at her until Allie took her by the hand. "We're not doing any good sitting here. Let's go see how we can help."

"Okay," Sophie sniffed. "We'll bake cookies, or make posters, or whatever." They filed silently to the door, Doppler circling them in confused agitation.

When they reached the driveway, Zimmerman's four-wheel-drive truck pulled in at the curb and Gina ran to hug Allie. "I'm coming. It doesn't matter how much overtime my babysitter racks up. She can buy herself a forty-six inch TV for all I care."

"Hi boss." Jimmy's fingers fluttered tentatively from the back seat. "Are you coming to grandma's?"

"Darn right, little man." Gina got in the front and dug through her purse. She showed Allie a paper map and orienteering compass. "With your built-in GPS, it's not like *you* need this, but look what Gunther gave me. See the blue lines? He's even drawn in all the animal trails he knows."

"Dad said Mr. Schmidt knew Davy Crockett," Sophie offered.

"Maybe. He's pretty old."

"Who's Davy Crockett?" Jimmy asked.

Gina smiled, sad lines creasing the corners of her eyes.

"Are you angry that Victoria ran away?" Sophie held one hand over her mouth but was unable to stop the words.

Allie looked at her in the rear view mirror. "I'm not angry. I'm worried. Why would you think your sister ran away?"

"She made me promise not to tell." Sophie hesitated as if unsure which information to divulge. "I told her not to sneak out to meet Rory any more. She goes almost every day and they kiss and stuff. The last time we had a fight, she said she wanted to run away and have an adventure."

"Rory? No, sweetie. This is not about him." Allie's heart caught in her throat. "This is not your fault."

Gina turned in her seat. "Victoria didn't run away with anyone. She was… she was… Chris said he talked to Victoria's boyfriend, and he's not involved."

"If she didn't run away with Rory—" Sophie began.

"Someone kidnapped my sister?" Jimmy shouted and the dog sprang off his lap.

"It looks that way." Allie hated that she had to be the one to give the kids such horrible news, hated that anyone else would have to do this, and hated that this world was not the place their circle of adults had led them to believe in.

"She's gonna kick their butts!" Sophie growled. This wasn't quite the response Allie had expected from the fashion conscious, nail polish aficionado. "She's the fastest runner in our whole school and she knows karate."

"No, she doesn't," Jimmy hissed.

Sophie punched a feisty eleven-year-old fist into her palm. "Yes, she does. She's been learning it from the internet. Last week, she kicked a board right off the backyard fence."

"I hope she can." Allie turned down the hidden driveway to Erin's parents' house on the river.

"And she has a knife like yours, Auntie Allie. She got it for summer camp, remember?"

Optimism thawed cold fear. Victoria was smart. She was resourceful and she might take her abductors off guard.

CHAPTER TWENTY-FOUR

"You better not be lying to me, Armand." Derek swished a mouthful of whiskey through his teeth and set the bottle on the hood of the delinquent rental car.

"I wouldn't lie to you, man. You said to call if I heard anything, so I'm calling. I don't think it's in my best interest to have you come and visit me in person again." Even on the phone, Armand was a weasel.

"I'm positive it was Tiffany's kid. She used to peek through my curtains all the time when Tiff was over. She's grown up some, but looks pretty much the same. Same skinny ass, same blonde hair, same eyes." There was a pause. "Same weird green color as yours." He snorted. "You're the baby daddy, ain't ya?"

Derek would have Armand's weasel throat in his fist if he was there right now. "What did she want? Was she looking for her mother?"

"Naw, didn't mention a thing about her. All she wanted was something to get high."

"Did you sell her goddamn drugs?"

"Course not, man. I'd never..."

"If this is bullshit, the next time I come over will be your last."

"Maybe I gave her some ADD shit for her and her boyfriend. Nothin' real serious. They make that for kids. It's totally safe."

"You're a freaking circus act, Armand. I suggest you consider moving out of Morley Falls. That's my kind advice to you, for your own good." Derek disconnected. Boyfriend. Lily had a boyfriend. She never did drugs before. A little beer once in a while was no big deal, but this was different. The boyfriend was a bad influence on his daughter. It was all the goddamn boyfriend's fault.

He picked up the whiskey bottle and heaved it at the nearest tree, regretting it the moment it smashed. Honey colored liquid drizzled into the grass and he closed his eyes until the crazy impulse to run over and lap it up subsided.

He tossed his cell phone on the seat and shut the car door. The rental was smaller than his Mustang used to be, but easier to hide, and he'd edged it further into the bushes, where a casual observer would never spot it. He hoofed it along the back trail to the dead zone. Electronic devices were useless here in Gunther's bog. The sun had come out and dried the trail enough so water didn't slop over his shoes.

At the edge of the clearing, he stopped dead in his tracks. He'd been enjoying the sensation of dry feet so much that he nearly missed the signs. The stillness of woodland animals, and the silence of the songbirds told him to be wary. He was not alone.

A dark sedan with government plates parked in the driveway, and three people exited. He ducked behind a thicket, heart hammering in his chest. It was too far to make out who the people by the car were, but that blonde hair belonged to Erin Ericsson. She disappeared inside the shed with one while the other kept watch in the driveway.

He wedged himself into a drainage pipe, sludge seeping through his clothes. If he twisted just right, he still had a decent view through the foliage screen of a wild columbine. A mental inventory of the shed's contents filed through his mind. Had he left anything incriminating?

His legs cramped and his neck muscles burned from the contorted angle by the time Ericsson stepped out with a handful of papers.

Aw, shit. He'd forgotten about the police reports he'd paid for. The requestor's badge number would be on them. He ground his teeth when she tucked them into her bag. Ernie, his last police ally, just got burned.

As if the planets had misaligned to shit upon his day, Ernie chose that moment to show up in his cruiser. Beside him sat the department's golden boy, Chris Zimmerman. Ericsson leaned down to whisper in Zimmerman's open window and the news was out. To Zimmerman's credit, he didn't betray his knowledge by turning to gawk at Ernie. He gave a nod and got out of the car. Chauffeur Ernie stayed put, working on a report, or a crossword puzzle, or some damn thing.

At least Ernie couldn't rat Derek out. He had no idea he was here, squeezed into a dirty pipe like a mole. He sucked air through his teeth. He was a better man than this. With elbows planted in front, he inched himself out and straightened his cricked spine. His back ached, his neck was in spasm and his knees trembled when he got his feet under him. At least upright he felt more like a man than a rodent.

He hunkered behind a nearby dogwood and did his best to listen as words drifted over on the breeze. The first word he made out gripped his throat like an angry fist.

"Schmidt. Lily Schmidt... Peterson is her father..." Ericsson had her back to him and the woman she was talking to must be FBI. "Might know where she is..."

"In the swamp... Not on my map... Not another kid..." The agent was all angles and rough edges, the kind of female who looked right through his charm. Like fuckin' Erin Ericsson did.

Keeping to the trail left by Zimmerman's boots, the male agent tiptoed through the weeds. Zimmerman kept his head down and Derek couldn't make out a single word of their conversation. He guessed the prissy agent's side of it went something like, "Slow down, I'm getting my shoes dirty. Are we going to be late for evening cocktails at the club?"

It's not that Derek had trouble with authority figures, he didn't trust a man in a suit. A man without dirt under his fingernails had no business out here. A man with soft hands would never understand him.

Zimmerman completed his circle around the shed and stepped toward the trail. He stopped and motioned to Ericsson who acknowledged him with a tip of her head, and leaned in to say something to the rough-edged female agent. Inside the car, sunlight glinted off a pair of binoculars in Ernie's hands. Had the little bastard spotted him?

Derek slowly turned and checked for an escape route. The path he knew best would take him to the old Johnson place. Sweat ran between his shoulder blades. He eased his weight onto the balls of his feet, ready to run for it, when the female agent suddenly broke away from Erin. She marched back to the car and got inside with the city boy in the suit.

Erin walked to the bog. He held his breath when she planted the toe of her shoe on the plank and drew it back. As if she was finished testing the waters, she pivoted on her heel and strode with purpose toward the car.

The planets had realigned and blessed him with a little luck. They were all leaving. He exhaled and slowly backed out of the bushes but worry nagged his subconscious. This was too easy. A branch snapped to his left and Derek's heart plunged. Zimmerman.

Erin exploded into action, sprinting straight for him. *Dammit!* Zimmerman sucked at clandestine work, but he was an excellent strategist. While Derek had been hiding like a child, and collecting prickly hitchhikers up his pant legs, Zimmerman had worked out the best way to snare a rabbit.

The FBI agents exited the car and closed the noose. Sitting in his cruiser, as if caught picking his nose, Ernie raised his oblivious head.

Derek made a run for it anyway. He didn't get half a dozen steps before Erin blocked his escape route. He'd forgotten how fast she was.

Well, if she wanted him, she'd have to work for it. Mud sucked against his shoes when he put his weight on the plank, and he shuffled sideways. He kept an eye on her when she skipped onto the end, nimble as a squirrel.

It wobbled with the added weight and Derek extended his arms like a tight-rope walker. The tremors made his knees weak, his balance tenuous. His entire spinal column was a tower of blocks, haphazardly stacked by a toddler.

Two more steps. Three. Out there was his sole clue to finding Tiffany. The more he'd thought about it, the more he'd convinced himself that it was truly her purse in the mud. Who knew what clues it held? His legs threatened to send him headlong, and he fell miserably to his knees. The corner of that horseshoe buckle poked out, still out of reach. So close, yet a lifetime apart.

"Derek." Erin's voice was soft when she spoke. "Don't make this harder. Let's talk."

The sheer misery of his situation hit him. "I didn't kill Badger. I didn't. I couldn't have."

"Come on in and we'll talk about it."

He wasn't a crying man, but a hot tear defied him as it rolled down his cheek. "Aw, shit. Look at me."

She looked at the mangled skin where his ear used to be and shook her head. "All I see is a guy I went to school with a long time ago, having a rough time."

Unable to hold her clear blue gaze, he dropped his eyes. She extended her hand and he shuffled toward her. He had shitty luck. That was all. Just a helluva lot of unfortunate incidents. It could all be explained away. Erin reached out and he gripped her hand, her skin smooth under his calloused palm.

He glanced back at the buckle. If he allowed himself to be taken in, would he ever get his answers? Would they believe him or would he wind up back in Stillwater? His body shook and the walls closed in on him. He tried to pull away but she held tight. She was stronger than she looked, but didn't weigh enough to anchor him when he dove.

Darkness overtook him. His body shuddered when he hit the mixture of mud and rotted organic matter that made up the black soup where the excavator had dug. He couldn't breathe. This was the end. He imagined himself being dragged to hell by his ankles and tucked his arms in for the ride. He'd make such a tragic figure in the afterlife.

* * *

Erin released Derek's hand when the plank began to tip. She wasn't going in there with him. Last year, he might have completely submerged. It might have been a life-threatening situation. Now, with most of the water pumped out by misguided developers, it was a much denser goo. All Derek managed to do was wedge himself, headfirst, in the spongy muck. She tipped back and forth before she regained her balance enough to retreat to shore.

Zimmerman shrugged his wide shoulders in the universal gesture of *what the heck?* and stomped after Derek. He yanked him by the ankles, pulled him onto firmer ground and released him with a soggy thump.

"Where am I?" Derek sputtered. He coughed brown water from his nostrils and struggled to sit up.

Zimmerman ignored the squawk of his radio. "I'm about done dragging your hind end out of the mud, dumb ass. Every time I see you, I'm knee deep in the loon shit with you." Zimmerman brushed clumps of muck from his trousers and frowned at his ruined boots.

Lockwood joined them. "Messy, but effective, technique."

Derek rubbed mud from his eyes and squinted up at her. His entire body vibrated with the shakes, like an alcoholic going into DTs. "You look like an angel."

"It's not the first time I've been told that." Lockwood purred in her gravelly voice. "So, you're the guy causing all the ruckus? Go figure."

Gonzales grinned at Erin and she stifled the urge to smile back. Delirium tremens, potentially fatal, were no laughing matter, if that's what this was. For all she knew, he had low blood sugar. Either way, Derek needed medical attention before they could have a coherent conversation with him.

She shot a glance toward Ernie, who silently watched from the driveway. By now, he'd probably figured out that he was in trouble. He was probably calculating how much cash he had in savings and if that would last until he got another job.

Zimmerman's radio squawked again and this time he thumbed the mike. "Busy here. One in custody. Can I get back to you?"

"Why don't they text you or something?" Gonzales mumbled.

"No service." Zimmerman clipped the radio back onto his duty belt. "Our radio repeater gives us coverage as far as this point, but not out there." He vaguely pointed to the miles of dense bush.

"Oh. I figured my GPS was glitchy."

"Officer Jenssen!" Zimmerman called, and Ernie's posture snapped erect. No one used his real name unless it was serious. "Bring the blanket from the car." Ernie bolted up to the driveway to do his bidding.

"I'll cut a couple of poles," Erin knew exactly what he needed. "We'll haul him out with a travois."

"And it'll keep him warm." Lockwood nodded her approval. Before she'd joined The Bureau, her bio included a number of years on San Diego PD's Harbor Patrol Unit. No doubt, she knew how fast someone could get chilled if they were wet. Stress and alcohol abuse compounded it.

"We need to be able to talk to him as soon as possible." Erin helped fashion a makeshift stretcher and secured it around the poles with cable ties before they loaded Derek.

Zimmerman's radio squealed unintelligible words, and then the dispatcher used plain speak. Ten codes were becoming more and more a thing of the past anyhow.

"Sarge, I really need you to get back to me on this. It's important."

"Fine," Zimmerman yanked the radio from his belt. "Go ahead, but be advised that I've got company."

"Boss wanted me to let you know right away. A lawyer's down here with a prison guard from Stillwater. Uh, Deputy Chief is with them now. The guard has just confessed to the Lewis murder."

Lockwood cocked her head. "This place gets stranger and stranger." She hoisted the travois. "Let's get him up to dry ground so medics can have a look at him. Maybe then we can get some answers on the whereabouts of our fugitives, and your missing niece."

"Wasn't me," Derek moaned. He rolled to his side and extended his hand toward an unreachable spot somewhere at the end of the wooden plank. "Tiffany…"

CHAPTER TWENTY-FIVE

"Slow down, you little shit." I stop filming and put my phone away. I know what that kid is up to. T has her on a leash, using his belt and a piece of rope from the truck, but she's stretched it to its limit up ahead. With his messed up knee, she probably figures she can get him off balance and do a runner, but I'm onto her. At the sound of my voice, she turns her blonde head and the rope sags between them.

"How long is this gonna take? I thought you said this place was nice, not a hut in the swamp." T's face is flushed and he's panting like a dog. "I gotta sit down."

Sweat rolling down the back of his neck reminds me of the greasy plumber back in juvy. The toilets backed up every second day, with some kid or another plugging them, and you'd be amazed how much crap he hauled out. Toothbrushes, bars of soap, underwear, you name it. Watching that sweat roll down, I can still smell it.

"It's not in the swamp, but we have to get past it to get to my place." I don't want to think about the sweaty plumber, or the stink of the backed up toilets. "What's your real name? Tell me."

"Call me T."

"I'll tell you about the first time I killed someone." I pull the gun from my waistband and turn it over in my hand.

His head comes up.

"All the gory details." I've hooked him.

"Really?"

"Absolutely. Swear to God."

He sighs and looks at his shoes. "T is short for Trenton Leslie

Madison."

"Those are girl names."

"No, they're not. They're family names."

"For girls." I knew he must have had a rough time in juvy because he was a skinner, but a skinner with girls' names? He would have had to hide every single day. How did I not know he was a pedophile before? "No wonder you wouldn't tell me."

"Now *you* tell *me*."

"I stepped on a bug when I was three." I slide the revolver back into my pants. I am not telling him about my mother. I'm not telling anybody.

"Aw, please, sugar-baby."

"Let's go." I turn to leave.

"I'm not going any further until you tell me the real story."

"Come on, T. It's not that much farther. All you're gonna do if we sit here is feed the skeeters. Keep moving."

He grinds the crust of blood off his nose with his fist and glares at me. "You're always telling me what to do. If I say I'm taking a break, I'm taking a goddamn break." He plunks down on a rotted stump and gingerly stretches his knee. It's fatter than the last time, all knobby under his jeans. "Where are we going? What if they come for her?" He juts his chin at the kid who's crouched in the grass as far from him as she can get.

I tug the rope to make her waddle closer, and she turns her back when he gawks at her as if he's got x-ray vision.

"Fine, you big pussy." I toss him a beer and explain it like I'm talking to a baby. "I told you. I've got a place on the river. It's all mine." I promised him heaven on earth, and a place of our own at my bog, but I need to scout it out first. Make sure no one else is there. Besides, the shack is good too. A home away from home. No one would hear a scream for ten miles.

The kid shifts her weight and slowly glances at the grip of the revolver sticking out of my pants. She's planning something. I can't believe I didn't see the resemblance the second T pointed her out on the side of the road. She's Erin Ericsson's niece, of course she's planning something. The excitement of that knowledge wiggles in my belly like a tadpole, all eager to sprout legs and break free. Something's about to happen, and it'll be wild.

A twig snaps somewhere and a bird flashes by. "Goddamn

whiskeyjack!" I holler, tossing a stick after it. It hops from branch to branch, challenging me. I throw another stick, but it dodges at the last second and yaks at me.

The kid gets to her feet and stares up. "Priya? Is that you?"

"Are you so stupid you're talking to a bird?" She must be half insane. It's just a freaking bird. "I hate birds. If I catch it, I'll kill it."

She squares her shoulders and narrows her eyes at me. That's ridiculous because she's just a little kid.

The bird swoops so close I feel it split the air by my face. I duck into a ball and the kid covers her mouth. Is she laughing at me? I ought to...

"Someone's back there." T straightens his sore knee and staggers upright. The break hasn't made him any calmer and he's still sweating like the stinky plumber. "They're coming for us, Lily."

"Bullshit. No one can find us out here. They probably have no idea she's even gone." When I was her age, I wandered all through these woods, day and night, and nobody ever noticed. Nobody missed me and nobody will miss her. We can do whatever we want. I take out my phone and turn the camera on her. "Do you have any last words?"

This gets a rise out of the kid. She stomps her foot and her eyes flash anger. "Auntie Erin *and* Auntie Allie are going to..."

I laugh. She's like a pipsqueak mouse yapping at a panther. I reach out to swat her but T steps in my path. He's a paranoid freak.

"She's right. They're coming. I can hear them back there. Hundreds of 'em, with tracking dogs, and the S.W.A.T. team. Is that a search plane? Oh God, they're coming."

I zoom the camera to his face. I can see the whites of his eyes all the way around, and his chest heaves like he sprinted a mile. He's so pathetic.

I remember when I made my ex-friend Nina watch a slasher film. I had to walk her all the way home afterward, right up to the window, and then wait until she'd crawled inside. Nina, who turned out to be not who I thought she was. She was like all the rest. *Loser.* I hope she's enjoying her life behind bars.

"You're going crazy, T. How many of those ADD pills did you take?" I shouldn't have let him hold the bottle. He's a pig when it comes to drugs, and he'll swallow as many as he thinks he can get away with.

"Not enough." He pops another in his mouth before I can grab the bottle. The kid's edging away, trying to use this distraction to escape. I grab the leash and yank her, gagging, to her knees.

"You ain't goin' nowhere. You're my revenge. I'll film every single thing T does to you and send it to your stupid family. Let's see how your FBI aunt likes that." I look in the lens and hold up the gun. "I could shoot you but I don't have to kill you to destroy your life. When I deliver this to you, it will be the best day of my life." I throw the rope back to T. "Guard your own prisoner, loser."

He snatches it out of the air and drags the kid down the trail, willow branches whipping behind them. He's a man on a mission, but he doesn't last long before the pills get the best of him. My own heart is hammering in my chest with only one pill. It's unreal that he's still walking around.

When I catch up, he's bent over, hands on his thighs. "Are they coming? Give me the gun and I'll take them all down."

"No. There's only a couple of bullets left. I need them." He's one paranoid fucker on this shit. I've got the perfect buzz, but I don't want to take so many that I end up with mashed potato brain, like T.

"I have to pee." The kid tugs the leash toward the nearest clump of bushes. "Really bad."

"No. Hold it." I don't have time for this. "Let's go. We're getting close."

"Aw, let her take a piss." T strokes her hair. "You're gonna be a good girl from now on, aren't you?" After what she did to his nose, he shouldn't give her any sympathy. He lets her squat behind the bush and eases the weight off his swollen knee, rope held loosely in his fingers. "It still hurts like a son-of-a-bitch."

Stealthy feet across moss-covered tree roots make surprisingly little sound. T is still moaning about his knee when I notice the tension in the rope is gone. It hangs from his wrist like a dead worm.

"You let her go!" I punch him square in the mouth and the pain shoots from my fist to my elbow.

"I didn't!" His jaw slackens, as if he's been sacked in the balls, lifeless rope dangling.

I grab it up and examine the end where it's been cut clean through. "The little shit had a knife. Didn't you check her pockets when you were trying to feel her up? Go get her back!"

He leaps over the bush and stumbles on his bad knee. "Where'd she go?"

There's a flash of light where movement has parted the branches. "There! To your left."

He crashes forward and, not smart enough to keep to the more solid footing offered by tree roots, sinks to his hips through the moss. His thrashing and swearing drives him in to his chest.

"Lily. Pull me out." He tosses the free end of the rope and it lands at my feet.

When I was a kid, I watched my mother die. It was a lot like this, but I helped a little. I twist a dead branch loose. If I smash him behind the ear, he'll go under too.

"Lily? What are you doing?" T's eyes are round with fear and that excites me a little. "Help me!"

I step back to consider my options. He was fun for a while, but now he's a freakin' lunatic. If he drowns, the fun will be over, and I'll be standing here alone with my beer. If I get him out, we can still catch the kid, and I can film him doing what he does. I'll get my revenge.

"All right." I put down the stick and bend a willow branch over so he can reach it. "Pull yourself out."

I squat on my haunches to watch. The muscles in his wiry forearms tremble with fatigue by the time he's out. "You're an evil bitch, Lily. You really are." He flops onto his belly. "It kind of turns me on."

"Keep it in your pants until we catch the kid. Then you can do what you want with her, and I'll make you a big star."

"Gimme a beer. I earned it."

I'm feeling generous because he's provided me with fifteen minutes entertainment. I twist the cap off one and hand it over. "Fill yer boots."

"How are we gonna find her?"

"Don't worry. I know every single trail around here, and it'll be dark soon. Panthers can see in the dark. We'll get her."

"You're not a panth—"

"Shut up, Trenton."

CHAPTER TWENTY-SIX

Allie gathered an armful of flashlights from Erin's mom and carried them outside to the makeshift table. "Where did you get all these supplies so fast?"

"Scouts. One phone call and we're swamped with volunteers." Ellen's face was pinched with worry, but she was not a complainer. "This is a good town."

Like an assembly line of elves, Jimmy and Sophie sorted matches, bottled water, whistles, and first aid kits into piles, while Doppler trolled beneath the table for interesting things to chew on.

Buzzing with energy, dozens of people waited for search instructions. Little kids had been left in charge of the group as a whole, while their parents attended to urgent business. They played on the lawn in packs of two or three, obediently staying within sight of the house. Ladies from the church prayed in a football huddle with their hands on each other's shoulders.

Allie skirted around them. Neither pleasant nor unpleasant, that kind of energy always buffeted her like a gusty wind.

Gina laid out a series of maps, each with a different grid outlined in red marker. She'd copied the animal trails from Gunther's map onto them with a ballpoint pen.

"Yo, Tom! Little to the left. Keep 'er comin'. That's it," someone called out as Erin's dad backed his truck up to his new boat trailer. "Walter's gone down for his boat too. We'll launch it right here, if that's okay with you."

"'Course it is," Tom hollered back. "It'll be dark before we know it. Let's get this show on the road."

"What about the National Guard?" The man in the bright orange jacket and matching cap would be visible a mile away. "Can't they bring in air support?"

"Naw," said a woman with an eager hunting dog. "Too many power lines. Dangerous for choppers."

Choppers. Aircraft. Allie turned to Jimmy, who rocked on his heels in anticipation. That was what they needed.

"We should use my drone to find Victoria," he said. "It can fly closer than airplanes or helicopters, and it has a great camera."

"You're right." Allie's pulse quickened. There was something more they could do, something vital. She motioned for Gina to join them. "Every member of Morley Falls PD is searching the town, but I don't think that's where we'll find her. She's out there." She pointed to the forest. "Somewhere downstream, but they won't find her by boat either."

Gina lowered her voice. "Do you *know* where she is?"

Allie shrugged. "I don't have an exact location, but I can feel if we're onto something, or not. Jimmy's drone is a good choice. It's a step in the right direction."

"You want to use his toy helicopter?" Gina tilted her head as if she hadn't heard quite right.

"It's not a toy helicopter." He crossed his arms. "It's a professional grade aerial drone, and the video images are high definition. I can control it with a smart phone."

"But there's no cell service past town," Gina said.

"It doesn't matter. It establishes its own connection and orients itself using satellites."

"Don't you sound like a little pilot." She tousled his hair.

He stopped her with a stern look. "I'm not so little."

"You're right. I've been noticing that you're getting more grown up."

He blushed.

"Is that a mustache on your upper lip?"

"Boss! Come on. You know I'm only seven."

"Seven is the right age for this." She mussed his hair before he could dodge. "So, will you lend us your professional grade magic flying machine?"

Allie rested her hand on his shoulder. "Please show me how to fly it."

This was likely the hardest decision of his life, to part with his prized possession, a grownup purchase he shared with his uncle Thomas. Finally, he straightened his hair. "It takes a lot of practice. I need to come with you."

"You know I understand a lot of what you do when you fly. We can't let you come. Not this time. It's too dangerous and I won't put you at risk."

He shuffled his feet. "But Uncle Thomas said..." Doppler circled him and sat on his foot, wagging his tail.

"What would Uncle Thomas want you to do?"

He looked at the little dog. "He would say we need to do everything to help my sister."

Allie exhaled. "Yes, I'm sure he would." She'd have to be a quick learner.

"But you have to take Doppler with you."

If those were his terms, she'd accept in a heartbeat. "Let's unpack that drone and you can give me some pointers."

After most of the volunteers had left for their respective search grids, Jimmy cleared an area on the far end of the lawn. He held his smart phone out in front of his chest. "You have to wait until it establishes a GPS connection with at least six satellites."

"Six!" Gina peered at the illuminated screen. "There are that many up there?"

He nodded, and snapped the phone into its onboard bracket. "Eight is better." He flipped a switch up and down a dozen times until the LED light turned solid yellow. "This is how you calibrate the compass."

The futuristic little machine rested on the lawn a few feet away, green lights blinking. He raised it horizontally, and rotated it in a full circle until the light switched to solid green. He repeated the same thing vertically. The light went off.

"It's ready." He placed it on the ground and switched on the remote controller, pulling both sticks to the bottom corners to start the motors. Like a tiny alien spaceship, it lifted off the ground. A few years ago, neighbors would have called in UFO reports if they spotted something like this in the sky. An aerial view of the property showed up on the smart phone's screen.

"Cool," Gina said, leaning over his shoulder. The image detail was impressive.

Doppler ran to where it had taken off and circled, barking at the white dot against the sky. Jimmy shrugged. "He always does that. Maybe he wants to catch it." He reluctantly handed the controller to Allie.

"I've seen you do it many times, but remind me how the fail-safe works." She manipulated the controls to rotate the airborne drone, and Gina waved when the video camera looked down on them. She decreased motor speed until the machine softly landed.

Jimmy nodded his approval. "On a full charge, you get about twenty-five minutes flying time and we already used four, so…"

"I won't waste time," Allie finished.

"I've never flown more than a mile or two." Jimmy packed it up and reverently handed over the box. "Please be careful."

With equal respect, she placed it on the Jeep's back seat. She would do her best to return it to him undamaged.

Doppler sat on Allie's lap and lolled his tongue out the window while Gina drove the Jeep. North was all they knew, so Gina hit the old logging road until it narrowed into a double set of tire tracks through the field. The jagged fingers of stunted trees scraped paint from her doors.

"Faster. Drive faster." Like smoke trails hugging the ground, Allie envisioned the urgency of Victoria's fear mingled with the dark oily smear she recognized as Lily's hate. There was one more trail, male, whose energy vacillated. Disorientation, paranoia, and a driving desire for the child. A sour taste rose in Allie's throat. He meant to do Victoria harm.

A pointed rock screeched when it scoured the bottom of the Jeep, and suddenly she knew exactly where they were. "I've been here before."

"Is this the blueberry picking road?" Gina swerved to narrowly miss a boulder, like an iceberg jutting up from the dirt. Foxtails, with their bristly heads, swished against the undercarriage.

"No, but the river is up ahead. I came out here with my Mini Cooper once."

"The same car that got fried when my store burnt down?"

"Uh-huh, and then your light-up fish sign crashed through my sunroof when the fire truck backed into it." Sometimes Allie missed that car, missed cruising down Toronto's Yonge Street, dodging traffic and sipping a frothy latte. She didn't miss the virtual cacophony of noise in her head from so many human beings. It was much quieter here, easier to think, to focus.

"Yeah, that."

They had a shared experience in common. Lily had permanently scarred them both. Over coffee, they'd talked it to death, going over the details until, one day, they'd decided it was enough.

Bonded as friends, Allie confided in her about her gift. How her mind was a wide-open receiver, collecting unbidden signals like so many radio waves bounced off the ionosphere, how she was left to sort through the atmospheric noise, and somehow make sense of everything. The frustration of her gift's unpredictable nature.

They'd leaned on each other and healed, physically and emotionally, but now Lily was back and the scars were torn open. She could tell by the lines creasing the downturn of her mouth that Gina felt the same.

Foliage swept overhead as they passed through an overgrown section of the path. Doppler, head out the open window, yelped when a branch snapped his muzzle.

"Sorry," Gina muttered.

The dog withdrew his head, tucked it under Allie's arm, and she riffled her fingers through his fur, warmth seeping to her core. She closed her eyes. *Which way do I go?*

If she believed in God, or some supreme being, she'd pray for Victoria's safety right now, but she'd never been sure, never felt that spiritual pull the way others described. What she felt was constant, and unyielding. Sometimes a pull, and other times, more of a push. Right now, it was as if she were drawn, at breakneck speed, by a powerful magnetic force. Fear crawled across her scalp and made the little hairs on the back of her neck prickle. Was it Victoria who drew her in, or was it Lily? Was there such a thing as destiny?

They reached the end of the road and stopped. Ahead was the boat launch, a dirt road that disappeared into the water. Anyone could drive straight in, and Allie had once done that, in this very spot. She'd needed to find Erin, and had driven her Mini Cooper into the river until it had sunk to its hood in the mud. The fire and the falling sign had damaged the car, but it had been the mud that had finally rendered it irreparable. That had been a hard one to explain to her insurance company. Afterward, she'd taken then four-year-old Jimmy's advice and purchased a vehicle more suited for the local terrain.

She stepped from the Jeep and followed Doppler to a clump of weedy poplar trees with an odd shape. The very air jittered in anticipation.

Gina hurried to follow. "Where are you going? Should I bring the pack? The bug spray? Hey! Wait up, girl." She dashed through the grass to where Allie stood, inches from a shiny bumper protruding through the mound of hastily thrown tree branches.

"This is it." Allie grabbed the first branch and heaved it aside. Together they uncovered the rest of the stolen truck.

"She's not here," Gina called out when she pulled open the door. She picked up a coil of rope. "They better not have..."

Allie ran to the Jeep for the walkie-talkie Jimmy had tucked into their back pack. He'd told her it had a range of ten miles, but probably less in the woods. She clicked the button and waited, as he'd instructed, for two seconds before she spoke. "Jimmy, are you there?"

"Home base here." He sounded like a professional.

"Can you get a message to Erin? Tell her to come to the public boat launch."

"Which one?" He was so excited to have such important news to relay, he forgot his own radio rules and spoke too soon, cutting off part of his first word.

"Tell her it's where I drowned my car. She'll know."

"Ten-four," he chirped, this time a little more controlled.

"We're going to send the drone up soon. Yes, I'll be careful. Over and out." She tucked away the radio.

"That direction." Allie pointed north. Somewhere out there, sweet little Victoria, whose only misdeed was sneaking out for candy with a boy, was in danger.

"Do you want to find a path, or try the helicopter thing from here?" Gina took the pack from her.

Dread shrouded Allie's body. Her beloved dog's final resting place was in these woods, marked by a rock cairn to keep out predators. Predators like the wolves that had killed Fiona. Now there was a different kind of predator stalking through the forest. A predator with no boundaries or conscience. Nothing good happened in this neck of the woods. She backed away.

"Let's fly it from here."

CHAPTER TWENTY-SEVEN

"Derek, did you hear the radio transmission?" Erin tapped him on the shoulder. Curled on his side, sweating like that, he worried her. He'd perked up since consuming a bottle of water and two energy bars, but he still trembled like he was coming down from an adrenaline rush.

"You're in the clear. Z-man said a guard from Stillwater's in custody for Badger's murder."

Derek blinked and he focused on Erin, straining at the cable ties that bound his shaking wrists to the poles. "I friggin' told you I didn't do it, Ericsson, and you can tell Lizard Boy I've got no idea how my name got into Badger's pocket. I wouldn't meet with that bastard even if hell froze over. He had it in for me since I was inside."

The note in the dead man's pocket had been confidential information gleaned from the unlawfully obtained police forensics report. Bert in Ident would not be pleased that his best friend Ernie had compromised the case.

Zimmerman slitted his eyes, ignoring the dig about his reptile collection. "The guard had been working with Ethan Lewis to smuggle drugs inside, and when Ethan started a side business, he decided to take out the competition. His lawyer turned over a handgun and blood spattered expandable baton." The tall officer towered over the hastily constructed stretcher. "By the way, Lewis was coming for you. The guard who killed him might have saved your life in the process."

"Lucky me." Derek tugged his wrists against the restraints. "Now let me loose."

"This confession hasn't been verified, and we still need to have a chat, you and I." Zimmerman poked a finger at Derek's defiant chest. "Once the medics have a look at you, that is."

"I ain't gonna say a damn thing. Remember what happened last time I had a run in with you two yahoos?"

"You may be clear on the murder, but what about this?" Erin pulled the police report from her bag.

By the car, Ernie craned his neck to see what she was holding. He stayed put, smart enough to have figured it out.

She had no business speaking on behalf of the local police, but right now, she didn't care. "The department might be willing to cut you some slack for bribery of an officer if you cooperate." All she wanted was to get Victoria back, safe and sound. "If you don't, you might wind up in prison again."

Derek eyed the papers in her hand. Sweat beaded his forehead.

She leaned in, her voice sharp. "Where's Lily? Where's she taking my niece?"

"How the hell should I know? I ain't seen her." He glanced at the report again. "Maybe I could remember, but my wrists hurt so much I can't think."

"All right, no ties." Zimmerman snapped out his lock blade knife and sliced through them. "But you're not going anywhere." He crossed his arms, muscles bulging under uniform sleeves.

"Where's this place?" Erin resisted the urge to grab Derek by his lying throat. "Stop wasting our time."

"Remember the spot on the river where we, uh, *danced?*"

"Danced? You asshole. You gave me this." She pulled up her sleeve where the pale scar snaked across her bicep. "And you nearly brained me."

"Yeah, well, you did this." Like siblings one-upping each other, he lifted his chin to show the permanent flattening of his trachea. "You messed up my singin' voice. The church choir won't have me."

"Church, right," Lockwood huffed behind them. "Come on kids, can we get past this?"

Gonzales chipped in his two-bits' worth. "She doesn't want to find another missing kid dumped in a plastic bag."

Lockwood stiffened and Erin shot him a look that would have melted iron. If missing kids were Lockwood's kryptonite, he should know better than to mess with old wounds.

Derek pointed to where the late afternoon sun still glinted off the metal at the end of the plank. "You dig that buckle out for me and I'm yours, gentle as a lamb."

"I'll do it," Zimmerman growled. He stalked out and got to his knees. With his expandable baton, he lifted a mud-covered item into the air. "Is this what you wanted?"

"Awww." Derek's chest caved in as if his lungs had collapsed. He sank back on the stretcher, skin pale.

The urgency in Zimmerman's voice brought Erin running. "What is it?" She tightrope-walked down the plank until it threatened to overturn with their combined weight. Lockwood and Gonzales stayed behind, their frowns keeping Derek in his place.

Zimmerman held up an object, a bag of some sort. On the strap was a metal buckle, the horseshoe-style westerners liked. Clots of muck plopped onto his shined boots. "It's a ladies' bag." As if the taboo about men looking into women's purses still applied, he tossed it to Erin.

She nearly tipped them both into the swamp when she grabbed the bag and her weight shifted. "It's full of mud, but there's something inside." She smeared black ooze from a plastic covered folder and slid out a single card. "It's a Minnesota Driver's License." Much of the surface had been destroyed but, notorious for its resistance to the degradation of time and elements, the plastic card still held the image of a young woman. Beside the smiling mouth, Erin read the owner's name aloud. "Tiffany Schmidt."

Derek's howl, a feral keening, reverberated through his damaged vocal chords, and sent goose bumps across Erin's skin.

Zimmerman knelt and scooped handfuls of mud from the hole with his bare hands. "There's more," he whispered. "I think..."

"You can't dig that by hand. It's too much."

His head swung around to the heavy duty machinery trapped in the bog. "I played with one of those once. My uncle had a contract to demo a building. What if I can get it started?" He stood and, without warning, vaulted across and attached himself like a spider to the side of the cab. Erin dropped to her knees to avoid tipping. He beetled over, yanked open the door, and folded himself into the driver's seat.

"The key's in it!" he called out. "Hope there's gas."

"What's he doing?" Lockwood hollered, likely none too pleased at having to babysit a sweaty, howling alcoholic.

"Starting the excavator!" The machine squealed and coughed once before going silent. Zimmerman whooped. "Come on, baby." The engine sputtered and turned over. He tried again and it caught, an erratic rumble that threatened to quit if challenged.

Erin dashed back down the plank when the boom came around and the bucket shuddered on its arm, inches from her head.

"Sorry!" he yelled. This time, the boom rose and traveled smoothly toward the little hole he'd dug with his hands. He worked the levers to scoop out sludge.

Erin edged back out for a better view. Something was dangling from the bucket's steel teeth. "It's a stick, or a branch or something. Try again!" she shouted.

She peered into the ragged hole as he was preparing for a second pass. It was slowly refilling with water, but protruding from the bottom was a distinctive shape that made her pulse skyrocket. She waved her arms like a flight deck crewman trying to abort a carrier landing. "Stop!"

The boom halted mid-air, bucket gently rocking above her. Zimmerman poked his head out. "What's wrong?"

"You need to stop." She motioned him over with a subtle shake of her head.

He killed the motor, and she crouched low to brace for impact when he made an awkward leap back. One size-fourteen boot beside the other, he shuffled over and gave a low whistle. He glanced over his shoulder at Derek.

In its boggy grave, a human skeleton rested on one side, arm extended as if to ward off death. A crack zigzagged across the skull from ear to forehead, the temporal area, she was sure a pathologist had once called it. "I think the skull might be fractured," she whispered.

Derek sat up and wiped his eyes with grimy fingers. "What did you say?"

Zimmerman hooked a thumb through her belt loop, and she stretched as far as possible, but could not quite grasp the glimmer of gold encircling the skeleton's left ring finger.

"He gave her an engagement ring," Erin breathed, "right before she disappeared."

"You realize that this makes him a suspect," he whispered back.

"Technically." She shrugged, but she knew who was really responsible. Allie was always right. Heel to toe, she walked back to solid footing with Zimmerman right behind her. Derek raised teary eyes when they approached.

She wiped muddy hands on her pants and tried not to think about all the swamp creatures teeming in the organic matter now seeping into her skin. She'd become a petri dish. She'd turn over her entire bank account right now for soap and water. How would she make it back to town like this? How could she concentrate?

She scraped her fingernails with the seam of her pocket, hoping it would remove most of the grime. "You told me you gave Tiffany a ring the last time you saw her. Can you describe it?"

Derek pounded his fist in the dirt. "Tell me, goddammit."

Zimmerman stepped in. "There are what appear to be human remains. We won't be able to make an ID until we get a proper recovery team out here. You'll need to stay in custody in the meantime."

"Da fuck I will," Derek muttered, eyes hard as flint.

Zimmerman stepped back and thumbed his mike to call it in.

"What the heck?" Deputy Chief Williams bellowed back, loud enough for everyone to hear. "You'd think this was New York City, with all this *shee-it* goin' on. Are you sure?"

Lockwood smirked. It sounded like something she might say.

Zimmerman lowered the speaker volume, but Erin had a pretty good idea how the conversation went. *The corpse isn't going anywhere. Put a man on it. We'll get to it when we get to it.*

Erin needed information before Derek completely melted down. She touched his shoulder, and he kicked out in animal fury.

"She killed her!" he screamed, voice crackling with the force of his words. "She killed her own mother. I should have known. All the lies upon lies."

"Derek. Calm down, we won't know what happened until…"

"Oh, everything's gone to hell."

"We need to find her, Derek. Where's Lily?"

"I've got nothing left."

"Where is she?" Erin snarled in his face. "You owe me. Now tell me!"

One eye on Zimmerman, Derek whispered. "Only place I can think of is about a quarter of a mile from the spot where we *danced.*

There's a little creek that empties into the river, with an old trapper's shack hidden a ways in beside it. It's half fallen down but she liked it there." Tears streamed down his cheeks, and he mumbled through trembling hands. "You can reach it through the woods, but it's rough going. Boat is easier."

"I know where to look." Erin remembered when she had chased Derek down the river. There were footprints in the sand beside a tributary creek. She'd almost followed them before Allie had insisted they press on in their pursuit of Derek. That was back when they were under the awful misconception that Lily was a victim. A victim! Not for one second was that kid a victim. After that day, everything had changed.

Zimmerman shook his head at the man bawling at his feet. He turned and signaled Ernie, who was probably still calculating how many days' suspension he'd get, or if he'd be fired outright, for what he'd done. Ernie jumped to attention and came within earshot. "Cuff him." He jerked a thumb to Derek.

Given a chance to redeem himself, Ernie gave a curt nod and assumed a position beside his previous mentor turned prisoner. The FBI agents backed off, eager to be free of their informal sentry duty.

The radio squawked and a seven year old boy's voice came over, loud and clear. "This is home base with an urgent message for Z, um, for Sergeant Z."

"Jimmy? What are you doing on the police channel? You shouldn't be playing with this." Zimmerman exchanged a questioning glance with Erin, who shrugged her shoulders.

"But I have an important message for Auntie Erin." The boy sounded offended that his hero would ever think he'd mess around.

"What's going on, buddy?" Erin spoke into the mike when Zimmerman held it out.

"Allie said she needs you to come to the place where she drowned her car. She said you'd know."

Erin sucked in her breath. "That's not too far from the place Derek told me about."

"I'm going with you. I have to." Zimmerman considered the man on the ground and hauled him to his feet. "You're looking better, Derek. Maybe you were hungry." He cuffed him, and locked him in the back of the cruiser.

Then he took Ernie aside. "Officer Jenssen. You will guard him and wait for the ambulance. They should be here any minute, and so should Rickby. He'll take custody of the prisoner or escort the ambulance to hospital, if that's the way it goes."

"I understand." Head down, Ernie was a man seriously worried about his future.

"When Rickby's gone, you will stay here and guard the scene until a team arrives. Give me your radio. You can use the one in your car if you need to order a pizza." Neither laughed at his joke. "We'll discuss the issue of the wayward police report later, but I don't need to remind you that the rest of your career is hanging in the wind."

"No, sir."

Zimmerman slid into the back seat with Agent Lockwood and exchanged opinions on a printed map while Erin drove, tires bouncing from pothole to rut on the dirt road. Quiet, and nearly invisible as usual, Gonzales rode shotgun up front.

Gina waved Erin down when the FBI sedan, with its enhanced suspension system, ground its way over the last of the rocks embedded in the dirt road. They'd left a trail of engine fluid in their wake and might never get this car started once it seized up.

Zimmerman was first out the door. "Darlin' what are you doing out here? It's not safe." He scooped Gina in his arms and hugged her tight.

"We had to help." She pointed to Allie who was staring at the smart phone controller. In the sky, a high pitched mosquito buzzed, and the aerial drone obediently rotated side-to-side in a search grid.

"Good idea, ladies," he said, peering at the screen, "but I'm not sure how useful it will be in this dense bush."

"Like finding a needle in a haystack, I'd say." Lockwood spotted the truck in the trees and hurried over with Gonzales to examine it. "There's a purple bike helmet on the floor. She's been here."

Zimmerman's radio squealed an alert that was reserved for emergencies, and Erin's posture straightened.

"Sarge. Do you copy?" It was Rickby, the officer assigned to take custody of Ernie's prisoner.

"Go ahead," Zimmerman replied and everyone else fell silent.

"Uh, when I arrived, I found Ernie, uh, incapacitated."

"What the heck does that mean?"

"Uh, he was, uh, handcuffed to a tree."

"What about the prisoner?" Zimmerman could guess where this

was going. He'd seen stupid cop movies too.

"The prisoner's gone, escaped in Ernie's squad car."

He looked at the sky, at the moving dot, and kept his thumb off the mike. "He had one task to keep his job. Ten minutes prisoner supervision."

"Ambulance has come and gone, Sarge. What do you want me to do?"

Zimmerman scrubbed his forehead with his knuckles, and then brought up the radio. "I need you to take over scene control out there, and I'm asking you to relieve Officer Jenssen of his sidearm and his badge. He is to present himself in the Chief's office first thing tomorrow morning."

"Uh, how will he get home? It's five miles to town."

"Tell him to walk." Zimmerman jammed his radio into its holder and took a deep breath. "Where were we?"

"I trust that Allie's idea will be useful," Erin said. "But I think we also need boots on the ground. There is a shack they may be headed for and I'd estimate it at between two to three miles in, beside a tributary creek. I'll try to find a path along the river and it might be a good idea for at least a couple of us to take the car and backtrack to the next forestry road. The map shows there's a trail from that direction, so you should be able to find another route."

Zimmerman handed the radio he'd appropriated from Officer Jenssen to Erin. "Let's split up. Agent Lockwood can ride with me." He addressed her like a southern gentleman. "I don't expect you to trudge through the mosquito-infested swamp, ma'am. Gonzales can go on foot with Erin."

His sincerity disarmed her, and Lockwood practically curtsied like a lady. "Why, thank you."

Gonzales' jaw dropped. "Does anyone have insect repellant? I get these really itchy—"

"We'll walk fast," Erin said and started toward the river. "It'll be dark soon." Animals needed water, and there was almost always some sort of trail to give them access. She stopped to examine a cluster of broken branches at the entrance to an overgrown trail. Yes, they'd come this way.

Gonzales slapped at his neck and skidded after her in his leather-soled shoes.

CHAPTER TWENTY-EIGHT

"Leslie is a girl's name." I like to make T's neck flush red so I can zoom in on it with my camera phone. He's still covered in swamp goo from the chest down and his mood is getting darker by the minute. They say you should never poke the bear, but panthers aren't afraid of bears. "So is Madison." The mottled color spreads to his cheeks. "And Trenton, that's kinda pussy too, isn't it?"

His jaw muscles ripple and he glares at me through bloodshot eyes, curling his lip. A crow caws somewhere in the distance. He shoots a glance over his shoulder as if he's expecting company, an imaginary search team busting out of the trees, or a band of guerrillas lying in wait.

"What are you so worried about, Trenton? Ain't nobody here but us chickens." The pimp dealer I got the drugs from used to say the same thing when my mom told him she couldn't stay, couldn't do the nasty things he wanted, because she had a kid waiting. He knew I was watching through the window. I wonder if anyone is out there right now, looking in.

I remember the stories I made up about all the people I'd killed, a half a dozen lies I'd counted off on my fingers. Most of them were bullshit. There was only my mother, and the lady I blew up by accident. I'm not sure if I should count Nina's father. Her hand was on the knife when I pushed it in.

This is different. Now the corpses are real. I swear, my mother's voice howls on the wind. I can almost see moss drip from her bones. Right behind her is the church lady, screaming in a blaze of fire.

Shoving through them is the angry spirit of the old lady I stabbed in the neck, and the man we killed at the gas station. I'm sure they're dead too.

A shiver that's half pride and half fear slithers up my spine. Fear is a new sensation for me. I don't like it. In the movies, girls run screaming from spiders and ax murderers. What should I do when my chest feels tight and my throat runs dry?

"Fuck you!" I spin the camera in a circle and record the angry shapes hunting me from the dark places. "You can't touch me." On the screen, it all looks normal, innocent. There is nothing out here but moss, trees and bugs. Beneath the layer of moss is swamp water, sometimes deep, sometimes just enough to wet your shoe. You never know until you put your weight on it. Any minute I could step off this path and fall through.

"Aaagh! I am a badass panther." Furious blood pumps through my veins, warming me and chasing away my mother's imaginary ghost.

T eyes me with his head cocked. "Anyone ever tell you that you're a bit crazy?" His balance sways. "You really believe you're a panther?"

"If I had my knife, I would hack out your heart."

"Aw, sugar. You're dangerous, and that's the kind of crazy I like." His lips curve upward, the little mustache bending at the corners. Even soaked to the skin in swamp shit, his hair greasy and his eyes bleary, there's a certain smarmy appeal to him. That must be how he gets the kids. *Trust me, sweet girl. I won't hurt you. Can you help me find my puppy?* He's so pathetic that I can't stay mad at him forever.

"Whatcha gonna do about your prize, Trenton?" We haven't seen the kid for at least fifteen minutes, and it's all his fault. He was too friggin' polite to watch her pee, and now she's gone, along with my perfect revenge.

He's such a pussy. I don't get how he was ever gonna bring himself to do anything to her once we got to the cabin. Maybe there's a line he needs to cross before there's no going back. He juts his chin at me and pops another pill in his mouth. That must be what takes him over the line.

"Trenton Leslie Madison, gimme one of those." My buzz is almost gone. I might as well take another pill too.

"You know you're not really a panther, don't you?" He walks

away, careful to keep both feet on solid ground.

I ignore the panther comment, for now. "Come on, T. I'm just messin' with ya. You shot the gas station guy. You're not such a pussy."

He swings around and his huge pupils are as dark as the hidey-hole under my grandfather's shed.

"Give them to me."

He holds my gaze with his weird eyes, and reaches into his pocket for the bottle.

I pop one in my mouth and wonder if my eyes are like his. I look into the lens and make faces. When I watch this later, I can say *Holy shit. I'm the star after all.*

"There are two places that kid can go." I click the camera off and put it away. The battery indicator is low and I need to remember to save some juice for the final scene. "Along the river, or out to the power lines. If she's got any brains, that's where she'll go, but she has to make it through there. It's hard to cross that shit."

T shudders. He probably inhaled a half gallon of green water before I rescued him.

"There's a shortcut and I bet we can beat her there." I point to the swamp and he backs up a step. "But you have to stop pissing around."

He adjusts his cap, leaving muddy fingerprints across the brim. "I'm ready."

Running down a bush trail with a case of beer in my arms will slow me down, but I'm reluctant to leave it behind. Finally, I convince myself that we'll be back with the kid in a few minutes, and cram it under a tuft of cow parsnip.

"You run funny," T says behind me. "Stiff like a scarecrow. I never noticed before." He falls into step when I jog, his breath wheezing in his chest, and his sore leg hitting the ground with a *clumpity-clump*. I find the side trail and turn right. It's overgrown and takes imagination to follow.

I keep my head low but T is upright, and branches whip him square in the face. He's lost his polite facade, using words that would make my grandfather blush.

When the trail firms up under our feet, soggy moss, birch and willow give way to thick grass and knobby brush. Ahead, the power line pyramids stand tall. We're close. Stealth is more important than speed. I turn to him, my finger across my lips. "Shh."

Between ragged breaths, he manages a smile, white teeth glittering like fangs.

The birds have stopped calling. Animals have gone silent. Are they reacting to her, or us? I perk up, turning my head to catch any sound. Leaves tinkle, and fragments of bark drift through the air in my peripheral vision.

"There!"

* * *

"There!" Allie nearly dropped the controller and the drone spun sideways. The video image became a sea of green. Was that Victoria? She thumbed the toggles until it navigated back to the clearing that carved a swathe across the land. The setting sun sprayed the sky with color, and dappled the earth with elongated shadows. Which shadow had caught her eye? The high definition camera had recorded it all, sending the image feed to the smart phone, but she couldn't waste time reviewing it now. She had to keep looking.

"You found her?" Gina squeezed beside her. "I don't see anything but trees and the power line."

A tiny figure wearing a blue shirt came into view. Little more than a dot on her screen, it ducked in and out of brush under the towers.

"There she is!" Gina shouted.

Allie's body shivered with hope. "Victoria knows this area." She'd walked that grassy line with her last year, searching for blueberries. It led all the way back to Morley Falls.

"Run home now. Run." Gina whispered, careful not to bump Allie and lose the image. She watched a few seconds longer and then ran for the radio.

Victoria whirled, and Allie wanted to reach out, to touch the blonde hair flying in the wind, to reassure her that everything would be okay. The dot froze, and dissolved into the grass.

"No!" Two more figures approached from the woods, and she imagined them sniffing the air for the scent of their prey. One went left, the other right. She dropped altitude.

"Gina! Tell them to hurry."

* * *

T takes off, crashing through tall grass like a moose, all long legs and bizarre angles. A squirrel scampers up a tree to yip down at us. That's all it was, a squirrel. "Argh!" he growls. "We should make a fur mitten out of it."

If the kid is nearby, she'll be on her belly in the grass with all the racket he's making. We need to flush her out. I send him north and I go south. It's a matter of time. We'll find her.

"Come out and play!" I try the sing-song voice my mom used on me when I was young, but it sounds stupid coming out of my mouth. "Get out here, you little shit. If I have to come and get you, you'll regret it."

Past the first transmission tower, T imitates me, hunched over as if he's searching for a lost kitten, but his backbone is tense. I'm not the only predator here. That kid doesn't have a chance.

Soon, she'll bolt from cover, a rabbit making a zigzag into my trap. This panther will stalk her like easy prey, snatch her off her feet and sink my fangs into her throat. Hunter's blood pumps in my veins, faster and faster, fueled by the extra pill in my gut and washed down with beer.

As if I've run a mile without stopping, I can't catch my breath. Sounds magnify, twisting themselves into images from a horror movie. A slight breeze ruffles the tops of the grasses and I imagine the suspense music starting. Grasshoppers grind out their diabolical mating call, sawing one jagged leg against the other. In the sky, an ominous speck draws closer, sun glinting off one buzzing eye, its shadow tracking me.

"Come on out, sweetheart. We won't hurt—" T goes silent. He sees the speck too. He cocks his hat on his head and stares like an old farmer watching a storm cloud take form.

Something's coming. I feel it in the marrow of my bones, leaching into my flesh. The buzz becomes a whine, high-pitched and insistent. This might be the end. My mother is here. She wants her revenge too.

T takes his eyes off the orb and turns them on me. He's right there but I'm alone, powerless. My skin cracks, like pottery dried too fast, and splits from my powdery bones. I crumple to my knees.

The sun is going down but my mother's vengeful eye still tracks me, radiating angry light. She's coming. My heart, wrapped in old leather and rusted steel, peels away from my ribs and tumbles to the ground.

"What's wrong?" T squats beside me but he's not real. He's a hollowed-out version of himself, pale and colorless. The real T is tall and dark, with a baby mustache and a man's lean muscles. "Are you tripping?"

"I'm sorry!" I shout to my mom's shining eye, watching me, plotting her punishment.

"It's okay. It was my fault she got away." T wraps his arms around me and squeezes, his heart hammering against my ribs. The buzzing of my mother's ghost vanishes. *Good riddance.* Was it my imagination?

"Don't touch me!" I twist away from his sweaty embrace.

The bush behind us vibrates, and T lunges for the flash of blonde hair. Long arms extended, fingers grasping, he gets hold of her shirt sleeve and reels her in, a fish on a line, one inch at a time. The intense fire in his eye tells me to get the net because he's ready to land her. Right before I can, she drops to her back and kicks his groin like a mallet smashing rotted wood. It takes him to his knees.

"Aww." Guttural wind vibrates through his throat and he curls onto his side, a dying insect.

The girl's running, and streaks toward the woods, feet kicking up behind her. There is no rabbit zigzag, no hesitation. She's fast.

I propel myself into motion, my feline hunger for revenge a wonder drug for my empty bones. I mean to catch her but I can't. Before I reach the trees, I'm winded. My lungs burn, and my heart hammers harder than it should. The kid outruns me, backtracking into the swamp.

"Fuck!"

I'm losing her. In the muggy green jungle, where I have to step carefully, her little feet skip from tree root to tree root, careful not to linger in one spot. "T! She's getting away."

He's on his knees, crawling after me, black eyes wild. He pants like a dog, chest heaving with the effort.

"Get her. I *need* her." My jawbone aches with hunger. The cop needs to pay. Her girlfriend needs to pay. Goddammit, everyone needs to pay. I don't even care what they did any more. I want them to bleed. "Trenton, get up."

He staggers to his feet, spine cockeyed, hat sideways. The knuckles of one bony fist dig into his chest. "Lily, I think I'm having a h-heart attack."

I pull the revolver from my pants and point it at him. "Trenton Leslie Madison. Go get her."

His eyes roll, and flick forward like the possessed doll in that movie. "I-I can't." He drops his fist to his side, watery eyes on mine. "This is the worst birthday ever." He's about to collapse.

"You useless fucker." I pull back the hammer, even though T told me they only do that in movies. With my other hand, I click to record video. This is gonna be a helluva movie.

"You're not a man. You're a pussy." The barrel of the gun looks ten feet long from this angle, and it's pointed right at the middle of his old-time cowboy shirt. A gurgle starts in my belly, and matches the crazy rhythm my heart's making.

"Please, no."

"So long, sucker." I tense my finger on the trigger like he showed me. How many bullets are left? Two? Three? I can't remember, and it doesn't matter. I have enough. Don't pull it, just squeeze, nice and smooth.

"But I love y—"

BAM! The grip bucks in my hand when the bullet explodes. T drops and crumples backward, a drizzle of dark blood oozing from the hole in his shirt. This is nothing like the movies. There is no kicking or screaming, no dramatic music. He falls back and his whole body deflates into the weeds.

I stand over him, camera on record, but I'm not sure what to say. *Goodbye* might seem as if I liked him, and I can't say I did. He was exciting sometimes. I wanted to, but I couldn't like him.

Maybe I should have thought this scene through, or rehearsed. I poke him with the toe of my muddy shoe. Nothing happens. Why couldn't there be screaming, sprays of blood, a gushing wound, something more fantastic?

When the barrel cools enough that it won't burn my ass, I tuck it back into my pants. At the edge of the swamp, I straighten my shoulders as the earthy smell of moss and stagnant water summon me. A frog jumps across my path. On the hunt, I follow the little muddy footprints into the darkness.

CHAPTER TWENTY-NINE

Allie shook the drone's controller, as if that would magically send the machine back into the air. The last thing she'd seen before she lost control, were the two figures advancing on Victoria's hiding spot. The image had spun and the screen went black.

Then there'd been the loud bang, a noise that traveled through the forest and ricocheted off her synapses. She prayed it had only been a tree falling, a distant thunderclap, anything else.

"Did you hear that? It sounded like a gunshot." Gina was on her toes, tense with nervous energy. She looked at the smart phone's screen. "It's gone. Did it crash?"

Allie wanted to hurl the controller into the sky and will it to make Victoria safe. Doppler jumped up and put his paws on her knee.

"We might have lost power, or it tried to return to its origin." She didn't want to talk about the gunshot. "I need to go out there and find her before it's too late."

Gina answered a squawk on the radio. "Chris heard it too. He told me to wait right here. He's going in on foot with that FBI lady. Erin's trying to come from the river trail, but the guy she's with is having trouble keeping up, something about his shoes."

"I can't sit here and wait." Energy quivered against the darkening sky, as if electricity leapt to bridge the space.

"Chris told us to stay." Gina's brown eyes flashed. "Dammit. Let's go get Victoria."

Allie ran for the Jeep, and Doppler launched himself onto the seat as soon as she opened the door. "I know a road that parallels the transmission towers. We can hike in." A single unbreakable thread pulled at her heart like a spelunker's safety line, a thread that stretched all the way to Victoria. Branches scraped at the sides of the vehicle, and rocks assaulted the undercarriage. She pressed the gas pedal harder. The dog whined.

Gina gripped the door handle and hastened to put on her seatbelt, anything to keep her from slamming into the dash. "I hope the FBI man with terrible shoes doesn't mistake us for the bad guys."

The automatic headlights activated when they plummeted down a dip in the road. They clicked back off when they crested the next hill and the last rays of sunlight blinded them. Allie held up her hand to shield her eyes.

"Watch out!" Gina yelled.

A deer crossing the road startled as they rounded a bend, her graceful posture turning to alarm. Allie swerved and nearly lost control, the Jeep spinning sideways. It was a sharp drop into the ditch, and the tires ground to a halt inches before going over the edge.

"Holy crap!" Gina yelled, clutching the dog tight to her chest. "Could ya get us there in one piece?"

"I'm sorry. We're so close." Adrenaline sizzling nerve endings, Allie reversed and backed out.

In front of them, the panicked deer galloped one way, and then the other, blocking them from passing. Finally, she laid on her horn and the deer bounded sideways into the trees, white tail raised like a flag.

They drove for another quarter of a mile, until the road was blocked by a Morley Falls PD patrol car. Allie stopped behind it and they got out. Both of the cruiser's front tires had gone over the shoulder, its bumper ground into the ditch, rear tires suspended mid-air.

"Unit forty-one is the car Ernie drives." Gina peered through the driver's window to the empty interior. "I heard them talking on the radio. Derek stole this."

Allie squeezed her eyes tight. So much conflicting energy vibrated through this area that it confused her.

"Derek." Gina looked into the woods. "Where is that crazy son of a bitch?"

"I can't figure him out. Is he really dangerous?"

"I thought he was only a pathetic drunk, but…" Gina's hand went to her throat. "I don't know any more."

"He went that way." Allie pointed to a trampled spot in the grass. Beyond, weedy poplars gave way to a canopy of birch and pine that filtered out what was left of the light.

"Isn't that swamp past there?"

"Yes, but there's a trail that leads to the power lines. I think I can find it."

"I trust you, Allie. I don't totally understand what's going on in your noggin' but I know it's something special, something good, and you're stronger now than I've ever seen you." Gina's chest rose sharply and fell. "But Lily's not the same kid that used to shoplift in my store. Derek's different too. And there's the boy. I'm a bit scared."

"Me too, but I don't sense any danger from the boy. I don't sense him at all." The thread that connected her to Victoria pulled with urgency. "I have to go." For the first time she realized that she wasn't ill, did not have a headache and wasn't losing control. She was focused and confident.

The trail through the swamp beckoned. Colors clung to the grass like smoke, lazily swirling downward. Doppler barked and bounded after them, as if he scented the vibrant blues and greens she saw, the colors that dissolved when she walked through them. An acrid tang stung her nostrils, and her stomach rebelled against the metallic taste on her tongue. She spat it out.

Gina whispered their location into the radio, and got a squelch of alarm back. "Stay in the car and wait," was all they understood.

Allie shook her head. "I can't." She turned to follow the dog, his tail sticking straight out behind him. "Maybe you should stay," she called over her shoulder.

Gina tucked the radio into her pocket, and was beside her with a crash of brush and a hastily-muttered curse. "No way. I'm scared shitless, but I'm coming. What if this was *my* kid?"

They ran after the dog, leaping fallen trees and dodging branches. Doppler whined in anticipation and Allie felt his energy pull her as much as Victoria's. An ominous thrum, dark and oily in the back of her mind, reminded her that Lily too was out there.

The light was faint under the cover of trees, but she found the path she knew was there and they followed it as it wound its way over higher ground. All around them, a chorus of frogs and insects joined in one last deafening tribute to daylight. There was a subtle change in the air, as if the forest sounds sharpened, and separated into individual voices. The cushion of moss beneath her feet transitioned to solid footing, grass brushed her pant legs. She stopped when they got close enough to see the towers, steel arms outstretched like sentinels.

The sky flushed muted sunset colors but, above the clearing, anger churned like black clouds, like hate.

"What's happening?" Gina whispered. Tail drooping, Doppler whined and circled them.

"Something terrible." Allie turned away, couldn't bear to feel it. She had to block it out or she'd never be able to find Victoria. Icy fingers traced her spine when she ran the opposite direction.

A few hundred yards further, they found another trail into the woods. Well-worn, Allie recognized it as the one she'd taken last year to come berry picking with the kids. Last year, when the sun was shining, and no homicidal lunatics were stealing children.

Their biggest worry was the hungry bears lumbering along the edge of the blueberry patch, looking for the best spots. They'd never encountered one, but had an emergency plan in place if they ever did. 'Put down your pails, kids,' she'd say. 'Leave them right there and, quiet as you can, follow me back to the car. Stick together and we'll be fine.'

The kids loved the adventure, made a game out of practicing to walk silently in a pack. Now Victoria was out here with a predator worse than a hungry bear. She was in the hands of a soulless monster.

Allie clutched her stomach as she ran. The scar burned as if it had opened wide, raw and angry. When she'd been stabbed, Lily's face had been oddly devoid of expression, as if she had no idea what to do until Allie reacted. Was Victoria seeing that face right now?

When she couldn't hear Gina's ragged breath, she turned to see that she had fallen behind. She waved her arm in a *hurry up* gesture.

"Go," Gina panted. "I'll catch up."

Allie didn't want to leave her, but the thread's pull was insistent. With Doppler at her heels, she let it lead her.

The sunset faded, leaching the remainder of light from the forest. Branches tore at her face, tugged at her clothes. Doppler yelped when she struck him with her heel, but she had no time to stop and reassure him. One misstep might land her in the swamp, twist an ankle, or worse.

The trees parted, and she found herself at the side of the road. She bent to catch her breath, to check if her belly really was bleeding. The jagged scar looked the same as always. A growl rumbled from the dog's throat and she pulled her shirt back down.

"Why didn't you die?" Lily stepped out, her arm crooked around Victoria's neck. In her other hand, the shiny barrel of a gun pointed at the frightened girl's head.

Doppler barked, his little legs bouncing off the ground with the effort.

Lily narrowed her eyes. "I think I've met that dog before. At your friend's house in Winnipeg."

"He bit you, didn't he?" Allie shifted her weight and took a step forward. The blood droplets on the cereal box in the cupboard. Doppler had bitten Lily out of fear. "I won't let him bite you again, if you let Victoria go."

Lily threw her head back and laughed. "Let him try. I'll shoot him on the spot." She swung the revolver toward Doppler and a strange gurgle bubbled in her throat.

Victoria's eyes were wide, cheeks flushed as if she'd been running too. She coughed at the pressure on her throat.

"Should I shoot her?" She pressed the barrel into Victoria's temple and the girl winced, clenching her jaw tight. "This little shit gave me a world of trouble today. Thanks for the knife, by the way. It's mine now." She jostled Victoria as if they were old friends exchanging a joke. Victoria turned her face away.

"Or should I shoot *you*?" Lily swiveled the gun to Allie and bared her teeth. "Are you gonna put a hex on me? A witch spell or something? I wish I could record this with my camera. It would be awesome, but I'd rather kill you."

White hot energy surged through Allie's veins, pure and focused. Doppler whined and peeped from behind her leg. "Put the gun down." The words came out of her mouth, but it sounded far away. Motion slowed. There was time. "You can run, you can escape."

A siren wailed in the distance, then another. Gina had the radio. She'd called for help, but did they know which way to go?

Lily loosened her grip on Victoria's neck and a flicker of doubt crossed her face. "Why didn't you die?" A moment of fear. "Why does my mother haunt me?"

"You do that to yourself." Allie didn't believe in ghosts, not the kind Lily was talking about. Regrets of the past, memories of terrible things, those were the ghosts she believed in.

The jagged edges of Lily's energy wavered. "How do I kill her if she's already dead?"

Allie narrowed her eyes. "You can't. Let go of the girl and run."

Lily flinched. "I-I'm not running. I'm the badass panther!" She twisted a handful of Victoria's hair in her fist, and brought the revolver up.

Allie wanted to leap at her, to tear the gun from her hand, to put her arms around Victoria and make her safe. *Wait. Wait a moment longer.* She clenched her fists and stood motionless on the road.

"Stop!" A man's voice boomed from the dark. Derek. Would he help? Something terrible was about to happen.

Lily hesitated, twisting the handful of hair until Victoria cried out. Doppler exploded from Allie's safety, a snarl on his tiny muzzle. He leapt into the air and sank his teeth into the soft flesh inside Lily's elbow, twisting and thrashing. She howled and the gun thudded onto the road. The dog hung on until she swung her fist at him.

Go. Go. Go! Allie rushed in and blocked her punch until Doppler released and skittered back to his feet. "Let her go!" She pummeled Lily with her fists in a tidal wave of protective instinct.

Lily sagged under her onslaught. "I'm sorry mommy." She crouched in the dirt, arms covering her head while Doppler barked in her ear.

Victoria tugged at the back of Allie's shirt until she backed away. Allie grabbed her hand and gripped it tight. No matter what, she would keep this child safe.

Her twin sister had been right when she'd said Victoria was a fast runner. The girl matched Allie pace for pace as they sprinted with Doppler at their heels. They didn't stop to catch their breath until long after Lily was out of sight.

Victoria hiccupped a sob. "Auntie Allie, I tried to be brave like you."

"Oh, sweet girl. I was so proud of how brave you were." She drew her into her arms.

"You were like a mama bear. Better than Auntie Vicky's stories."

Allie hugged her again. They were safe but Lily was still back there, and the sirens were getting closer. "Gina's coming for us. We need to meet her."

They hurried to a fork in the road and arrived moments before the headlights of an unmarked car, with her Jeep on its tail, flooded over them. Victoria waved, and they skidded to a stop. Gina exited the Jeep at the same time Erin leapt out her door.

"You're safe!" Erin reached for both of them.

They threw their arms around each other, cheeks colliding in a flurry of relief. When Gina cried, tears rolled down Victoria's cheeks too.

"Did you radio Chris?" Allie lowered her voice. "Did he catch the boy?"

"He's with him now." Gina gave a small shake of her head. Lily's boyfriend was dead.

"Where's the female suspect?" Gonzales called out the open door.

Allie pulled out of the hug and pointed down the road. "She was a half mile that way. We'll go with Gina to your parents' house. Victoria's mom and dad should be there soon, and they'll be so happy to see her." She wrapped her arm around the girl's shoulder and met Erin's eye. "Go catch Lily."

"I will," Erin assured her. She got back behind the wheel. "Is she armed?"

Allie nodded. "She has a gun."

"Let's go." Gonzales racked the tactical shotgun in his hands.

"Be careful, Erin. Derek is with her, and…" Allie bent to whisper in her ear.

CHAPTER THIRTY

"Lily! Stop!" Derek squinted through the dusk at the figures on the road. He hadn't even been sure it was his daughter until she spoke. She'd been talking about killing whoever was up there with her, and she had a gun. Where the hell had she gotten a gun? The last time he'd seen her, she'd been a child, not unlike the one she was holding by the hair.

A dog barked and someone yelled. Two people ran away, leaving Lily standing alone. He hurried across the grass and through the ditch. If he'd known she'd come out here, he could have stayed on the damn road, instead of trundling his ass through the swamp. The back of his neck was a mass of insect bites, but he didn't bother to scratch them, not now, not when he'd finally found his daughter. "What are you doing, sweetie?"

Lily turned, one hand squeezed over her opposite elbow, dark blood dripping through her fingers. "A demon bit me. I tried to kill it." She wiped her hands on her pants. "You got a cigarette?"

What had happened to make her like this? Was it his fault? Was it the fault of *both* her parents? That left the blame squarely on his shoulders. He'd failed, in so many ways. Tiffany was gone. Dead. Her cracked skull dumped with her bones in Gunther's bog. How was Lily involved in that?

Somewhere far away, a woman shouted. Lily picked up the revolver, holding it in her palm as if she was considering its weight, its ability to wreak destruction despite its size. She curled her fingers around the grip and pointed it directly at Derek's chest.

"Dad?" She didn't appear surprised to see him, as if she'd expected it. The skin of her face was smooth, as pale in summer as in winter, no matter how much time she spent outside. He used to joke that the sun bounced right off her. Her cool green eyes regarded him from beneath colorless brows, the resemblance to his own somewhat disconcerting. It was as if she were the younger, female version of himself. Where he was thick and muscular, she was slim as a willow, and just as resilient. The biggest difference was that he burned like a hairless pig. Burn, peel, burn, peel, all summer long.

"I shot T, out by the power lines. It wasn't like I thought it would be," she said.

"Okay, we can talk about that, sweetie." Derek held out his trembling hands, palms up, the way you'd calm a small child or wild animal. She was neither. Both. She'd killed her boyfriend. "Why don't you put the gun down first?"

"But I need a climax before the credits roll."

"What?" He took a slow step toward her. His alcohol-starved brain screamed for caution. Lily had always been unpredictable, and now she held a gun.

She reached into her pocket, brought out a cell phone and thumbed a button on the side. Lens turned to her face, she addressed the camera. "Okay, so the battery is dying. I need to hurry and film my final scene. It was gonna be different, but this will have to do. And... action!" She turned it around toward Derek and held out the gun so it would be in the shot.

He took a step back, his shaking legs threatening to buckle. "Whoa! No. Let's not do this."

Lily giggled. "Good. That was good. Reaction. I love that." She closed the space between them. "Hey, dude, did you know your ear is missing? Did the monster bite it off? He bit me too." She showed him her elbow with its tiny drizzle of blood.

"Yes, the monster bit me. Look, we have something in common. Let's talk, sweetie. Put the gun down and I'll help you make your movie, or whatever you're doing with that camera."

Lily narrowed her eyes. "Whatever I'm doing? Don't talk to me like I'm a kid. I've never been a kid. I'm making the best action movie of all time. You should be grateful that I'm putting you in it."

Derek could have sworn that his stomach had emptied hours ago, but now fiery whiskey burned his throat. "No, you're making a mistake. It's not too late."

A high-pitched wail sounded in the distance. Goddamn Ericsson, or Zimmerman. They'd never stop dogging him.

Lily's spine straightened. "This keeps getting better."

"It's time to do the right thing, sweetheart. They want me too. Let's turn ourselves in. We'll go together and sort everything out. I'll stick by you, you know I'd do anything for you."

"Would you die for me?" She thumbed the hammer back and tensed her finger on the trigger. "Bang!"

His intestines twisted sideways and he nearly passed out.

"Ha, ha. You flinched." She eased the hammer forward. She was toying with him. Trying to get her old man to wet his pants out of fear for her goddamn video.

"That's not funny." He'd always been a permissive father. It was time to be a real parent. He reached for the gun.

Her eyes narrowed. "Here comes the climax."

His fingers closed around the cylinder as she squeezed. It rotated and bucked in his hand when the firing pin struck the primer. A molten hammer pounded Derek's upper thigh, taking the strength of his leg out from under him. He groaned and fell to his side. Heat spread to his groin.

Lily leaned over him, camera in his face. "Aren't you gonna do something? Scream, or fight?"

An unmarked car rounded the bend in the road, and its siren abruptly halted when it came to a stop.

She panned over with the camera, "Fuckin' Ericsson's here," and panned back. "You still wanna turn yourself in?"

There was yelling, and a flurry of activity as Erin and the male FBI agent exited. They took cover behind the engine block. She'd called him Gonzales, like Speedy Gonzales. Derek smiled at the thought of the fast little Mexican mouse and wished Lily could have had a normal childhood, watching cartoons in her pajamas with her parents. Things might have been different.

"Drop your weapon!" Someone called out.

His life was spilling from him, but he willed himself to stay conscious when his body yearned to curl into a ball and, what? Die? Maybe death didn't scare him as much as it used to. Hopes for a family were gone, but he had to know.

"Tell me what happened to Tiff— to your mom."

Lily's jaw twitched. Was she smiling?

"Step away from him!" Erin shouted. "We can talk."

Lily bent as if all her bones melted at once. She pressed the gun to his forehead. "That's what we're doing, right? We're talking. We don't need her poking her nose in our business."

"Tell me," he said. His vision fogged, and despite the summer heat, his feet were cold. "It was an accident, what happened with your mom, wasn't it?

"I wanted it to happen. I made it happen." She pointed the camera at the hole the bullet had torn in his pant leg. "That's awesome."

Blood gushed every time his pulse pounded. Here he was, bleeding out, and she was talking about shooting him the way another kid might talk about homework, or a decadent dessert. She enjoyed watching her father bleed to death.

Erin was still yelling but he couldn't make out the words. Why was she here? She would never leave him alone.

"It was... an accident. You were... a child."

"I told you. I was never a child," Lily spat. "Mother said you were gonna marry her. Talked about it like it would solve all her problems, my problems. Did you know she was afraid of me? Who's scared of their own kid? Anyway, she always liked drugs more than she liked me. She said she stopped, but she would have used again, you know."

Derek's throat closed, his lungs grew heavy. He was so tired.

"I wanted to kill her and the opportunity appeared, out of nowhere. She took me for a picnic, but I pushed her in the swamp and smashed her head. I hated her. I thought she was gone, but she haunts me." She looked at her phone's screen. "Scheisse, my battery's dead."

* * *

"Dad?" I don't remember if I ever called him that. He was more like a servant. My minion. He'd do anything I told him. His blood squirts between my fingers and drips off my elbow. The greedy dirt drinks it up, leaving a stain that will be gone with the next rain. If we were in a movie, the pool of blood would be big enough for us both to lie in, on our backs, laughing and making cherry-colored angels.

Fuckin' Ericsson has been yelling at me since she got here but I don't want to hear her. I'm not even totally sure what an *artery* is, but that might be why there's so much blood. Go ahead and call an ambulance if you want to, but don't come over here. Not while I have a gun pointed at my father's head. My dad.

"Daddy?"

I hadn't really planned for him to die right away. We never talked like this before. I never told him the truth about anything, only what I figured he wanted to hear. What would I need to say to get him to give me another cigarette, or maybe twenty bucks? Finally telling him about my mom felt good. Like the very first buzz I got with T in the library of the correctional center. Before the headache hit. Before I went to the infirmary. Now the buzz is gone and here comes the awful *after* feeling.

He's the last family I have. The last person who pretended to like me, who didn't want anything, or jam his hands down my pants when I passed out. Maybe he even loved me. "Daddy? Daddy!" I push harder, but the blood no longer flows, and I can't stop from blubbering. "Daddydaddydaddy!"

I raise my head when Ericsson comes. What's her problem? I still have a gun. I could shoot her between the eyes before she grinds me into the dust, but I realize that I don't care about her any more. I don't care about anybody. Everyone leaves me anyway. I lean against my dad's chest and put my mouth around the barrel of the gun.

She digs her heels into the dirt and stops out of arm's reach. "Lily! Don't do it." Her big black pistol points at me, as if I give a shit.

I'm not going back to juvy with that pack of losers. My grandfather hates me, my parents are dead. Even T. He's in the grass, flies buzzing around his corpse by now. My fun's over. They'll make a movie out of my videos and I'll be famous forever.

Fuckin' Ericsson never learns. She grabs for my gun.

I smile and squeeze the trigger.

CHAPTER THIRTY-ONE

Erin tore the sparkly gift wrap open and took the lunch box by the handle. "Wonder Woman, nice." She unsnapped the tiny pink latches, and smiled at the fast food gift card.

"Because you're always hungry." Agent Gonzales stuck out his hand and she shook it. He wore brand new shoes with oversize treads, not at all like the slippery leather-soled ones he'd cursed the entire time they'd run through the forest. Here he was, back in The Bureau's air-conditioned Minneapolis office but now he was prepared for bush trails. He probably had a bottle of insect repellant in his briefcase.

She laughed. "The gift card's awesome but I'm not sure about the lunch pail."

Agent Lockwood chucked her on the shoulder. "Nah, he got it right. Wonder Woman is so much better than what they used to call you." As if setting the scene, she cleared her throat and held up a hand. "You missed your official Academy graduation ceremony to come help us out. I know The Bureau did that little presentation thing for you after the fact, but this is something extra."

Erin shrugged. "Aw, I'm not a big fan of ceremonies. I skipped my own high school grad, and only showed up at the one for university long enough to grab the certificate and run."

"Shush, girl. You're ruining my speech." Lockwood produced an unusually wrinkled envelope and plopped it on the desk. "I bet you're impressed with how it's wrapped, but don't let your admiration get in the way of your excitement. Go ahead and open it."

Erin grinned. "All right. At least you didn't hire confetti throwers, or a mariachi band or something." Lockwood had certainly grown on her. She opened the wrinkly envelope and withdrew a computer USB drive. "What's on it?"

"Connections. The finest contacts I've developed during my career, categorized by field of expertise, and if they owe me a favor. Those are gold. You need anything, mention my name and you'll get assistance, no questions asked."

Gonzales adjusted his necktie. "That information carries with it a huge responsibility."

Erin's fingers closed around the storage device. "Are you sure I'm the person you should entrust this to?"

Lockwood snorted. "I was sure the day I met you. Keep it confidential. Some of these are just point people for their agencies, but others are safe houses and covert contacts. The information can boost your ability to solve challenging cases, and might be instrumental in saving lives."

"Thank you. You have no idea how much this means." A lump formed in Erin's throat.

"I almost wish I wasn't retiring, so I could do a few more investigations with you." Lockwood blinked misty eyes. Was the venerable crocodile about to cry? "I'm glad you talked your way onto this task force, and I'm glad your niece is safe."

"Victoria's an amazing kid. She's going to be okay." Erin snapped the USB drive into the lunch box. "I'm sad to see you go." She met Lockwood's vice-like handshake with equal pressure.

"Tell me, did you think Lily wouldn't shoot herself, or did you know the gun was empty?"

"It was something Allie said."

Lockwood tilted her head with the unspoken query.

"She just knew."

The retiring agent gave a single nod. "Well, I'm glad she did." She put a hand on Erin's shoulder. "I'll be following the court case from my new villa in the Bahamas. With her own video evidence stacked against her, there'll be no more sad-eyed sympathy crap for Lily Schmidt. They'll be trying her as an adult, and she's not getting out."

"Is Marty meeting you at your new villa?" Gonzales dodged Lockwood's swipe in his direction.

"Maybe he is." She winked.

"Marty? As in Marty the state trooper?" Erin stared at her. That was a quick romance. Hadn't they just met at the roadblock in Utah? Lockwood was still very much an enigma.

Gonzales eased his weight off the corner of the desk. "Your friend Zimmerman said Lily's grandfather bought back his property by the bog, at a quarter of the price he sold it. Donated it to the state as protected wetlands, or a memorial or something."

Erin pursed her lips. Big city developers never should have tried to build condos that destroyed natural habitat, but they wouldn't have solved Tiffany's disappearance otherwise. Like Allie said, sometimes it was fate.

"Did they officially identify the remains out there? Did Lily really kill both her parents?"

"Yeah, autopsy report confirmed Tiffany Schmidt's skull suffered blunt force trauma, exactly how she described," Erin said. "Forensics lab dates the remains at around seven years. They're working on pinning that down, but it's close."

He winced. "She would have been eight at the time of her first murder. I still feel sick to my stomach after seeing the videos on her phone. I hope the evidence is sealed, so it never sees the light of day."

Lockwood snorted. "Me too. She might get her wish to be famous, but not how she hoped. Wait until the press gets wind of this. Killer kid destroys everyone around her. Some bloodsucker will want to make a documentary."

"I won't be watching that horror flick," Erin said.

"No, but you'll be keeping an eye on the whole thing from right here, won't you?" Lockwood picked up her jacket and folded it over her arm. "I heard you actually requested this godforsaken field office."

"But, I like Minnesota." Erin's jaw tensed before she realized that Lockwood was teasing. "And it's close to home, to my family."

"You're right. The Bureau has changed from the old days when I joined. Nowadays, agents are encouraged to have a life, to be well-rounded people." She eyed Erin. "You'd better marry your girl if you're gonna keep her around." She chuckled when Erin's face flushed. "I suppose you'll send me an invitation to the ceremony, and I'll buy you something frilly from the Home Depot catalog."

Gonzales' eyes bugged out. "Married? That's right, that whole

Supreme Court thing. You can get married anywhere in America, can't you?" He rotated his wedding band so the inset diamond faced forward. "Count me in, too. I'll come."

"And don't forget to pencil me in for the position of godmother to your kids." Lockwood was on a roll, but she wasn't far off. Erin had been thinking about how Allie was with children, how she needed them in her life, full-time.

"Kids!" His mouth dropped. "How would you…?"

Erin grinned. "Turkey baster."

Gonzales' Adam's apple bobbed.

Lockwood pounded her on the back. "That's the spirit."

"Um, we might consider fostering." Erin said, seriously. Where was this coming from? Getting married? Becoming foster parents? The words had come out so naturally that she realized it had been on her mind, but it wasn't until this very moment that it all made sense.

There were so many children who needed help, whether temporarily or long-term. Allie's childhood had proven that it could work, and the two of them, together, would make a great team. She looked at her hands, at the spot on her finger where a ring could sit. "I guess I'd better call my girlfriend."

Lockwood nodded. "Good luck, Erin. I'll be keeping in touch." She ushered the stunned Gonzales out of the office and left her alone.

Erin took a deep breath and retrieved her phone.

Allie was cheerful when she answered, as if this was the best day of her life. "Hi Honey! When are we going apartment hunting in Minneapolis?"

"Uh, about that…"

"What is it?" Allie shushed the dog's barking. "Will you be going to a different field office?"

"No, that's not it." Her heart thumped as if she'd run two miles. "I think an apartment might be too small."

CHAPTER THIRTY-TWO

Jimmy held the aerial drone up to the web cam so Allie could see. "This is the brand new model! Ooh, look at the gold stripes and the advanced camera. Uncle Thomas will have a heart attack when he sees this!"

Two hundred miles away, Allie squinted at the wiggly image. He had the same frenetic energy as his auntie Erin. "Happy birthday, Jimmy. I'm sorry it took so long to replace, but I wanted to wait until the new model came out. I hope you like it. There are some pretty cool features."

"I love it!"

Sophie nudged him aside and took over the spotlight, a close-up of her nose and grinning mouth consuming the camera's field of view. "We're going to Disneyland."

"Disneyland!"

The image tilted as Victoria picked up the laptop and looked directly into the lens. "Dad got two whole weeks off work, and we're going to celebrate Mom. She's all done her treatment!"

"I'm so happy," Allie said.

"And there's a drone competition," Jimmy chimed in. "It's on the way. I get to compete."

"Anyway," Victoria continued. "We're going to ride Space Mountain, and—"

"No," Sophie interjected. "Rollercoasters make me sick."

The image on the laptop swiveled to their mom's face. "Hi Allie. We're going, on one condition, if my kids do all their chores and get along. This trip will be epic." Erin's sister Liz smiled. Her face had regained its healthy glow after she'd finished the last grueling round of chemo. Since the doctor had declared her cancer free, it was as if she'd begun a whole new life, with energy to match.

"Aw Mom, you can't say epic. Nobody says that anymore," one of the girls grumbled off-camera.

"Mom's going on all the rides with us!" Jimmy shouted.

Liz smirked at the camera. "Yeah, no more nausea. I sure don't miss chemo."

Victoria's face appeared on the screen again. "I miss Doppler. Can you bring him for a visit?"

"I promise. As soon as we can."

"It's suppertime," Liz announced and the kids said their goodbyes.

Allie closed her laptop and Wrong-Way Rachel grumbled, hopping off the desk. Despite everything on her mind, she'd gotten a great deal of work done today. Ciara and Raphael had taken over the business, and she remained as consultant. Her hours were flexible and her stress level low. That helped a lot.

She got up, and Doppler followed her to the kitchen where Erin sat with the newspaper. She squeezed in beside her and took a sip from her flower-painted mug.

"Yuck. You need some cream in that, or—"

"Sprinkles?" Erin pulled her into her arms. "Do I need candy confetti in my coffee to make you happy?"

"I am happy." She leaned on her shoulder and held out her hand to examine the shiny ring on her finger. "Thanks for not getting me the Cinderella diamond. These little sapphires are so much prettier."

Erin brushed her lips against Allie's forehead, breathing her in. "You smell good, Baby."

"You're always thinking about food! What do you think I smell like? Bacon?"

"No. You smell like rain," Erin murmured. She took Allie's hand in hers, "and sometimes strawberries."

They kissed, soft lips brushing, energy mingling in harmony. Today was a big day. The start of something new.

"Don't be nervous," Erin said. "We completed all the training. You asked your mom for every piece of advice she had. You know what to do if a baby gets sick, if a toddler flushes everything in the house, or even if a teenager sneaks out late at night. You'll be the best mom ever."

"Foster mom," she corrected.

"A foster mom's still a mom, sometimes the one most needed."

"You're right. I learned a lot from mine. A kid can never have too many people in her life who love her." She sprang to her feet, and then the doorbell rang.

Erin set her mug on the table. "I love that you can do that."

"She's here."

"She?" Erin put the dog in the yard before they answered the door.

On the front step stood a prim young social worker with a faux-leather case, and a world-weary expression, even though she had to be still shy of thirty. She extended her hand. "Hello, I'm Cassandra, with Child Protective Services." The social worker's reticence made it sound like a question. "I called about placing Willow in your home."

Beside Cassandra, at elbow height, was a serious-faced girl with black curly hair, and a baggy dress that hung from her thin body as if it had been hastily borrowed. She gripped a plastic shopping bag with meager possessions to her chest.

Willow needed a bath; her skin was the mottled brownish color that Allie's foster mom had joked about when she'd called her in for an overdue bath. 'That's not a tan, that's tanned-in dirt!' she'd laugh, and send her directly to the bathtub for a good scrubbing.

Allie met the girl's clear, bright eyes and her breath caught. Despite her neglected appearance, there was a serene intelligence about her, as if her exterior condition mismatched her interior. Her energy was familiar, like they'd been waiting for each other. Bright and clean, it filled Allie like fresh air.

She breathed it in and squatted to Willow's eye level. "I'm Allie, and that's Erin. Would you like to come in?"

"Okay." The girl shrugged and stepped over the threshold. She surveyed the living room as if she were an approving interior designer.

Erin nodded to her and led Cassandra to the kitchen. "I'll take care of the paperwork while you two get acquainted."

"Would you like to see your room?" Allie opened a door decorated with dancing cats wearing parkas, showed her the newly painted room, and kids' bed they'd stayed up late to assemble the night before. New pajamas, size six, were laid out on the bed.

"I dreamed of coming to a place like this." Willow picked up the pajamas and nodded her approval at the elephant pattern.

"How old are you, Willow?"

"I turned six right before school started." She held up the corresponding number of fingers. "This is nice, but where are they?"

"Who do you mean?"

"The animals."

"Oh," Allie smiled. She must have seen the dog toys and the photo of the cat. "Would you like to meet them?"

The little girl nodded vigorously. Allie led her to the back door where the dog bounced, each time high enough to peep through the glass. His tongue lolled out the side of his mouth. "This is Doppler and he's a Chihuahua."

Willow smiled, and her energy flashed bright orange. She was happy to see him. That was good. Doppler missed Erin's nieces and nephew, and he'd be a good little buddy for her. Allie opened the door and the dog bounded into the girl's arms, him wiggling excitedly, and her struggling to hold him. She giggled and finally put him down where he raced circles around her legs. "He's cuter than I thought."

"He's adorable, isn't he? But he isn't really supposed to jump up. We need to work on that. Later, I can show you where his treats are and you can help him, if you like."

Willow nodded again, and peered into the kitchen where Erin spoke with Cassandra.

"You'll like Erin. She's fun and she loves kids. She can teach you how to make a whistle out of a piece of willow branch, a tree with the same name as you." Allie grinned and held her hand up to her mouth. "But tree bark tastes bitter." She made a face that she'd intended to be funny.

Willow gave an earnest nod as if she would file this information away for future use, but she was distracted. She examined the closet.

The social worker laughed about something when Erin escorted her back to the front door. Cassandra stopped long enough to pat the child on the head, and reassure her that everything would be okay before heading off. Erin returned with a stack of documents, and an overwhelmed expression.

She put the papers down, and forced a smile. "Your name is Willow, right? I'm Erin." She held out her hand.

The girl's face clouded with confusion for a moment before she extended her own, and they shook firmly, arms swinging up and down. "It's very nice to meet you." She let go and laid on her belly to peek under the closet door, left open a crack. Tail wagging, Doppler wiggled in beside her. Side-by-side, they maintained vigil.

"What are you doing?" Erin asked. Laying on the floor and staring into closets, this one wasn't on the list of things kids did.

"Where's the kitty?"

"Oh!" Allie exclaimed. "You're looking for Rachel. You're close." She teased open the door. "Shh." Curled on the bottom shelf of the linen closet, the cat slept, her fluffy tail swept across her nose, paws tucked into a massive ball of fluff.

"Ahhh." Willow whispered in awe. She reached in and touched Rachel's soft fur. "There you are."

The cat purred and Allie's chest vibrated from the energy being generated between the child and sleepy feline. The way sunlight glistens through icicles, light twinkled around them, beautiful in its simplicity. From the moment she'd seen the girl on the step, there had been an undeniable connection, but she hadn't expected this. This was meant to be.

"Oh," Willow whispered, surprised. "I forgot you only had three paws. In my dream, you had all of them." Wrong-Way Rachel lazily stretched out her single front paw, and rolled over for the little girl to stroke her furry belly.

Erin shot a glance at Allie. "How did she know?" she mouthed. "Did you...?"

Allie shrugged and reached for her hand, intertwining their fingers.

Willow glanced back at her new foster parents, a tentative smile on her lips. "I think I'm gonna like it here."

THE END

ABOUT THE AUTHOR

Makenzi Fisk grew up in a small town in Northwestern Ontario. She spent much of her youth outdoors, surrounded by the rugged landscape of the Canadian Shield. Moving west, she became a police officer with patrol, communications and forensic experience before transitioning to graphic design. She now works for herself.

Her first novel, Just Intuition, earned her Debut Author in the 2015 Golden Crown Literary Society Awards. Just Intuition was also a Mystery/Thriller Finalist in the 2015 Golden Crown Literary Awards and the 2014 Rainbow Awards. She is a Canadian Lesfic author, a member of ARWA, and GCLS.

Website: makenzifisk.com

Books in the Intuition series:

Just Intuition - Book One

Burning Intuition - Book Two

Fatal Intuition - Book Three

Made in the USA
Charleston, SC
04 September 2016